If At First…

If At First…

2nd in the Brad Hastings series

J. Burnett Smith

Writers Club Press
San Jose New York Lincoln Shanghai

*This project would not have been possible without the
encouragement of my family, and especially the help of
my daughter Camille Bea Smith for her assistance in preparing
the manuscript for publication and designing the book cover.*

CHAPTER 1

Brad Hastings opened his eyes slowly. Even that small movement sent a stabbing pain from his forehead to the back of his neck. Through blurred vision, he discovered this was a hospital room and there was someone seated near a window a few feet away. The form rose and approached the bed, leaning over to look into his eyes.

"Hey, Bud. You awake? Talk to me."

It was Doug's voice.

"Dad? What happened? Why am I here?" His father gradually came into focus when he backed away with a look of surprise on his face.

"*Dad*?" Doug chuckled. "You ain't called me nothing but 'Doug' since you was ten years old!"

This topic was never openly discussed between the two. With his father slipping in and out of their lives throughout his rodeo years, Brad automatically became the man of the house in taking care of their small horse ranch with his mother. Up to age twenty, when Brad himself became a professional bronc rider, his role in the family consisted mainly of keeping Doug out of jail and trying to keep him moderately sober when he came home for a few days between shows.

Brad struggled to recall why he was in a hospital. It must have been a car wreck. He and Doug were supposed to go fishing near Paul Gorman's cabin. That much he remembered. Then what?

Doug stepped forward again and placed his hand on Brad's arm. At five-eight there was little family resemblance between the two men except for the Hastings' red hair and blue eyes. Doug's square jaw, thick neck and wide back in no way resembled Brad, who was tall and broad shouldered, with slim hips, more like Grandpa Hastings.

"Did we wreck the truck, Doug? Is Skeeter okay? What about Smoky?"

Doug seemed to choose his words carefully. "No, Bud. No car wreck. My roping horse and your Aussie dog are okay. You had an accident in the saddle bronc riding…"

"Oh, come on, Doug. You know I don't ride broncs any more. What's the real lowdown?"

Doug went back to the window and retrieved a chair. He pulled it next to the bed and sat down. He seemed reluctant to answer.

"Well," Brad asked impatiently, "what really happened?"

Doug seemed relieved when a blonde student nurse peeked through the doorway and smiled in response to seeing the patient awake.

"I'll get the doctor." She disappeared as quickly as she had emerged, but not before Brad saw the room number on the door. Number 23. Small hospital? Not 123 or 223. Just plain 23.

"Quit stalling, Doug. Give me some answers."

Brad would have recognized Doug's pained expression as a reluctance to answer had he not been in so much discomfort himself.

Another reprieve for his father intervened in the person of a small, bespectacled doctor who rushed into the room as though a brain transplant patient awaited him in the operating room.

"So!" the doctor exclaimed in a high pitched nervous voice. "How's my patient this morning? Ready to get back to your *broncos*, I suppose."

The man's sarcasm came as no surprise, so Brad remained silent. This attitude was familiar from past years when Brad was rodeoing full time and he or one of his friends found themselves under the care of a "civilian" medical man. For some reason quite a few doctors seemed to resent caring for patients who, in their collective opinions, went out of their way to put themselves in danger. There also was the added fact that in the past, amateur riders generally were not covered by medical insurance. To hospital personnel this apparently made the recurring episodes even more unacceptable. What this doctor probably did not realize was that even the amateur rodeo hands were now offered the opportunity to buy medical insurance, and members of the Professional Rodeo Cowboys' Association were actually required to do so.

One thing Brad could not fathom was why the man referred to "your broncos." Since his retirement from the rodeo business at the ripe old age of twenty-seven, when he became a small town deputy sheriff in New Mexico, Brad had no aspirations to return to competition except for an occasional team roping event with his father.

The doctor impatiently took Brad's blood pressure, listened to his heart, peered into his eyes and ears as though searching for signs of anything tangible, such as a brain, inside his skull. Before skittering out of the room, he prescribed a pain reliever in response to Brad's obvious discomfort at the not-too-gentle probing.

Brad wanted to elicit some answers from Doug before the nurse arrived with the sedative but again the grilling was delayed. This time it was their friend Tooley who came bursting into the room and rushed to Brad's bedside. A small red faced Irishman with graying hair and pale blue eyes, he was dressed in his usual off-work wardrobe of coveralls, baseball cap and hiking boots. Tooley always leaned forward at an eighty-five degree angle when he was in a hurry, like he was climbing uphill. In his haste, he slammed into the bed with a thud.

Brad flinched.

Even in times of stress, the way Tooley's mouth curled up at the corners, he generally seemed about to laugh out loud. This time his face showed only concern.

"Brad. Sorry I couldn't get here sooner. Had to work the night performance. Talk to me, Son. What happened?"

Tooley was a former rodeo clown/bull fighter who now performed with three Australian Shepherds in an act displaying the dogs' ability to manipulate twenty or thirty sheep around a rodeo arena. To all who knew him, Tooley, whose real name was Sean O'Toole, distinguished himself primarily by his unintentional habit of completely butchering any expressions and/or proverbs he attempted to quote.

Brad looked from Tooley to Doug and back to Tooley.

"Why don't one of you fill me in? Where's Smoky? What the hell's going on?" His head began to throb again. Smoky, his Australian Shepherd, was from the same litter as Tooley's performing dogs and the two of them were almost never separated except in an emergency situation.

Brad caught the puzzled look exchanged by the two men.

Doug was the first to speak. "Remember signing up for bronc riding at Bear Claw, Colorado, don't you, Bud? You claimed you might as well give it a try if you was gonna travel with me for awhile..."

"Broncs? I don't understand! What happened between our trout fishing and this hospital bed? You're not ribbing me are you, Doug?"

"Sure not, Bud. It's a true fact. You and me was gonna team rope and since we're here anyway, you decided to try the saddle broncs just for the hell of it. This show's too small to be sanctioned by the Pro Rodeo Association and all the stock is local..."

"That right, Tooley?"

"Right as rain, Son." Strange that Tooley always referred to Brad as "Son," even though their only relationship was based solely on many years of friendship and Brad's closeness to Tooley's daughter, Angie. This was in contrast to Doug always calling his son "Bud."

"You knew this stock wasn't too tough," he continued, "so I guess you wanted to test their air. Don't know why you'd have some gunsel belting you down, though, the way these range-land broncs are likely to go over backwards in the chute. You were lucky to get out of there in a nickel of time, especially with some yahoo helping you that don't know what he's doing."

Brad was so preoccupied with this puzzling turn of events, he was barely aware of the nurse's presence until he felt the prick of a needle in his upper arm and almost immediately experienced a warmth permeating his body from his arm to his other extremities. Relief from the pain in his head was welcome, but he still fought complete unconsciousness. There were too many unanswered questions.

As he drifted to the edge of total blackness, Brad was aware of the conversation going on between Doug and Tooley.

"Doug, you got any idea who the hell that joker was that was beltin' him down today?"

"Not a clue. All I heard was his name. Stokes, I think someone said. He's in a room down the hall. Brother's there with him."

"So what happened?"

"Seems that bronc reared over backwards in the chute and instead of pulling Brad out of there, this dummy just hung on and they both ended up under the horse! Lucky they weren't killed."

"How bad was the gunsel hurt? Did you ever hear?"

"Not bad enough, I'm sorry to say. If his brother didn't watch him every minute, I'd go over there and knock the shit out of him myself. Somebody like that oughtn't be allowed around the arena."

"Well, you can't always judge a book under the covers. If this was a pro rodeo, he wouldn't have been allowed. Even then, why would Brad let him…?"

Those were the last words Brad heard before he was completely swallowed by a wave of darkness.

CHAPTER 2

Down the hall in room number 18, Orville Stokes straddled a straight chair and rested his chin on his forearms. As usual, he wore faded green chinos, a bleached green T-shirt under a nylon Chicago Bulls jacket and high-top Reeboks. He tipped his red baseball cap back so it would not obstruct his view, and stared at his brother, Homer. He tried to will his brother awake from his drugged sleep so they could discuss the events of that afternoon.

Just then Homer stirred. The cervical collar around his neck prevented any head movement but his glazed eyes appeared to focus on Orville who was facing him near the foot of the bed.

"Hey, there, little brother," Orville straightened to be sure Homer could see him. "Wish you'd come out of it long enough to explain what you was doin' in the chute with that bronc rider…"

"Gimme my shades first. Lights are killing me…"

Orville stood up and came around to the side of the bed where he carefully placed a pair of dark glasses on his brother's face.

"There you go. Now explain."

Homer, unable to nod his head, wiggled the fingers on his right hand to indicate he heard the order but he still seemed unable to fully understand what was going on. Orville returned to his chair and studied his brother's face while he waited.

Homer's pale green eyes had always been sensitive to any kind of bright light so he was forced to wear dark glasses, even indoors. When upright, he was medium sized with skinny arms and legs, hollow cheeks and bushy eyebrows. He never wore a hat because he felt it mussed his hair. In Orville's opinion, the way he parted it in the middle made him look like Dagwood Bumsted, anyway, but he never had the heart to say so. It was kind of like the situation with his nickname from grade school. Orville always felt that the kids called Homer "Gopher" because of his thin face and extreme overbite, but when Homer mistakenly assumed that the name referred to his being the one who was always sent to "go fer" this and "go fer" that, Orville again protected his younger brother's feelings by agreeing with that opinion.

Orville was so intent on getting an explanation out of Homer that he barely heard the knock. The door opened slightly and a face with small dark eyes topped with a flat brimmed black hat appeared.

"Hey there, Dude? Can we come in…?"

At first Orville did not recognize the intruder until he saw the complete picture: snakeskin hatband, leather pants, sheepskin vest and beaded moccasins. He jumped out of the chair and rushed forward.

"Papoose! You sonofabitch, where'd you come from?"

The door swung open wider and the small wiry Blackfoot Indian entered. He was followed by a larger, more muscular man with a broad face and sloping forehead, a non-Indian who appeared to be uncomfortable in this room with strangers. The big man was hatless and wore a plaid shirt, denim vest, and unlaced sneakers. He lumbered into the room with his hands in the hip pockets of a pair of faded levis.

Papoose came toward Orville, hand extended. "Hey, Dude. After that mess at the rodeo today, I thought I'd better check up on you two. I seen Gopher hanging around the bucking chutes, looking' as out of place as a Brahma in a pettin' zoo, and I had to find out what the hell he was up to. He hurt bad?"

Their last meeting had been five years before. The Stokes brothers were released from prison at Deer Lodge, Montana, on the same day as their Blackfoot Indian friend. They were serving a three-year term for petty theft while Papoose, on the other hand, was incarcerated for an illegal scam he pulled on two Chicago cattle buyers. Apparently the swindle occurred outside of the reservation or he would have had to serve his time in a federal prison. During their stay, the three men spent many hours in the prison library, the one place they could hang out without being spied on by other cons. Homer used his interest in plant life as an excuse for being there and Papoose always had his nose in one book or another about herbs and different types of medicine. Orville was there simply to plot various ways to get rich without expending a great deal of physical energy.

With a glance toward the bed, Orville said quietly, "I ain't really sure how he's doing. He just woke up a minute ago…"

Homer strained to observe what was happening but again the neck brace restricted any movement.

"Orvie! Who's there? What's going' on?"

"Just friends, Homer. Remember Papoose?"

The Indian approached the bed and leaned over to peer into the dark glasses. Homer, unable to nod his head, made a slight movement involving his forehead and eyebrows that indicated his awareness of another being in front of his face.

Orville tugged on Papoose's arm and pulled him away from the bed. "Let's give him a little time. He'll come around pretty soon when the dope they gave him wears off…"

The two men moved toward the window and sat in straight-back chairs facing each other.

Papoose nodded toward the man who had accompanied him to the hospital. "That's Ted. Goes by the moniker of *Pinto*."

The larger man simply shrugged his shoulders. Leaning against the wall, he still appeared ill at ease. Without moving his feet, he slid down the wall into a squatting position and wrapped his arms around his knees. At this point, an apple-sized patch of white hair on the back of his head was visible. Pinto.

"You wanna fill me in on what you're doing here?" Papoose asked.

"It's kind of a long story but it all boils down to a kind of mess we got ourselves into with some stolen bearer bonds."

"*You* stole them?"

"Not exactly. We heard about the deal from a couple of guys in a jail cell next to ours in L.A. They tipped us off to a way to make contact and buy them for twenty percent of face value. We were supposed to handle it from there."

Papoose, ever skeptical, asked, "Why didn't they do it themselves?"

"They were both headed for the joint on a five-year stretch and said they hated to see such a good deal fall into the wrong hands. Besides, we agreed to give them a cut if it works out…"

A moan from Homer caused Orville to rush to his bedside.

"Orvie! What're you telling him?" Homer asked hoarsely. "We got enough trouble without you blabbing it all to somebody else."

Orville leaned over to whisper in his brother's ear. "I won't give away anything important, but Papoose might be just the one to help us find those damned bonds that we lost…"

Homer was beginning to twitch, and in a body that was predominantly immobile from the waist up, this was a scary sight for Orville.

"Okay, okay, okay. I won't say no more for now. You just relax and we'll talk as soon as they leave."

Orville returned to stand beside Papoose. "I think we need to give him a chance to rest. Maybe I can meet you later for a beer. By then I should know more about the accident."

Papoose looked puzzled. "You don't know what happened, either?"

"Not really, but I'll fill you in as soon as I learn something. You live around here?"

"Denver. Pinto and me got an apartment in the 5100 block, just north of the intersection on West Colfax where we do most of our work. We stuck around for tonight's performance or we'd a been here sooner. At one time, I rode a few bareback broncs in small shows on the reservation but I kept getting bucked off so fast they had to roll me out of the way to close the chute gate. Since then, I figured I'd rather watch somebody else take the punishment. Now I just *spectate*."

Papoose started toward the door and Pinto slid back to an erect position, following with his hands in his hip pockets.

"Where'll you be later, Papoose?"

"There's a little joint called 'Bar&Q'. Just drinks and pool cues, *not barbecue*. We can pick up a few bucks shooting 8-ball while we wait for you." He glanced toward the inert form on the bed. "Take care, Gopher. You'll be out of here in no time..."

As soon as the door closed behind the two men, Orville returned to his brother's bedside. Homer's upper body had stopped twitching but he continued to clench and unclench his fists.

"Now you wanna tell me what you were doing in the bucking chute today?"

Homer's whining voice reminded Orville of when they were small boys and his brother did something wrong. He always depended upon Orville to cover for him and the little-boy voice generally worked.

"I just thought it was a good chance to get rid of him, Orvie. I saw it on TV once where the guy helping a rider get down on the bronc didn't let go of his belt and the cowboy fell back into the chute and broke his neck."

"But why in hell would you want to kill some yokel you don't even know?"

"But, Orvie," he whimpered, "I *do* know him! Remember that thing at the lake?"

"You mean the day we drowned that FBI agent and I had to fish you out of the water? What about it?"

"Well, it was just bad luck that I got tangled in the anchor chain wrapped around his body. When I got pulled under and you had to drag me back into the boat, this cowboy was joggin' along the shore and I'm pretty sure he seen us. He stopped to tie his shoelaces or something, and he looked right at us."

"So how come you never said nothing?"

Had it been physically possible, Homer would have hung his head. "I was so 'shamed of botchin' that deal I didn't want you to know that somebody maybe could identify us. I was afraid you'd yell at me for makin' it worse."

Orville pulled a chair over to the foot of the bed and straddled it, again in a position where his brother would be able to see his face.

Orville kept his voice deceptively calm, to avoid yelling. "So what happened to your big scheme for getting rid of this yokel?"

"Jeez, Orvie, I don't know. I guess when that horse fell over in the chute, I was tryin' so hard to hang onto the cowboy's belt, the horse came over on top of *both of us!* I had my gloves on, like always, and couldn't let loose of his belt. Somebody helping load me in the ambulance said if the chute had been bigger, him and me would both have been smashed, instead of just banged up a little when they dragged the horse out of there…"

Orville shook his head. He always tried to find some kind of logic in Homer's brainstorms, but as usual it was difficult. His obsession with those damned gloves, for one thing. It was good to wear them when they were on a job, or when he stole a new car, but then he would turn around and leave fingerprints all over the inside of the vehicle, anyway, once they drove it away. This time he had no idea his brother was even near the rodeo arena until the announcer asked for "someone named Orville" to come to the bucking chutes immediately, that his brother had been injured.

"How did you get him to let you help? You don't even look like you belong around a rodeo! And where'd you get that damned dime-store cowboy hat?"

Homer's voice was so weak that Orville had to lean forward to hear his reply.

"I was wearing them new cowboy boots you bought me and when I recognized that man, I figured I could pass as a rodeo hand so I bought the hat off of a hot-dog vendor. I just climbed up the back of the chute like I knew what I was doing. Maybe I shoulda waited..."

"Maybe so." Orville realized that Homer had gone back to sleep so he stood up, moved over to rearrange the bed covers, and quietly slipped out of the room.

Just as he stepped into the hallway, Orville caught sight of the man he had been following earlier in the day. This man, in his fifties, was the reason the Stokes brothers came to the rodeo in the first place. He and a man in coveralls were emerging from room 23 and heading for the exit at the rear of the hospital. Orville dropped in behind them and stayed within earshot until they reached the parking lot. With any luck, they might lead him to the horse trailer now and he could search it after they headed downtown for some chow. No doubt they, too, had missed their evening meal during the hospital vigil and he wanted to inspect the trailer before the evening performance.

"What d'you think, Doug," the man in coveralls asked, "Brad going to be okay?"

"I think so, Tooley. The doc says he has a couple of cracked ribs and he got whacked on the head pretty hard..."

So the man with the pickup camper was named Doug. That was the first clue Orville had as to the identity of the person who now had possession of the bonds. All he knew was that he and Homer had to hide their cache in a hurry when the FBI man showed up. It was all pretty involved after the bonds were passed on to them near Little Bear Lake. They had met in a cabin belonging to a mobster known only as the "boss man" who had financed the transaction because of the investment/payoff ratio. During the arrival and disposal of the stranger that they assumed was sent to arrest them and confiscate the bonds, the hiding place selected for their "booty" was the manger of a horse trailer parked behind a cabin a few hundred yards from their own location. The bonds were originally in a brown leather briefcase until Orville transferred them into Homer's Acme Boot box.

Since that time, not one single opportunity had presented itself for them to retrieve THE BOX as they now referred to their loot. Either this man Doug was loading up his gear or his horse was already in the trailer nibbling hay that was frighteningly close to the Acme box filled with one hundred grand in bearer bonds. Orville had been following Doug and felt he was closing in on the now empty trailer at the very moment when he heard the announcement about Homer being injured. Now he would have to start his search all over again by waiting for Doug to lead him to the loot. All of those horse-hauling vehicles looked alike to Orville and he couldn't take any chances by pawing through every horseless trailer parked at the rodeo grounds.

Orville hated driving. Homer was the automobile man with his expertise limited to stealing cars, some of which were barely an improvement over walking from place to place, and seeing to their upkeep. He piloted the various machines from one "job" to the next.

Orville took care of all other plans, including execution of same, but at the moment he simply bemoaned his bad luck that their current vehicle turned out to be a beat-up old Chevy with a stick shift. With his cursing vying for dominance over the noise of grinding gears, he followed Doug's pickup-camper as closely as he felt was advisable, only to discover they were headed toward the center of the town instead of to the rodeo grounds.

The small hospital was located in a wooded area on a hillside south of town. From the parking lot, it was possible to view the entire village, (population 1,401 according to a sign on the highway). A narrow road called Gravel Alley wound its way down to where it crossed Colorado Highway 119 to continue on toward the rodeo grounds. Although the street was now paved, it was apparent that the improvement was not considered sufficient cause for replacing the original name.

Orville kept an eye on the pickup truck when it turned left on CO-119 and proceeded along the five-block main street, passing Bear Cave Drive and a cross street with the optimistic name of City Center Avenue. Doug turned right at the next intersection, Cattle Drive Road, and pulled into a space in front of the Bar&Q.

Orville drove on to the end of the block where he made a U-turn at the next corner. He came back to park the Chevy three cars away from the pickup, only slightly scraping the side of a Ford Taurus in the process. He stepped out of the Chevy and saw the two men entering the pool hall.

Doug and his companion nearly collided with Papoose who pushed through the front door at that exact moment with Pinto lumbering closely behind him. Papoose was talking into a small cellular phone when they stopped in front of Orville.

Papoose closed the phone with a snap and shoved it into the pocket of his sheepskin vest. "Sorry. Gotta head for the city. Big order for some of my home-grown grass and they want it tonight…"

"You into that stuff now, Papoose? Make much wampum or is it just a sideline?"

Papoose's reply was muffled as the two men hurried past.

"It's a living. See you tomorrow, Dude…"

They disappeared into the darkness.

The Bar&Q was a narrow pool hall wedged between a hardware store and an auto supply business. Orville eased through the door and stepped to one side where he could survey the room in semi-darkness. This was a long-standing habit developed through years of casing possible robbery sites and/or checking for lawmen after the fact. The familiar odor of stale beer and second-hand smoke made him feel comfortable with the surroundings even though most of the customers in this small town bar were either rodeo cowboys or local residents.

Makeshift lighting over the pool tables consisted of two inexpensive Tiffany-type fixtures above each playing area. With a total of four tables along the left side, this arrangement offered very little illumination to the booths at the far end of the room. Neon beer signs and black-and-white TV sets at either end of the back-bar gave off enough light for Orville to locate the man named Doug seated beside his companion, so he eased onto a stool two seats away from them.

"So what d'ya think, Tooley?" Doug was saying. "Brad don't seem to remember his accident."

"Damned if I know. I've heard about things like this. I think they call it some kind of *magnesia*. Give him a couple of days, he'll come out of it. You got somebody else to team rope with you or will you just drop out?"

"Do me a favor, Tooley? You said you already put Skeeter in his stall and fed him, right? After we finish our beer, let's pick up a couple of tacos across the street and I'll take you back to the fairgrounds where I need you to tell the rodeo secretary I'm defaulting in the roping event. Will you do that for me?"

"Sure, Doug. What else you sign up for?"

"Just hazing for Tom Lizenbee in the bulldogging, that's all. Anyway, for now, I really need to spend the night at the hospital with Brad. When he wakes up he's going to want some answers. Maybe I ought to take him some chow, too, for later."

"Sure enough, Doug, if you just don't go getting' drunk tonight. Brad worries when you get into trouble…"

"Promise. Okay?"

Tooley put his hand on Doug's shoulder. "I'll keep Smoky there with my dogs, too, so don't you worry none. It's bad enough to have your kid laid up…"

Orville nearly spilled his beer when he heard the last statement. So the bronc rider Homer was after was Doug's son! Once they got THE BOX back from these yokels, he and Homer had better hit the road and get out of Colorado before the cowboy remembered what really took place when Homer almost drowned.

It appeared to Orville that there was nothing to be gained by tailing the pickup any longer so he headed back to the hospital. On the way, he stopped at a service station to gas up the Chevy.

"Looks like you got a low tire, sir," the teenage attendant said. "Right rear. Want I should put some air in it for you?"

"Sure. I guess so. Just fill it up." Orville noticed a puzzled expression on the boy's face but decided the kid probably wasn't too bright so he just paid for the gas and drove away.

CHAPTER 3

Brad's attempt to roll over onto his side caused such a spasm of pain he awoke with an outburst of, "Oh *shit*! What the hell's happening…?"

Doug jumped from his chair by the window and charged over to Brad's bedside.

"Hey, Bud! Glad you're awake. You had a good long rest after your last shot. It's almost midnight and the doc says you can get out of here tomorrow if you don't have no more headaches."

"And if I *do*?"

"Possible they might send you to Denver for a CT-scan…"

"No way! Just get me out of his place. All this confusion is driving me nuts."

"Tooley says you'll probably remember everything in a day or two and you shouldn't worry about it for now. He's taking care of Skeeter and your dog, so just relax."

"I'm sure you're right, but somehow relying on *Doctor Tooley's* medical opinion isn't very comforting…"

"Well, the law of averages, he's got to be right once in a while! Anyhow, can I get you something? Juice? Food? The taco I brought you is cold by now and you slept through your supper."

Brad fumbled for the crank to adjust his bed but finally had to give in and ask Doug to help him to a partial sitting position. He really wanted to talk to his cousin Gary, a Phoenix policeman. The two had been raised like brothers after Gary's father died in a car accident and his mother was hospitalized a great deal of the time due to various illnesses. They even attended Arizona State University in Tempe, Arizona, at the same time. Gary would tell him the truth about the recent *missing days* if he knew the answers.

"Doug, would you see if you can get me some toast and a glass of milk? I hate to ring for nurses at this time of night and maybe you can scrounge up something without causing too much of a fuss…"

"Sure, Bud. Anything else?"

"Yeah. How about handing me the phone before you go? I'm not sure where my cell phone is…"

"Phone? At *midnight*? I doubt if you can even get an outside line…"

"Well, I'll try. I need to talk to Gary. He won't care what time it is."

Reluctantly Doug moved the phone within Brad's reach and left the room, shaking his head. Brad had a direct outside line and the call was completed almost immediately.

"Gary?" he said, when he heard his cousin's sleepy consent to accepting a collect call. "Hate to wake you but I really need some answers…"

Gary confirmed that Doug had called him earlier with news of Brad's accident in the saddle bronc riding event.

"When did you decide to start that old shit again, Cuz? I thought you were just tagging along to keep Doug out of trouble, and maybe do a little team roping."

"Damned if I know, Gary. I'll clue you in as soon as I figure it out myself. I've been breaking a few colts in my spare time in New Mexico, but I'm sure not in any condition to try something as stupid as competing again." He hesitated. "Tell me something, is my truck at your place? I'm still trying to get things straight in my head…"

There was a pause at the other end of the line.

"That calico-colored junk heap? Nope, it's not here. Why'd you ask? Are you okay, Cuz?"

"Yeah, sure. Just confused. You're sure it isn't there? I don't remember bringing it to Colorado."

"You better get some rest, Cuz. You don't sound too good. Josie says to tell you to quit massaging your scar. She knows that ever since that doggin' steer stuck his horn through your cheek, you have a habit of rubbing that spot whenever you're worried. Oh, I forgot! After that little blonde groupie complimented you on your cute *dimple*, we're not supposed to refer to it as a *scar* any more!"

"You're sure a comfort." Brad jerked his right hand away from his face. "Besides, I'm not doing any such thing. And to get back to the subject of my truck, you're sure it's not there?"

"How many times you want me to tell you? I'm positive! Besides, if I had that patched-up pile of metal in my yard, I'd either hide it from my neighbors or give it a paint job…"

"Don't you dare. You'd spoil the effect of the four replaced fenders. "Hey, Doug's coming back so I gotta hang up. I'll call again when I get more info. Give Josie my love and tell her I'm sorry to call so late."

"Aw shit, Cuz. Don't worry about anything. Just take care of yourself…"

* * *

Orville slowly opened the door to Homer's room. His brother was awake and in approximately the same position as he had been earlier in the day with his chin resting on the cervical collar and his vision directed at the ceiling. The supper tray appeared untouched.

"Where you been, Orvie?" he whined. "I needed you to feed me. You know I can't do nothing' when you ain't around…"

Orville moved around the bed to see if he could salvage enough of the unappetizing food to get both of them through until breakfast.

"Sorry, Homer. I really needed to get out and do some snooping, and it's a damned good thing I did. Wait till you hear what I found out!"

"So tell me, Orvie," he whimpered. "Hope it's important enough to leave me here, starving' to death. I wouldn't let the nurse feed me. You never know what these small town hicks might be up to. Maybe someone squealed about that FBI man and the Feds are tryin' to kill me…"

"I'm here now, so don't worry. We can both eat something while I tell you about it."

While they nibbled on cold mashed potatoes, peas and sliced ham, Orville retraced his steps of the past two hours. He told of following Doug and eavesdropping on the conversation with his friend Tooley. When he reached the part about Doug being the father of the man Homer tried to kill that afternoon, Homer nearly choked.

"Jeez, Orvie. Now what do we do? We can't bump either one of them off until we get THE BOX back. Right? Maybe the cowboy knows where it is. What do we do now?"

"We're safe for awhile on that score. It seems the cowboy don't remember nothing for the past week or so. All I need now is time to figure out how to handle things. The old man dropped out of the steer roping but he's staying here for some 'hazing', whatever the hell that is, so we need to locate where the trailer's parked before the rodeo's over. Even if we find THE BOX, we might have to get rid of those two just to protect ourselves. It's possible that Brad, that's the cowboy's name, might get his memory back and we don't know but what the dad maybe even got a peek at the bonds. This is real bad…"

"What about Mr. Bossman, Orvie? Weren't you supposed to call him after we closed our deal?"

"Yeah. That's another thing. We've got to tell him something pretty quick or he'll send one of his thugs to check on us. And just a reminder, he *is* the boss man of the L.A. area but his name is not *Mister Bossman*, in case we ever meet up with him. I don't even know his real name, only where to phone him…"

"Sorry, Orvie. I forgot."

"To get back to our problems, if Papoose was here, he'd know what to do. Wish I could get hold of him but he didn't give me his cell number…"

"I know what it is, Orvie! I know! Will that really help?"

"Sure. But how the hell would you know it?"

"'Cause I remember things, Orvie. We were on E-block, cell number 26. Papoose was right next door in E-27." He sounded delighted for a moment, then skeptical. "But I doubt the warden'll cough up a forwardin' address, especially for you and me!"

Orville shook his head and took a deep breath before he answered, "You're right, Homer. Just eat your food and try to rest. I'll stretch out on a couple of chairs while I figure how to pay your bill and get you out of here tomorrow. Maybe one of them credit cards we lifted in L.A. will do the trick…"

CHAPTER 4

Brad was surprised that he had actually fallen asleep. He awoke to see the sunshine reflecting off of Doug's balding head where he was stretched out on a small love seat near the window. Before waking his father, Brad struggled to summon up even one small recollection of the past days.

How many days? One? Two?

He might bluff his way through if he could just pick up a single clue. Doug began to stir.

"Hi, ya, Bud." He moaned and groaned as he struggled to his feet. "Every day it's that much tougher to get these old bones moving, 'specially when my five-eight frame is jammed into a four-foot-six sofa!"

"We can take care of most of our problems this morning, Doug. My New Mexico sheriff's insurance is still in effect while I'm on leave, so let's get me out of here and go line up a partner for you in the team roping."

"Sorry, Bud. I told Tooley to default us when you got hurt. I can always pick up a few bucks hazing for Tom in the dogging, or by farming out Skeeter to one of the steer ropers. We'll worry about that when the time comes."

It was nearly ten o'clock by the time Brad was released. The mousy little doctor had flitted in, poked at all of Brad's sore spots and flitted back out after taping his chest so tight that the simple act of breathing was a real effort. It was agreed that a CT-scan did not seem to be called for at the present time.

Painfully, Brad managed to get dressed with Doug's help, putting on the Nike running shoes and navy blue warmups that his father brought to the hospital. Unable to tie his own shoe laces, the thought popped into his head that his daily run would no doubt be postponed for at least a few days. But how many? He was not even sure how long he had been in the hospital.

While Brad was waiting for a clerk at the front desk, he noticed two men in the lobby who were partially hidden behind a redwood planter overflowing with an enormous rubber plant. Doug nudged him and nodded in their direction.

"That one with the neck brace is the gunsel who almost got you killed," Doug whispered. "Looks like he's trying to avoid you, but it's me he'd better steer clear of. If we don't vamoose, I just might tear his head plumb off right now…"

Between pages of insurance instructions, Brad gestured toward the Stokes with his ball-point pen.

"That him? The runt? Looks like he's already hurting enough, and none of us needs any more trouble."

After signing the rest of the insurance papers, Brad stepped through the front door and paused for a moment to lean against a life-sized statue of a bear. He noted the "Bear Claw Hospital 1984" inscription and wondered briefly about the town's background. Was it a small town? Big? Any hotels? How far from Denver?

While he waited for Doug to bring his pickup around to the entrance, Brad realized he was able to determine an answer to at least one of his questions: Bear Claw itself. He gazed out over what was obviously a small town at the edge of a broad valley where grazing cattle dotted the fields on either side of a winding stream. A few fenced-in haystacks were visible and what appeared to be a narrow trail for horses or cattle led into the dense forest on the far side of the valley. While hoping for at least one thing that might seem familiar, the scent of the surrounding pine trees and sage brush stirred only distant memories but offered no clue to his immediate past.

Just before Doug arrived, Brad caught a glimpse of an old grey Chevy lurching around the corner of the hospital, gears grinding. Someone wearing a red baseball cap struggled at the wheel. At first glance Brad did not recognize the man as one of the two from the hospital lobby but the neck brace on his companion gave away their identity. The men must have slipped out through a different exit, apparently still anxious to avoid a confrontation.

First chance I get, I'll tell that gunsel there's no hard feelings.

Doug parked at the foot of the steps and Brad slowly climbed into the cab-over camper. Even with his father's help, he was too sore to crawl up onto the bunk bed so he stretched out on the sofa-seat of the breakfast nook.

"I'll rest in here until we get to my truck. I've got a bedroll in the camper and I can sleep there for awhile after I pick up Smoky from Tooley."

Doug frowned and seemed about to say something. Instead, he tossed Brad a pillow and closed the door. At the sound of the pickup engine turning over, Brad once again struggled to unravel the mystery of his missing days.

* * *

"Jeez, Orvie, see what I told you? That cowboy pointed right at us? I knew damned well he saw us dump that body!"

"It don't matter if he did. Like I told you, he don't remember nothing. It's the old man that's got me worried, but I am glad you ducked behind that damned bush, just in case."

"Okay, Orvie, but you gotta drive for the next day or so. I can't move my head too good."

"Yeah, I know. Let's find a place to stay in this hick town and we'll figure what to do next."

"Shouldn't we let them cowboys pass us so we can follow them to the horse trailer?"

"We could. But first we see about vacancies in this burg. We can locate them two later…"

"Jeez, Orvie! Can't you change gears without tearing' up the transmission? Maybe I oughta drive."

"No, I'll get the hang of it pretty soon. You can't even turn your head! How do you expect to drive?"

They reached the CO 119 intersection and turned left toward town.

* * *

Brad winced each time Doug's pickup slowed down, stopped and moved on. Since he did not remember the layout of the town or rodeo grounds he only assumed they had arrived a short time later when he heard his father call out to someone after they stopped and the engine was turned off.

"Tooley," Doug said, "you take care of everything?"

"Sure did, friend. Hated to default you out of the ropin', though. I had mixed commotions about you losin' your entry money but I did like you told me, anyhow. With a little more time I mighta found a sub for Brad."

The camper door opened and Tooley stuck his head in. "How you doin', Son? Ready to try another bronc?"

Brad suppressed a groan at the very thought of getting jerked around by some wild mustang. He assumed from what Doug told him about his decision to ride here, that this was a small local rodeo without sufficient funds to hire a major contractor to supply the livestock. Untried green broncs were much more apt to attempt to jump over the chute gate or fall over backwards, either there or in the arena.

Brad raised his head an inch or so from the pillow. He attempted a grin. "You bet I'm ready. Only one thing keeping me from trying: I can't get my ass off of this damn sofa!"

Doug appeared in the doorway. "Brad wants to sleep in his pickup but since he left it at Gorman's cabin, I'll just put him up here for a day or so." He and Tooley exchanged knowing glances.

They're trying to fill in the blanks for me. I guess Doug knows I'm still in a fog.

"There's somebody here…" Tooley began.

Just then Smoky crowded between the two men and leaped onto Brad's chest before anyone could stop him.

"Oh, *shit*!" The pain was so intense Brad felt he might pass out but he didn't want to scare his "calico" Australian Shepherd so he eased Smoky onto the floor beside him and rubbed the dog's ears. He consoled the animal by saying softly, "Hey, there pal. Been behaving yourself? I'm here now so everything's gonna be okay…"

Doug and Tooley stepped back and closed the door. Their voices grew fainter as the two men walked away.

* * *

Orville hurried from the office of the Cub's Den Motel and grinned at his brother. "Guess what? The owner has a small travel trailer out back and we can rent it for a couple of days! He even let me pay with one of them credit cards. Maybe our luck's changing. Suppose?"

Homer had to turn his entire upper body toward the car window to look in Orville's direction. Despite his discomfort, he was able to offer a faint smile. "Jeez, Orvie. Ain't it about *time*? Nothing's gone right on this whole trip and on top of that, if we don't tell Mr. Bossman somethin' pretty soon, we're gonna end up D-E-D, dead!"

"Not to worry, little brother. I already got a call in to him, and the motel manager said he'd let us know as soon as there's an answer."

Orville climbed into the car. He turned on the ignition without depressing the clutch. The Chevy, still in third gear, lurched forward and only an iron railing around the front steps prevented the car from plowing into the motel lobby.

Homer slammed into the dashboard. "Jeez, Orvie. Can't you see I'm *hurting*?"

The engine stalled and Orville began cussing the car. "Why'd you steal a goddamn freak like this in the first place? I never know what this fucking car is gonna to do next!"

Homer tried to shake his head but the cervical collar prevented any side motion so he just stomped his feet. "I don't care what you say, tomorrow *I'm* gonna drive!"

The trailer was small, about twenty feet long. The inside appeared to be clean, furnished with one high-backed chair near the front door, a small Formica table and chairs in the center, and a fourteen-inch TV on a shelf that was visible from any of these locations, including the one double bed across the front end. Once the Stokes brothers had stashed their gear inside, they walked around the corner and crossed the street to get something to eat at the Come-N-Get-It Café. Orville became impatient with Homer's whining about the meager selection offered on the menu and was about to tell him so when the son of the motel owner rushed in to say that the long distance call had come through.

"You stay here, Homer, and order us some chow. Get me a hamburger steak, medium, and some fries. Black coffee. I'll be right back."

"But Orvie…" Homer began.

"Just order. And *shut up!*"

"How can I do *both*?"

As he hurried toward the front door, Orville could hear his brother still muttering.

When Orville returned, he was experiencing a strange combination of relief and concern. "Well, I told them. I said we'd been robbed and that two rodeo hands had the bonds."

"Did they buy it?"

"Damned if I know. All they said was to keep an eye on the cowboys and if they hadn't heard anything in three or four days they'd help us check things out."

"Why'd they say that?"

"Guess they're not too happy with the way we handled this deal."

"You never told them about the FBI man, did you?"

"Shit, no! If they knew the feds almost had us cornered, they'd *never* trust us again..."

"Well, anyway, Orvie. The rodeo'll be starting in a couple of hours so lets get out there and find THE BOX. Maybe if we got good news for Mr. Bossman the next time you call him, they'll figure we're okay. Huh, Orvie?"

"Yeah. Right. So eat up, and let's go bond-hunting..."

CHAPTER 5

Orville and Homer yelled at each other all the way to the rodeo grounds.

"Why don't you just let *me* drive before you tear all the gears out of this rig?"

"Sure! That'd be real smart to give you a chance to run over somebody. Dammit, man, you can't even turn your head to check traffic and all we need is for you to crash into the local law or something…"

"Okay, okay, okay," Homer whined, "but for chrissakes *use the clutch!*"

They turned left off of CO-119 to the rodeo grounds. The entire area was encircled by a pole fence topped with three rows of barbed wire and the only entrance was through an archway that consisted of two large poles set about fifteen feet apart with a "BEAR CLAW RODEO" sign hanging on a chain between them.

Two men, wearing money-aprons over their western garb, held up signs stating that a two-dollar parking fee was required for any car not designated as a "contestant vehicle."

"Tell 'em I been working here, Orvie!"

"Naw. It's easier to pay the two bucks than attract any attention." Orville exchanged two one-dollar bills for a car sticker and a program then drove on through with the Chevy lurching and grinding.

To the right of the entrance was the rodeo arena. It looked much larger than it did the day before, now that the place was relatively empty, but as they drove around they saw some men who were handling the stock for the roping events at the north end and others with the bucking stock at the south end. A few contestants were visible, mostly men exercising their horses on the race track. Orville presumed these horses were to be used for the roping and bulldogging events but there was no sign of Doug.

A few early birds were already taking their seats in the grandstand that faced toward the east to avoid the afternoon sun but the free bleacher seats across the way were practically empty.

"See our man anyplace, Orvie? If we could locate that horse trailer we could search it while the rodeo's going' on."

"Yeah. We'll find it today. I know we will…"

A narrow stream bordered the far side of the arena. A row of cottonwood trees furnished shade for the various campers whose small trailers or Indian-style tepees were scattered along the fence. While slowly driving by, Orville noted there was a narrow foot gate allowing access to the creek and one cowboy was in the process of bringing two buckets of water back to his pickup camper. A teenage boy appeared to be teaching two youngsters seated along the bank how to bait their hooks with worms and cast their lines into the open water. Women and children milled around the area.

One cowboy practiced roping by throwing loops over a wooden replica of a calf's head attached to a bale of hay. A few feet away, a small boy who looked to be about four-years-old (no doubt the cowboy's son), had his own target. A midget "calf" had been built using four pieces of two-inch pipe for the legs; it appeared that these were then welded to a three-foot length of pipe (the spine) to which a set of steer horns were attached for the "head." The youngster looked every bit as serious about his workout as did the adult roper.

A young cowboy, probably in his late teens, was braiding strands of rope together, apparently in preparation for the bull riding event. Orville was fascinated with coverage of rodeos on ESPN, especially the riding events. While they cruised the area, he explained to Homer how the bull-riding rope was used, and how the cowbell hanging beneath the animal was put there for the purpose of dislodging the rope at the end of a ride and had nothing to do with the noise from the bell during the event. Orville specifically remembered one closeup showing a bull rider in the chute, just before the gate was thrown open. The rider slid his gloved hand, palm up, under the braided rope after it was pulled through the noose end and doubled back. At this point the cowboy took a single wrap around his hand with the loose end, gripped the two layers of rope stretched across his palm, and with a nod of his head the lopsided challenge began of a man against a one-ton Brahma bull. Orville had never done anything remotely courageous in his life but vicariously he felt a strong need to watch another human going against such uneven odds. Somehow he also felt the need to try and live up to Homer's unrealistic opinion of his big brother's infallibility. To Homer, Orville's only flaw was his inability to master the workings of the automobile. Orville sincerely hoped his brother would never come to realize that this was simply one of his *many* weaknesses.

They moved slowly around the north end of the rodeo grounds, trying to pick out Doug's camper among the twenty or so parked along the tree-lined fence. Orville hoped his brother would be able to recognize the vehicle since he was always aware of the vintage and model of nearly anything on the road, but even Homer was stymied by so many look-alikes crammed into such a small camping area. They circled to the north of the stables and were just turning south again past a row of about thirty-five horse trailers when Orville spotted Doug and his friend Tooley heading for the stable entrance.

"There he is, Orvie! I bet that's where he keeps his horse, the one he had at the cabin, remember? It's red colored with white hair on its face and legs."

"They're called sorrels, Homer. I learned that much watching TV. Anyway, all we gotta do now is wait 'til he goes after his saddle. We're almost home free!"

Orville slowed the Chevy as much as possible to keep pace with the two men who were now leading the horse toward a tank of water. He forgot to gear down and when the engine died, the car lurched to a stop about twenty feet from Doug and Tooley.

"That does it! Get out from behind the wheel. *I'M GONNA DRIVE!*" Homer climbed out, banging his head in the process, and circled around to the driver's side.

"Get back in the car, you dumb shit! They'll wonder what we're doing here…"

Orville realized it was too late. Doug and Tooley had already stopped and turned around to see what was causing the commotion. He heard Doug say, "*That asshole better stay out of my way or we're gonna tangle yet…no matter what Brad says…*"

Rather than call any more attention to themselves, Orville quietly circled around the back of the car and climbed into the passenger's side. He was so furious at Homer by then he could barely speak.

"Just drive this fucking-assed vehicle down there where they're parking the cars. We'll *walk* back over here and follow them when they ain't watching." Orville bit off each word in a hoarse whisper. He knew it was imperative to control his anger or they could forget ever regaining THE BOX. So far, it appeared no-one was aware of their underlying dilemma and it was important to keep it that way.

* * *

Brad and his dog stepped out of the camper slowly and looked around at the various activities of the contestants and their families. Smoky seemed aware that Brad was moving slower than usual and he cautiously followed at his master's heels. Several rodeo hands called out greetings and/or words of concern for Brad's condition.

"Anybody seen my old man?" he asked of anyone within earshot.

"He's over by the horse barns. I saw him and Tooley watering Skeeter a while ago." It was Tom Lizenbee. "Doug's hazing for me in the doggin' today…if he stays sober, that is…"

Brad looked at Tom, expecting to see some sign that the man was joking but soon realized the sarcasm was intentional. He remembered, then, that Tom had been left without a hazer at the rodeo in Arizona a couple of weeks before when Doug ended up in jail for starting a drunken brawl at a local bar. It was a surprise that they were working together again but no doubt Tom figured it was worth giving Doug another chance since he and Skeeter were considered top notch hazers when Brad's father managed to stay sober.

"Thanks, Tom. I'll find him…"

As he turned toward the horse barn, Brad noticed six Ben Hur style chariots lined up along the north fence. He turned back to Tom and pointed in that direction. "What the hell are those things, Tom?"

"Some rodeo promoter in Wyoming added chariot racing as a special event a couple of years ago and one of the locals here in town has been training to compete this summer. He got a few of his friends to dress up in short skirts and helmets and they do four laps of the race track while they try to keep them things right-side-up. They keep running into each other and falling out of their rigs. It's gets pretty wild…"

"I can see where it might!"

Brad approached the stable from the east side and saw Doug leading Skeeter by a halter rope with Tooley trailing along behind them, apparently talking to no-one in particular.

"Whatcha doing wandering around out here, Bud?" Doug asked. "I thought you'd sleep through the rest of the day. Need anything? We can go up town and get some chow or get a hamburger at one of the concession stands over by the arena."

Tooley caught up with them. "I can rustle up some grub in my *castle* if you'd like."

He had remodeled a moving van into living quarters several years before, after his wife died. Even with space in the back to store equipment needed for his sheepdog act, he still managed to design a fairly comfortable interior for himself and his three Australian Shepherds. He often bragged that his daughter Angie had "womanized" the place with the addition of curtains and a few other accessories.

"No, I don't need anything right now. Thanks anyway. I'm just prowling around, getting a little exercise. I doubt if I'll be up to jogging for a few days yet..." Brad still avoided mention of the fact that he was desperately trying to find something familiar about the rodeo grounds. "Tom says you're hazing for him today. Right, Doug? I'll go to the arena with you, when you're ready."

"Okay. But first we need to stop over at Tooley's. He didn't have a key to the front compartment of my horse trailer so he put my saddle and the rest of my gear in his van when I went to the hospital with you."

"Sure, Doug. You two go ahead. Smoky and I are moving kind of slow right now but we'll catch up with you in a few minutes..."

By the time Brad reached Tooley's *castle* where it was parked in the shade of a large cottonwood tree at the northeast corner of the rodeo grounds, Doug had already saddled Skeeter and was tying him to a nearby fence post. Tooley's sheepdogs were romping in an enclosure that he referred to as their "playpen," an expandable fence that formed a round corral which he always set up next to where he parked his rig.

Brad attempted to leave his dog outside with his "cousins" but Smoky persisted in following right at Brad's heels, even when they climbed the steps into Tooley's kitchen.

"Take a seat, Bud. Want to leave the mongrel in the playpen?"

"No. He'll be okay. He's kind of looking after me..."

Doug came through the doorway just then and came over to sit beside Brad in a breakfast nook next to a side window. He glanced toward where Tooley was lighting a gas burner and fussing with a coffee maker anchored to the counter.

"Don't go to no trouble for us, Tooley," Doug said. "We can pick up something over at the arena."

"No trouble. I'll just brew us some coffee and grill some ham and cheese sandwiches. We can relax for a little while before I have to unload the sheep for my act. This is such a small setup here in Bear Claw that the man I rent them from has to haul the sheep in from his place every morning because there's no extra pens for them over-night."

"Want me to put Smoky outside, Bud?"

"No thanks, Doug. He's pretty much glued to my heels for now. Maybe he and I'll help Tooley with the sheep…"

"Just don't try to rush it, Bud."

Brad was looking around the small kitchen at the blue and white checkered curtains with matching covers for the coffee maker, toaster and blender. He again thought of Angie's hand in decorating her father's living quarters. Only a couple of weeks ago Brad, his cousin Gary and an FBI friend called Laredo had saved the life of Angie and her husband. *That much he remembered!* They had also been instrumental in having them placed in protective custody with changed names, location, and all that goes with such an arrangement.

"Hear anything about where Angie and Chip ended up, or how they're doing?"

"She's called me a couple of times but she has to be pretty careful. A rodeo clown I know thought he spotted her in Florida hustling some joker in an 8-ball game!"

"That sounds familiar. She say what they're doing for a living?"

"They're both workin' for some kind of magazine. Chip's a book-keeper, y'know, and Angie's a pretty fair photographer. Sounds like their boss must be a nice friendly Italian guy 'cause she said she worked for 'Papa Ratzi.' That's about all I know."

"Think they'll ever be able to come back to a normal life, if you can call rodeoing *normal*? It must be tough on you not being able to get in touch with her."

Tooley turned and looked out of the window as if he thought he might actually see his only living relative loping by on her palomino trick-riding horse like she had so many times throughout the years. Without answering, he self-consciously brushed his eyes with the sleeve of his flannel shirt and continued fixing lunch.

"Got any cream'n sugar?" Doug asked when Tooley set three mugs of steaming coffee on the table.

"Nope. Sorry. I like my coffee *barefooted*, so I never keep any fixin's around."

"I could go for a little Irish coffee, Tooley. Got any booze hid around here someplace?" Doug asked hopefully.

Tooley and Brad exchanged glances.

"Not a drop, Doug. Not a drop."

CHAPTER 6

Orville and Homer discovered Doug's present location when they saw his horse, already saddled and tied to the fence next to a large moving van. The red and white lettering "SEAN O'TOOLE'S FAMOUS SHEP-HERD DOGS" covered almost the entire length of the side visible to them so they knew it belonged to Doug's friend, Tooley.

"See what you *did*, Orvie? If you knew how to drive a damned car, we coulda followed 'em when they went for the saddle and we wouldn't have been spotted. Now whadda we do?"

Homer's whining seemed more irritating than usual but Orville was too tired to argue any more. After they parked the Chevy, they had hurried back on foot for the full length of the rodeo grounds only to discover they were too late and would need to reconnoiter (a word Orville heard recently on TV and considered it a clever addition to his limited vocabulary). Puffing and panting, the two men went through the foot-gate to sit by the creek in the shade. One of the small boys was showing off a trout he had just pulled out of the water.

"Pull my shoes off for me, Orvie? I want to soak my feet and I can't bend over far enough to untie them…"

"Sure, Homer. Sure."

* * *

Despite protests from Tooley, Brad offered to help with the sheep when they had finished their lunch. With Smoky at his heels, he soon regretted the decision because any move to climb a fence or even open a corral gate caused more pain than he had anticipated. Doug rode past where they were unloading and apparently sensed Brad's discomfort because he dismounted and handed the reins to his son.

"Why don't you hang on to Skeeter for me, Bud? I'll help Tooley finish up."

"Whatever you say, Doug..." For once it felt good to be babied.

When the sheep were locked in a holding pen at the south end of the arena, Tooley left to change clothes and get his dogs. Doug walked back to bring his pickup over and park it near the bucking chutes. He said this way Brad could watch the rodeo in considerably more comfort than would be afforded by grandstand seating.

With Skeeter tied to the fence, the two men and Smoky climbed into the cab to watch the Grand Entry of local riders, rodeo entrants, flag bearers and clowns. One of the chariots, pulled by two grey horses in ornately decorated harnesses, joined the procession but since the strange contraption spooked all of the other horses, the driver trailed about thirty feet behind the rest.

As soon as the arena was cleared, pickup men loped their horses around, preparing for the bareback riding which was the first event. As usual, Brad enjoyed watching the bucking horses, and for today at least, was glad to be on the sideline. At these smaller rodeos, there were a few of the untested broncs that did not buck as hard as the riders would have liked, but also due to these horses being green off-the-range mustangs, sometimes they put on a wilder show than the more professional stock.

Several riders bucked off. Two horses tried to jump over the arena fence and one came out of the chute without a rider.

"Did the announcer say T.D. Rollins was next? Is he still trying to make a living out of these little shows?"

"Sure is, Bud. He makes most of his money by feeding the locals a line about how good he is and getting four or five of them to pay his entry fees. He uses cash from one of them to enter the event and pockets the rest. He always promises each man a piece of the purse but he never wins so nobody's the wiser…"

"There he comes! He's making a pretty fair ride. Looks like he'll make it." Brad leaned forward, watching in disbelief. "So what happened? He just flat let go of the rigging before the whistle!"

Doug snickered, "Figure it out, Bud. He probably had five or six sponsors that each gave him enough money to enter and if he promised every one of them the usual thirty percent, *he doesn't dare win!*"

"That's quite a racket he's got. Does he ever win an event on the square?"

"Not that I know of. He's kind of a joke among the real hands but I guess it takes all kinds. He's pretty much of a blow-hard and behind his back they call him 'Rowels' because even when he's around town after the rodeo, he never takes off his spurs. I heard one of the cowboys ask T.D.'s girl friend if he *ever* took them off. She said, 'Well, let's put it this way, he sure tears the hell out of a lot of bed sheets!'"

"When are you up, Doug?"

"Calf roping's next, then saddle broncs, then dogging. I'll sit here a little longer, then I'd better lope Skeeter around and loosen him up. I'd sure love a drink…"

"*Doug!*"

"Just kidding. I told Tooley I'd take it cool for awhile, at least while you're on the mend. Okay?"

"Okay. It's just that right now I might have trouble getting along if you get thrown in the can again…"

* * *

Orville and Homer hobbled toward the arena, puffing and wheezing. "Jeez, Orvie, can't we go sit down while you're figuring out what to do?"

"Sure. Why not? You take a seat over in the bleachers where you don't need a ticket and I'll get us a couple of burgers. Be sure to sit on the bottom row near the end so I can get out quick when I see that Doug person head for his horse trailer the next time."

"Be sure my burger is well done, Orvie, and get me some fries without too much salt…"

"Yeah, yeah, yeah…" Orville hurried away, afraid he might say something he would be sorry for. After all, Homer meant well, it was just that he kind of got on your nerves at times.

In a way, Orville was glad his brother remained on the far side of the arena. There was always a problem whenever Homer got within *smelling* distance of the popcorn, cotton candy and hot dogs; he always loaded up on so much junk that they could barely carry it all and with their bankroll pretty much limited at the moment, Orville tried to keep their spending under control. Stolen credit cards were of no use whatsoever as far as most food purchases were concerned, and certainly not at a rodeo concession stand. When he returned with their food, he found Homer in the center of the bleachers, at least thirty feet from either exit.

"Dammit, Homer, didn't I tell you to get a seat *near the end* so I could get out of here fast when Doug finishes whatever it is he does? We've *got* to find that horse trailer before somebody looks inside THE BOX!"

"Sorry, Orvie," Homer whimpered. "I thought you'd be pleased with seats on the forty-yard line!"

"This ain't a fucking football game, Homer. You gotta give me some help here or we'll never come out of this alive. Come on now, lets move down by the gate."

* * *

After watching the calf roping, Doug loped away on Skeeter. Smoky whined softly until Brad opened the door and let him in. The dog lay on the seat with his head in Brad's lap and only moved occasionally to look up at Brad as though checking to be sure everything was all right.

"I'm okay, fella. We'll be back to our Frisbee-catching games in no time…"

There were no real surprises in the saddle bronc riding. Some of the horses bucked, some did not; some fell over in the chute, and some tried to jump the arena fence. The local pickup men showed their inexperience by not being exactly sure how to retrieve the few riders who were still aboard after the whistle blew. At a small rodeo, it was sometimes almost as dangerous for the rider after the whistle as it was during his ride. Only four of the riders "qualified" by spurring the bronc for the required number of jumps out of the chute, while avoiding contact with the animal with his free hand, and still remaining in the saddle at the end of the ride.

Tom and Doug were next to the last in the bulldogging event that afternoon. The previous team was already departing through a gate at the south end of the arena as Tom and Doug entered from the north end. They backed their horses into the narrow stalls on either side of the chute where the steer was penned. Tom was on the left side so he would be in a position to lean to his right and grab the animal by the horns when it was released from the chute and crossed the line giving the steer a short head-start. His horse lunged out of the stall too soon but since the gate had not yet been opened, there was no penalty and he backed his mount into position again. It was Doug's job to ride on the right side and crowd the steer toward the left, in position for Tom to make his move. The timing was crucial and everything went like clockwork. From the time the steer was released until Tom had grabbed it by the horns, twisted it to the ground with all four legs straight out from its body, only 5.6 seconds had elapsed. Even at a larger rodeo this would have been pretty good "time," so for this show it should be fast enough to put him in first or second place. Doug would get a share of the winnings for being Tom's "hazer."

Tom remounted his horse and followed Doug who was already on his way out of the arena.

* * *

As soon as Tom Lizenbee and Doug Hastings had been announced as the next team in the bulldogging event, Orville jumped to his feet. He leaned over and spoke to Homer, much more harshly than he could remember having done before.

"You stay right here. Do you hear me? Right here!" He felt like taking his brother by the shoulders and shaking him to be sure he understood, but how can you mistreat a man who already has a six-inch-wide collar around his neck, who is tomato red from sunburn, and whose eyes (behind the dark glasses) you know are pleading for pity? You just hope that for a change he will follow orders. "I'm gonna be waiting for Doug when he gets through, and by damn, *this time* he won't get away from me!"

Orville ran around to the south side of the arena to the gate through which he had seen the previous contestants exit after they performed. He crouched down into what he considered a good "starting" position like he remembered racers doing on TV, and this time he felt he was ready. Nothing could stop him. During the time it took Orville to run from his seat in the bleachers to the gate at the south end of the arena, Tom had already bulldogged his steer and Doug was on his way out. Orville was surprised at Doug finishing so soon and he had no time to catch his breath before the gate swung open and Doug's horse loped through it and rounded the south end of the arena heading for the barns again. And, as Orville hoped, toward the horse trailer, which was the ultimate target.

Not until Orville ran the full length of the arena to reach the north end, gasping for breath, did it dawn on him that he could have waited at *that end* for Doug to ride past since their goal was at the north end of the rodeo grounds.

"Dammit!" he gasped for breath. "Why does he have to run that fucking horse all the way to the barn? Don't they ever just *walk* them animals?"

The horse barns and trailers were at least three or four football fields away and Orville began to slow to a walk. He felt like he wanted to sit down and give up. Just then he saw a chariot pulled by a team of grey horses driven by a man wearing some kind of a gold trimmed dress and a funny metallic-looking hat with pointed spikes on the top. The horses that pulled the chariot were walking slowly and the driver appeared to be casually looking around as though to see if people were impressed with his get-up.

Orville ran over to the chariot, jumped on the back to stand beside the driver, pointed toward Doug and yelled, "Follow that horse!"

The driver was so stunned, his only reaction was to try and push Orville out of the narrow one-man vehicle.

"Get away from me, you idiot!" the driver yelled. He grabbed a long whip out of its sheath on the right side of the chariot, and tried to hit Orville with the butt end.

As the two men struggled, the whip accidentally hit the rear end of one of the horses and he lunged, tipping the front end of the chariot upward. The driver was thrown out. By now the horses were racing toward the north end of the rodeo grounds, which was okay with Orville, except for the fact that the reins were dragging on the ground and all he could do was hang on to the front of the chariot to keep from falling out. Somewhere beyond the flying manes of the greys, Orville could see Doug, who by now had slowed his horse to a walk and was approaching a horse trailer where he dismounted. The left rein of the chariot horses' harness had become entangled in the wheel on that side and it was forcing the team to run in a circle which gradually became smaller and smaller.

Orville felt he was now close enough to his goal that he could ditch the chariot and walk the rest of the way, but he was not quite sure how to dismount from this strange contraption. As it gradually slowed down, he decided to leap out. When he thought about it afterwards, he could never understand exactly why he did it, but he pulled his red baseball cap down over his ears, hitched up his pants, *held his nose*, and jumped!

Orville could hear people yelling from somewhere in the vicinity of the rodeo arena and he knew he had better make himself scarce as soon as possible. He was not quite sure in what category of crime "chariot snatching" might fall, but this was not a good time to test the water. He got to his feet, escaped from the danger zone and sauntered away in the direction of the row of horse trailers. As soon as he was positive he could identify which one belonged to Doug, he stepped back between two other trailers and tried to make himself less recognizable. Lucky his Bulls' jacket was still in the Chevy. It would have been too obvious. He pulled off his khaki shirt and tied it around his waist, then carefully folded his baseball cap so as not to damage the beak, and tucked it into his hip pocket. With only a pale green T-shirt on his upper body, he felt confident that none of the local yokels would connect him with his most recent escapade.

The return jaunt to where he left Homer did not seem so unsurmountable now that he finally had something upbeat to tell his brother, so he ducked behind the trailers and followed along the fence to the arena without confronting any of the rodeo crew who were still trying to stop the two-horse merry-go-round.

CHAPTER 7

Brad rolled down the window to get some air and he saw Tooley heading for the arena, apparently in a hurry as indicated by his eighty-five degree angle of forward tilt.

Tooley had changed into the style of garb he created years before to portray a sheep man from the Australian Outback. The high-top boots with a leather tassel on either side and the leather pants with matching vest could actually have been representative of several parts of the world, but a western style hat with the brim on the left side clipped to the crown gave it the desired Aussie flavor. The three dogs trailing him completed the picture.

By the time Doug reached his pickup and crawled in with Smoky and Brad, it was nearly time for Tooley's act.

"Suppose he needs any help, Doug?"

"Nope, nothing we can do but sit back and watch the show. I never get tired of watching them dogs work."

The announcer began his spiel about the next act, explaining to the crowd that over twenty sheep would be turned loose in the arena with three Australian Shepherds to herd them. First the dogs would divide the sheep into three groups, one for each dog to maneuver. With just a slight motion of Mr. O'Toole's hand or a slight nod of his head, the dogs would move the three herds to separate areas of the arena, then eventually combine them into one group before driving them back into the catch pens.

"Smoky always runs back and forth outside the fence while they perform. I think he'd like to get in there and help." Brad opened the door on his side to allow the dog to jump out but Smoky simply looked up, put his head back down on his Brad's lap and closed his eyes. "Not today, huh, Pal?" He rubbed the soft fur behind Smoky's ears then slowly closed the car door.

"You see the ruckus over by the horse barn a while ago, Bud?"

"No, I was watching the trick-riding. There's a teenaged girl here that's really good. Reminds me a little of Angie when she first started. Anyway, what ruckus are you talking about?"

"Just a lot of confusion, but it had nothing to do with me so I stowed my gear and put Skeeter away. I'll go back later to feed him some oats."

"Ever see what the fuss was about?"

"Damned if I know. A team of them chariot horses got loose and when I came by, the damned fool animals were running around in a circle with about ten people trying to catch them…"

* * *

Orville arrived at the rodeo arena, out of breath from hurrying back to report his good news to Homer. Surprisingly, his brother was still sitting in the same spot where he had been instructed to stay.

"Where you been, Orvie? You sure been gone a long time. I was scared you might not come back for me."

"You know better, Homer. I'd never leave you even for a little while if I could help it. Anyway, guess what? I found the trailer!"

"You did? Can we go there now, Orvie? Can we?" Homer still had to turn his entire body sideways to look at Orville. "I seen that Doug person and his son sittin' in a pickup truck right over there by the fence just a few minutes ago." He tried to nod his head in that direction but finally pointed with his elbow when the nodding gesture proved impossible.

"Good! Give me a minute to catch my breath and we'll get the car and head over there right now. No use taking a chance that they might move that rig…"

Moments later the Stokes brothers parked the Chevy in front of Doug's horse trailer. They discussed the danger of someone seeing their car at the scene of a robbery but decided it was needed as a shield to hide their activity. Besides, they agreed, the whole project shouldn't take more than a couple of minutes, and anyway, it wasn't really robbery if you were just taking back your own property. Right?

There was one thing wrong with the plan. THE BOX was no longer in the manger of the trailer where they had left it! Homer, wearing his gloves for no particular reason, stood watch while Orville frantically pawed through all of the loose hay in the manger and even kicked at the straw under his feet in case THE BOX and been dislodged and had fallen over the edge.

"Sonofabitch! It ain't here, Homer. The goddamned thing ain't here."

"Jeez, Orvie. Now whadda we do?" Homer was nearly in tears. "You think they found it and turned it over to the feds? Maybe that's why that *feebie* showed up at the cabin. Suppose?"

Orville stepped out of the trailer's narrow side exit and rested his forehead on the door. After a few seconds he began banging his head repeatedly against the side of the trailer until Homer pulled him away.

"Don't, Orvie. Don't hurt yourself. We just gotta think this thing through. Maybe they put THE BOX someplace else without even looking' inside. Suppose?"

Orville stopped slamming his head against the trailer and stood quietly for a few minutes, thinking.

"I seen him open the front end of this thing once when he put his saddle away. It's kind of a storage area. Maybe you're right. They mighta moved THE BOX without looking to see what was in it. I did have it tied up pretty good with some twine string. Right?"

"Right, Orvie. Let's check it out."

Both men stepped around to the front of the trailer and stopped, staring at the front compartment.

"Jeez, Orvie. I seen people's houses with them kind of key locks but never a damned storage box! Now whadda we do?"

Orville just shook his head and slumped over the front fender of their car.

"You ain't gonna throw up, are you, Orvie? We'll figure somethin' out."

"Shit, no." Orville raised his head slowly and turned around to open the door of the Chevy on the driver's side. "We'll just have to reconnoiter and try again later. We better get out of here before somebody sees us…"

"Think we can locate this trailer at night?"

"Maybe not. You got anything I can mark it with before we leave? Some way to help us spot it later?"

"There's still a roll of reflector tape under the front seat. I used it a couple of times to mark cars so I could steal them when it got dark. Would that help, Orvie?"

"Just the thing. Hold on. I'll be right back."

Orville quickly grabbed the tape and used his pocket knife to cut a small piece off of the end. In seconds he had attached the strip to the trailer hitch and was back under the steering wheel of the Chevy, ready to leave.

Apparently Homer decided this was not the time to argue about who was going to drive because he removed his gloves and climbed into the passenger side of the car, quietly closing the door.

"There's no use hanging around here any longer, Homer. Let's go back to the motel and think things over. Okay?"

"Okay, Orvie. You know best…"

They rode in silence most of the way into town. Homer stood it as long as he could before asking cautiously, "You know how to pick a lock, Orvie? Maybe it ain't as tough as you think."

Orville just stared at the road.

More silence.

Just before they reached the center of town, Orville pounded on the steering wheel with his fist and turned to Homer. "Damned if I ain't got it figured out! Papoose used to rob houses all the time before his stretch in the pen. I'll bet if anybody could get into the front of that trailer it'd be him!"

"See, Orvie? You always come up with the answer, right?"

* * *

Brad was beginning to feel tired. The bandages around his rib cage were so tight they still caused him a great deal of discomfort, and now the throbbing head ache had returned for the first time since his release from the hospital.

"Maybe I'll climb in the back and lay down for awhile, Doug. Okay?"

"Sure, Bud, but we can just pull over by Tooley's rig and park for the night, if you want."

"Don't you want to watch the bull riding?"

"Naw. I'm ready to leave. These days the bulls are so rank, even in small-town rodeos, all you get to see is the chute gate swing open and some cowboy fly through the air. They tell me last year at the Nationals, if a bull rider made the whistle he'd be a cinch for first, second or third place, 'cause no more than two or three of them made qualified rides in each go-round." Doug started the engine and backed away from the fence before continuing. "I hear that one of the toughest Brahma bulls ever seen anywhere was retired in 1995 during the National Finals in Vegas. Bodacious was owned by Andrews Rodeo, Inc. and *Bo*, that's what they call him, had a hell of a record against the cowboys when Sammy Andrews said they were taking him out "while he was still on top.""

They reached the north end of the rodeo grounds and Brad opened the door to let Smoky jump out on his side. He was still curious to know more about the famous Brahma.

"I don't mind admitting that those bull riders have more guts than I do and I'm damned glad I never had any desire to go that route. At least a saddle bronc won't take out after you when he bucks you off! Anyone ever ride Bodacious?"

"I don't know a whole lot about him, Bud. Only what I hear around the arena. I do know the bull was not completely *unrideable*...."

Doug went on to tell about the few who managed to qualify on the famous bull were a cinch to have the high point ride in whatever go-round they drew him. An Oklahoma bull-rider named Terry West rode Bo in San Antonio. He scored 87 points, but he says he still has memories of the bull being responsible for his punctured lung in 1994 and said after the San Antonio ride, "I really don't ever want him again."

"Bo ever kill anybody, as far as you know?"

"Not that I heard of, Bud. Someone said that Tuff Hedeman, from some place in Texas, was one of Bo's latest victims. Hedeman was slammed in the face when Bo swung his head back just as Hedeman was being jerked foreward, and Tuff spent more than six hours in the hospital operating room for reconstructive surgery on his face."

Doug climbed down from his side of the pickup. "Ready to go inside, Bud?"

"Sure. Any time..."

Doug climbed into the camper first, and Brad watched through the door as his dad prepared a place for him to sack out. He removed Brad's Resistol hat from the top of the dinette table, crown down to protect the brim, and folded the table upward against the wall where it was held in place with a hook-and-eye latch. Before he pulled the dinette bench out to form a double bed, Doug started to toss the Resistol onto his bunk over the truck's cab.

"*Don't you dare!*" Brad yelled. "I've had enough bad luck without you putting my hat on your bed!"

Doug shrugged, silent. Since Brad only admitted to that one superstition, Doug apparently decided it was allowable. He spread out a large sleeping bag and got an extra bed pillow from his bunk before moving aside to give Brad a hand at climbing the outside steps.

Brad knew Doug was trying to avoid the implication that his son needed to be treated like an invalid, but he also appreciated the fact that his dad was aware of the discomfort caused by the strain of almost any movement. At this point, all he wanted to do was stretch out and rest. Once Brad had kicked off his Nikes and removed his sweat pants, he crawled into the sleeping bag. Smoky checked him out and seemed satisfied with the situation, then turned around and trotted back outside.

"I'll let you get some rest, Bud. Smoky'll be in the pen with the other dogs, and after I help Tooley load the sheep back into the semi, I'll take care of Skeeter. Tooley and me might catch a ride into town later on. That way we won't need to bounce you around in here. Need anything?"

Brad heard Doug's voice as though it were coming through a long tunnel. He wanted assurance that his dad would stay sober, and out of trouble, but there was no sense bringing it up now. Either it happened or it didn't…

CHAPTER 8

Orville decided to take Homer to the Bar&Q for a sandwich and a beer on the off chance that Papoose might drop in there when the rodeo ended. Although they had not seen him since the day before, the odds were in favor of his being present somewhere around the arena for every performance. When their ill-fated experience at the horse trailer proved to be just another in a long series of set-backs, they had wanted their departure from the rodeo grounds to be as low-profile as possible. Now, if they did not connect with Papoose at the pool hall, Orville decided they would just have to *reconnoiter* and try locating him later in the evening.

Orville played two or three games of pool while they waited for their food to be prepared, but Homer gave up after his first disastrous attempt to hit the cue ball. Because of the cervical collar, when Homer bent over to shoot he was unable to get his face out of the way when he stroked the ball. The cue stick banged against his chin so hard that he dropped the cue on the floor.

"I'll just wait for you in our booth, Orvie," he complained. "I can't have no fun at all no more."

By the time they were through eating, the Stokes had decided to go back to their motel and stay out of sight in the camp trailer they were renting. Before they finished their drinks, Doug and Tooley came in and sat down in the adjoining booth.

"Jeez, Orvie…"

"Shhh! Listen up. We might learn something."

"Let's just scram out of here, Orvie, before they see us."

"Why? We ain't done nothing…at least nothing they know about. We'll just sit tight and see if we can't pick up on what they're gonna do tonight."

After Doug and Tooley ordered, their conversation turned to Brad and his current condition.

"You headed for another show right away, Doug?"

"I told Brad we should go back to Gorman's cabin for a week but he insists we head for Estes Park tomorrow after I'm through here. Says it's good for me to stay busy. Sober's what he really means. Sometimes I get tired of staring at a glass of naked ice cubes, without a splash of booze, but I guess you can get used to anything…"

"It'll only be for two days so I suppose he's right, but you gotta admit, you're less apt to get into trouble out in the hills!"

"Yeah, but I don't like them *waterin' holes* so damned far apart! And what about you? You traveling north, too?"

"Nope. Angie's in-laws, the Olsens, live over in Golden so I'm going to spend a few days with them before I head for Elsie, Nebraska. I'll give you their phone number, though, in case you need to reach me. Like if Brad has any problems or anything…"

"Look, Orvie!" Homer was sitting sideways in their booth, facing the front entrance. Orville knew by his expression that he was wide-eyed behind the dark glasses, but he quickly motioned to his brother to be quiet. Orville had already spotted Papoose and Pinto shoving their way through the crowd at the bar as they headed for the pool tables and he had to avoid meeting them in full view of Doug and his friend.

"C'mon, Homer. You slip out the back door, down that hallway past the men's can. You're too easy to spot with that thing on your neck. I'll get the car and pick you up in the alley as soon as I give Papoose the high-sign not to let on he knows us. If we're gonna work something out with him, we better not be seen together."

Reluctantly, Homer followed orders. As soon as he was out of sight, Orville tossed a dollar bill on the table for the waitress and walked toward Papoose, shaking his head slightly to let the Indian know he was not to speak to him.

"Meet me in the alley in fifteen minutes," Orville said softly as the two passed each other near the bar. Papoose stared straight ahead and showed no obvious sign of recognition except an almost imperceptible wink. Orville left through the front door and drove around past the hardware store to the alley where Homer was waiting.

It was actually closer to thirty minutes before Papoose and Pinto approached the Chevy.

"Sorry, we had a trouble gettin' away from the pool game. We won a few bucks and had to promise we'd come back to give 'em a chance to get even. So what's up, Dude?" Papoose spoke for both of them as usual. In fact, Orville had begun to wonder if the man named Pinto ever talked at all.

The Stokes' dilemma had reached the point where it seemed necessary to share the whole story with Papoose, including the fact that Brad Hastings had witnessed the murder, if they were to ask for his help. Orville explained about hiding the bonds and then not being able to retrieve them after they got rid of the FBI agent.

"How'd you know who he was?"

"Had to be a fed," Orville explained. "Who else would be out there in the woods spying on two men with a hundred grand in stolen bonds?"

Papoose thought the part about Gopher getting tangled in the anchor chain, and getting pulled overboard with the corpse, was hilarious, but Homer became defensive at the laughter and pouted until they changed the subject.

The four men sat in the Chevy and discussed the pros and cons of how to burglarize the horse trailer. In fact, the irony of the situation was not wasted on Papoose. "Who better to handle this than a couple of burglary *pros* and four *cons*? My man Pinto here is one of the best lockmen I've ever worked with…"

For the first time, Pinto showed signs of paying attention. Following Papoose's accolade, there was a flicker of something that was almost a smile. In a flash it was gone.

When Papoose heard that the boss man in California already knew of the loss of the bonds, he began suggesting more profitable ways to handle the situation than to turn the loot over to the gangsters, if and when the bonds were recovered.

"Since you already told those dudes in L.A. that the bonds were stolen, why not just keep the stash for yourselves whenever you get it back? For a twenty percent of the take, Pinto and me'll help you get the bonds out of that trailer and unload 'em to a fence. Ain't that better than splitting with a bunch of dudes you hardly know?"

Homer had been facing forward, but now he managed to turn his body sideways in the front seat so he could look at Orville.

"Jeez, Orvie. I don't know. We got to think on this a little. We ought to give part of the take to those guys that steered us to the bonds in the first place…"

"Yeah, you're right. We got a lot of time and trouble invested in this thing, Papoose, and besides this is a big chance for us to get a foot in the door with them *biggies* in California. We can't just throw away something like that."

"Okay, but you think it over for a minute," Papoose reminded them, "if you let anyone know you've made money on this deal, word could get back to the big man that you recovered the bonds, or maybe never lost them in the first place! Then where'll you be?"

Papoose and Pinto climbed out of the back seat of the Chevy. Before walking away, Papoose leaned into the window on Orville's side. "Talk it over before tonight, Dude. We'll see you and Gopher next to the grandstand about eight o'clock and if all systems are go, we'll take it from there..."

* * *

Brad realized it was after dark when he awoke. He checked the small refrigerator for anything edible but outside of one slice of moldy cheese, he drew a blank. He opened the front door and looked toward the arena to see if any events had started yet. Because he heard Grand Entry music in the distance he knew the evening performance was underway.

Apparently Doug had been keeping an eye on the camper from Tooley's doorway because he immediately came down the steps and hurried toward where Brad was standing.

"Hi ya, Bud! Feeling any better? You had a pretty good nap."

"I'm not sure, Doug. I haven't been awake long enough to analyze *how* I feel. Except hungry. I just realized it's been a while since I ate anything."

"We've got time to run into town and get you some chow if you want. Need to go right now, though, so I can be back here to haze for Tom..."

"No, it's not that urgent. I can pick up a burger at one of the concession stands. That'll hold me over until you get through."

"They sell pizza, too, if that sounds any better. Want me to drive you there now? We need to take the rig to the arena anyway; Tom reminded me this afternoon that we have to pick up your Association saddle and buck-rein over there in the tack room. I put your chaps and spurs in my pickup but I forgot all about the rest of your stuff when you had your accident..."

Brad eased down the steps and closed the door behind him. "Pizza sounds good. I'll get Smoky, then I'm ready whenever you are."

At mention of his saddle, Brad had a *Twilight Zone* feeling that recurred each time there was talk of his bronc ride. The sore ribs were a constant reminder that there was, in fact, credence to the story, but so far nothing in his brain could confirm it. When they reached a small shed at the south end of the arena, both men went inside so Brad could identify his own gear. They found the saddle immediately, but it took a while to locate his buck rein which had been tossed into a pile of miscellaneous equipment in one corner. Most cowboys have their own preferred style of braiding the rope that is fastened to the halter of the saddle bronc he rides. These buck reins might all appear to be pretty much the same to an outsider, but for the bronc rider, it is his "life line," and being familiar with the size and texture could mean the difference between hanging on or having the rein jerked away from him.

Doug loaded the equipment into the pickup and said he would transfer it into the storage area of the horse trailer later. Brad held the camper door open and at that moment he had a brief flash of memory. Hadn't Doug or Tooley said earlier that Brad's pickup was at Gorman's cabin? Was that where they had transferred his equipment to Doug's horse trailer as he now seemed to recall? Or maybe he was simply stringing together a logical sequence of events after hearing Doug refer to the Association saddle that he always carried in the back of his Ford truck. Better not mention any of his feelings to Doug until he could get things straight in his mind.

* * *

Orville saw Papoose leaning against the counter at the pizza concession and signaled for him to meet them under the grandstand.

"What's up, Dude? You getting' jumpy in your old age?"

"Yeah. Only when I have to. That man in the jogging suit is the one Homer tried to kill. His old man has our bonds."

"You mean the character that was standing next to me at the pizza stand? He don't look like no cowboy to me…"

"Right! Now you see why I steered you away from there? Since he got hurt he ain't dressed like no rodeo hand."

"When you're right, you're right. So tell me, what's the verdict…we *on* or ain't we?"

"Pull your car over in back of the bleachers where we parked the Chevy, and we'll talk."

In a matter of minutes a plan had solidified. There were a couple of hitches that were not completely ironed out, but all four of the participants agreed that those decisions were not vital to the immediate plans. For now, breaking into the horse trailer was the big concern. The only concern.

Pinto grabbed Papoose by the arm and whispered something to him.

Papoose nodded. "We'll follow you over in my car. Best you don't hang around after you point out the trailer to us. It might attract too much attention. Once we get the bonds, we'll high tail it out of here and meet you in town. Okay, Dude? Gopher?"

"Sure. You won't have to break the lock, will you? Better if they don't notice right away that they been robbed..."

"Not to worry, Dude. Pinto could break into the White House and not leave a clue!"

"Super! You know where the Cub's Den Motel is? Just pull around in back of the office and Homer and me'll be waiting in the travel trailer. Any questions?"

"Not by me. How about you, Pinto?"

Pinto shrugged.

On their way to Doug's horse trailer, Orville was intent on locating the hitch with the reflector tape, but Homer apparently was concerned about something else.

"Orvie! I don't think you oughta just turn Papoose loose with them bonds. How do we know he won't take off? We might never see him *or* THE BOX again, once Pinto gets it out of the trailer. Didja ever think about that? Didja?"

"Yeah, I did, Homer. No matter how good a friend he is, we gotta protect ourselves. We'll just kind of hang around, out of sight, and be sure they don't take off on us."

Orville was surprised that only a few minutes elapsed from the time Papoose parked near Doug's trailer until Pinto jumped back into the car and they headed for the rodeo grounds' exit. As the white Mustang pulled out onto CO 119, their turn signals flashed to indicate a left turn, *away from Bear Claw!*

"See, Orvie! See what I told you? They're running away with THE BOX." Homer was screaming and stomping his feet. "We gotta catch him, Orvie. Go after him!"

At that moment, Orville smiled, realizing what had happened. The car they were following did not make a left turn as the signals indicated; instead, Papoose turned to the right and headed into town.

"You can stop yelling now, Homer. Papoose must'a seen us spying on him and he just wanted to give us a scare!"

Orville was chuckling quietly when they reached their destination and found Papoose and Pinto leaning on the front fender of the Mustang. Both men were grinning. Even Pinto.

No mention was made of the Stokes' suspicions, but at least a point had been made: Orville and Homer had no intentions of letting THE BOX out of their sight again until money exchanged hands (from *someone else* to *them*).

Orville unlocked the trailer and held the door open for Homer and the other two men to enter. As soon as they were inside, he eagerly reached for the package. Instead of handing it to him, Papoose took the Acme Boot box from Pinto put it on the dinette table within reach of each of them.

"Okay, Dude. Show me what a hundred grand looks like!"

It was almost as though all four men held their breath while Orville attempted to undo the complicated knots he had previously tied in the twine string. Quietly, before anyone realized what was happening, Pinto took one swipe with a switch-blade knife that appeared out of nowhere, and severed the triple layers of string.

Orville dumped the stacks of bonds onto the table and one by one the men reached out and touched them cautiously as though the loot might vanish if any rash movement occurred.

"I'll be damned! I never figured you two dudes to be smart enough to pull off something this big! No offense…"

Orville felt extremely proud at that moment, not only because he and Homer really had pulled off something big, but also because someone he admired, like Papoose, was witness to the fact.

"So whadda we do now, Orvie? We gotta figure a safe place for THE BOX until we can turn these things into cash. Huh, Orvie? Huh?"

After several minutes of complete silence, Pinto leaned over and whispered something to Papoose.

"Yeah, that's an idea." Papoose nodded. "Orville, why not see if the motel manager has a safe in his place? At least we could leave the box there until tomorrow when we can decide where to fence this stuff."

"Good idea," Orville agreed. "That'd give us time to reconnoiter…"

"To what?" Papoose snorted. "Where the hell did you come up with a word like that? You been going to college since I last seen you?"

Orville felt a glow of pride again. "Nope. Just a word I picked up somewhere." He leaned back in his chair and tipped the red baseball cap back off of his forehead. "I ain't no dummy, y'know…"

Someone needed to talk to the motel manager. Since there was an unspoken matter of trust, or lack of same, it was agreed that Orville and Papoose should go to the office, with THE BOX. In the meantime, Pinto could make a "beer run" to pick up some drinks and maybe pretzels or chips or something. Half way to the office, Homer caught up with Orville and pulled him off to one side.

"Jeez, Orvie! How do we know that Pinto person won't break into the safe? I don't trust him and his damned whispering!"

Orville put his arm around his brother's shoulder and spoke quietly, "Don't worry, Homer. If the safe don't look burglar-proof, all four of us will just have to sit up all night and watch over THE BOX, and each other. Then tomorrow we'll figure something out…"

"Okay, Orvie. Whatever you think's right." He returned to the trailer.

The motel owner did, in fact, have a fairly sturdy-looking safe and it was in the room where he and his wife slept, which made Orville feel more secure. It was agreed that they leave the package over-night but when Papoose requested that the box be sealed with wide packaging tape before he parted with it, the expression on the motel owner's face indicated that he had doubts concerning the intellect of two men who went to such great lengths to protect a pair of boots. He looked even more puzzled when they demanded individual receipts in each of their names (requiring *both signatures* on whichever receipt was presented) in order to recover the package.

"You know I gotta charge you extra for that trailer if you got more than two people sleeping over…"

"There's only two," Papoose assured him. "Me and my buddy are drivin' back to Denver tonight." He looked at Orville and added, knowingly, "But I'll be *back* first thing tomorrow!"

It was agreed by three voices and one shrug that the Stokes should stay out of sight for the rest of the evening, so they all sat around drinking beer and exchanging stories about their recent past since they were last together.

"Papoose, I don't think you ever did tell us just what kind of a scam you pulled on them cattle buyers," Orville said. "The one that got you sent to Deer Lodge when we was there."

"It was just a cattle deal. I'd pulled it before and got away with it, but this time the buyers wised up and they got us for fraud. I only had to serve a deuce at Deer Lodge."

"What was it you did?" Homer persisted. "I still never heard the details. All you ever talked about when we hung out in the library was all them damned drugs and stuff."

Papoose smiled slyly and tipped his black hat forward to touch the bridge of his nose. "Pretty simple, really. We had close to three hundred head of steers for sale but only about ninety of them were in real good shape...the rest were pretty scrawny from being on poor pasture all summer. What we did was take the buyers out to where we were *supposed* to have all the steers, but in fact we only had the fat bunch and the rest of them were at another location."

"Couldn't they tell the difference between ninety steers and three hundred? They musta been pretty dumb." Orville didn't figure anybody could be that stupid.

"It was pretty easy, really. We drove the two men out to where the ninety head were grazing behind a small butte covered with pine trees, and I told them my friends would drive all three hundred past us so they could look them over."

"And...?"

"And, my friends drove that same herd of ninety fat steers around and around the butte until we figured about three hundred had passed by and then they left them to graze out of sight on the other side of the hill!"

"So how'd you get caught?"

Papoose grinned. "We'd have been okay but I forgot about the two black steers in the bunch that were calves of a couple-a milk cows, and when those two blacks went past us for the third time, all hell broke loose!"

By the time Orville had related the history of the robbery that had been their downfall, all of them agreed that the rodeo had no doubt ended and Papoose wanted to leave town ahead of the crowd. He said he would pick up some food for all of them at a Taco Bell he saw at the north edge of town, and after dropping it off, he and Pinto would head for Denver. Homer was in the middle of telling Papoose exactly how he wanted his food prepared when the door closed in his face.

"Don't worry, Homer," Orville said. "They'll cook it just the way you like it…"

CHAPTER 9

At the rodeo that evening, Brad felt more like getting out and moving around during the performance. Smoky followed at his heels and even chased back and forth along the fence while Tooley's dogs were performing. In the bulldogging, Tom Lizenbee over-ran his steer and grabbed only one horn which resulted in his falling head-first into the dirt. The result was "no time" in the day money and took away his chance of remaining in the average (total "times" for all six performances), to qualify for the finals. With one more "go-round" left, he still had placed first on one steer and third on another which added up to a fair amount of prize money for both him and his hazer, Doug, even if they did not win anything else.

Doug rode over to where Brad was leaning against the fence talking to Jerry Tandy, a bull rider he knew from New Mexico.

"You feel like driving the pickup over to the horse barn in a few minutes, Bud? If not, I can come back and get you…"

"Sure, I can hack it." He grabbed the fence rail for support, feigning collapse. "Might need a boost getting into the cab, but after that I'll be okay!"

Doug laughed and tossed him the keys to his truck.

"You take in a lot of shows this year, Jerry? I noticed earlier you had on one of those elbow braces like most of the other bareback riders."

"Yeah, the stock seems to get tougher every year, and the judging is tighter. If you don't rear back and spur high right out of the chute, you won't get any kind of decent score, no matter how rank the horse is. Without a brace, your elbow might bend plumb backwards. Hyper-extension they call it. We've all learned to take advantage of this protection."

"Earlier Doug was telling me about that bull named Bodacious. You ever draw him?"

"No. I been lucky. Most of the time I just hit the smaller shows where they don't have top-notch bucking stock. I've heard a lot of stories about old Bo, though. They say a Montana bull rider, Scott Breding, rode Bodacious once and even wearing a protective mask, about two seconds into the ride he got knocked cold. He was treated for a concussion and several cuts on his face. Bo's busted so many heads, the boys that drew him started wearing football-type helmets!"

"Don't even mention getting whacked in the head. It hurts me just to think about it!"

"I gotta get ready for my own ride, Brad. He's nothing like Bodacious, but he'll be tough enough, anyway. Take it easy, man. Maybe I'll see you later…"

Brad drove the pickup back to the far end of the rodeo grounds and parked in the same space they had used before. Once Skeeter was put away for the night, and Smoky had joined his cousins in the back section of Tooley's van, Doug, Brad and Tooley drove into town in Doug's pickup to get some food. They saw a small café on the east side of the street next to the grocery store.

"I was going to get some grub to cook for our supper," Tooley said, "but that Come-N-Get-It sounds pretty good. How about letting them do the work tonight?"

"Okay by me," Doug answered when they reached the café, "but be sure and remind me to pick up a fifth of milk and a loaf of bread."

"A *fifth*?" Brad pressed against his ribs with both arms to ease the pain of laughing. "Milk comes in quarts or gallons, Doug. *Booze* comes in fifths."

His father looked sheepish as he pushed ahead of Brad and Tooley, mumbling, "Whatever…"

The smell of fried chicken and barbecue was overpowering as soon as they pushed through the swinging door of the restaurant. It was almost twenty minutes before the waitress showed them to a booth and brought their coffee. She was dressed in a white fringed skirt and vest, and knee-high white boots with red tassels. A red hat was held in place by a braided chin strap that matched her red shirt, and the whole getup pretty much mirrored the "costumes" worn by most of the town's citizens. She tossed three menus on the table and disappeared again.

While they were deciding what to order, Tooley again brought up the subject of the immediate future.

"You're definite about not taking a few days off, Doug? It might give Brad a chance to heal up."

Brad answered for both of them. "Nope. I'm not in that bad a shape, and besides, I figure Doug can win himself some team roping at Estes Park. He won't have any problem finding a partner to take my place. Plenty of ropers'll jump at the chance. Right, Doug?"

Tooley glanced toward Doug who continued to study the menu.

"We need to go back to Gorman's cabin, anyway," Brad continued, "for me to get my pickup. We can both rest up while I try out a new fishing pole I bought in Phoenix." He wanted to give the impression that he now remembered their time at the lake.

"So when is it you're leavin'?" Tooley asked.

Doug placed the menu on the table before answering. "Since there's only the one show on Sunday, I suppose it'll be getting dark by the time the doggin' is over."

"I can load Skeeter and get most of our gear ready while you're waiting for Tom to collect his winnings." Brad added.

"Forget it, Bud. I don't want you over-doing it. If Tom wasn't headed south after this show, I'd just wait and collect my cut from him later. Beside, there's no hellish rush about heading out. I only want to go as far as Nederland, anyway."

"What's in Nederland, Doug?" Tooley asked.

"When she was alive, an old friend of mine, Goldie Cameron, had a bar there for a lot of years. I'd like to see if it's still operating and who's running the place. You ever know her, Tooley?"

"Never had the pleasure, but I heard a lot of the old timers mention the name when I first started rodeoing."

"As a kid, she traveled around the Chicago area with her folks' medicine show, then, when she was seventeen, she joined Buffalo Bill's outfit, trick-riding I think. I met her in 1964 and she was still one pretty lady, running a place called *Goldie's Corral*. I was just a kid but I can remember like it was yesterday, her riding in that rodeo parade. She had on the same dress she wore to get married on horseback in Madison Square Garden in 1913. The local paper said the State Museum in Denver had loaned her the dress just for the parade."

"Ever see her again?" Tooley asked.

"I stopped by the next year when they had a two-day rodeo, and took her to supper. She was in her early seventies by then and I'm sorry to say I never got a chance to get up her way again." He paused and stared down at his hands crossed in front of him. "I'll never forget how she looked on that horse. Just like a queen."

Doug rose to leave the booth. "I'm going to pick up the Denver paper. See how the Broncos are doing."

As soon as he was out of earshot, Brad leaned across the table and asked, "What's the real problem, Tooley? Seems to me a lot of people are freezing Doug out, even at these small shows. Used to be he'd haze for eight or ten doggers at each performance and have ropers standing in line to pair up with him in the team roping…"

"Too much of the old demon *rumble*, I guess. When he's drunk, he either gets in a beef, gets in jail, doesn't show up for his events, or all of the above! Nobody feels they can trust him any more. I'm surprised Lizenbee sticks with him..."

Doug returned and disappeared behind the sport pages while Brad and Tooley changed the subject of their discussion to various fishing lures. At one time, when Tooley's wife was alive, the two of them used to camp out every time a rodeo was held in a town with a nearby trout stream or lake. In the past, he even spent a good deal of time tying his own flies.

The waitress returned and once they had placed their orders, buffalo wings for Brad and steaks for both Tooley and Doug, all of them headed for the mens' room to wash. Brad noticed a pay phone in the hallway, so when he was the first one in and the first one out of the single-sink area, he decided to give Gary a ring while he waited. As near as he could remember, his cellular phone must still be in his pickup truck.

"Operator, I'd like to place a collect call to Lieutenant Gary Hastings in Phoenix, Arizona. If there's no answer at his home, try the Phoenix police department."

Gary's wife, Josie, answered the phone. They chatted for a minute before he heard Gary on the extension.

"What's up, Cuz? You got yourself in some more trouble up there?"

"Not really, but I did get a brief flash of memory today and I have to admit, it felt pretty spooky. At first I had trouble believing everything they told me, but now I guess it's for real. I even know where my calico truck is! So what's happening with you? Anything special?"

"Not much. Of course you know I made detective since you were here..."

"The hell you say! As if you weren't already tough to get along with...now you'll be *impossible*."

"Hey, Cuz, you're in no position to talk. Our friend Laredo came through here today and he was telling me all about you. He still insists he had to do all the work when you two solved three or four murder cases on the reservation in New Mexico…"

"Damn his lyin' hide!" Brad tried to sound serious. "Next time you talk to that old reprobate, you tell him I can solve any case in the books quicker than he can!"

"You might get a chance to tell him yourself. He's flying to Denver next weekend for some kind of get-together of ex FBI men that used to work together and maybe you'll run into him while you're there."

"That I'll do. I can't wait to straighten him out! Anyway, congrats on your promotion. I'd better let you go for now. I've tied up this phone long enough."

"Adios, Cuz…"

"Back at'cha."

Brad was aware of someone in the shadows, apparently waiting to make a call. From what he could see, the man wore a sheepskin vest, levis, and beaded moccasins. Shoulder-length braids were visible, topped by a large black hat that shaded his face.

"Sorry I took so long," Brad said. "It's all yours now…"

The other two were back in their booth, already starting on house salads, with Doug barely picking at his food. No doubt most of his meal would end up in a doggie bag for Smoky. Brad sat across from the two men and shared part of Gary's conversation with them. "Can you believe he made detective already? He hasn't been with them that many years."

"Gary'll do a good job, just like his old uncle Doug!"

"Well, I don't think I'd go *that* far," Brad said, smiling. "Just because you two short husky bulldogs look alike, that doesn't mean either one of you are superior to me. Remember, Grandpa was the tall wiry *hardworking* Hastings that I took after…to say nothing of us being the good looking ones…"

"And don't forget the part about being humble," Tooley interrupted. "Maybe both of you ought to remember that actions are always louder than birds of a feather!"

That one was too much for Brad to decipher so he returned to the topic of his phone call. "Remember my FBI friend, Laredo? He's on his way to Denver next Saturday and Gary says I ought to try and get hold of him if possible. I need to straighten him out about murder cases..."

Brad heard the sound of glass crashing to the floor in the next booth. The man who had been waiting by the telephone, obviously an Indian from his appearance, jumped up and hurried to the counter where he tossed some money to the cashier and picked up two bags of take-out food. A large man in a plaid shirt shuffled behind him with his left hand in the hip pocket of his faded levis and his right hand clutching a half-eaten leg of fried chicken.

* * *

Orville heard the Mustang pull up and he had already opened the trailer door when Papoose charged in with braids flapping. He looked wild-eyed and panicky. He tossed the two bags of food on the table and stood in the middle of the room, arms crossed over his chest.

"You two are in deep shit, Dude! I mean *deep* shit!"

Homer jumped to his feet and nearly toppled over. He still had trouble getting his balance after any sudden moves.

"What's he mean, Orvie? Huh, Orvie?"

"Just be cool. Give the man a chance." Orville tried to sound calm but he knew his voice was getting shrill. "So what *do* you mean, Papoose? What kind of shit are we in that we weren't in before?"

"I'll tell you what kind. At that Taco Bell, there was such a long line at the drive-in window that we decided to get a take-out order of fried chicken from the Come-N-Get-It Café and grab a bite for ourselves while they were cooking it."

"So? What's so bad about that?" Orville prodded.

"Wait 'til you hear! I eavesdropped on that cowboy, the one wearing the jogging suit, when he called some cop in Phoenix and said he was starting to get his memory back! And on top of that, he told his old man and that sheepherder that he was going to meet some FBI man in Denver as soon as he got a chance, to talk about a *murder case!*"

Orville slumped into the high-backed chair and Homer toppled over backwards, trying to sit on the edge of the bed.

"We really are in deep shit, ain't we?" Orville whined. He realized he was starting to sound like Homer. "So what now?"

Papoose sat cross-legged in the middle of an oval-shaped throw rug just inside the front door. To complete the scene, all he needed was a tepee. Pinto did his slide-down-the-wall-to-a-squatting-position act under the TV shelf.

"I been thinking on the way over here, and it seems to me the best way to handle this is for all of us go into Denver tonight. In the morning we'll get a safety deposit box at the bank for the bonds, and come back here tomorrow night to waste them two dudes before they turn you in!"

"Waste them?" Homer's voice squeaked. "Both of them? But how?"

"I'm not sure yet," Papoose frowned. His expression indicated that several solutions might be running through his mind but for the time being, he obviously had not zeroed in on any one idea. "Whatever we do, it's gotta be in the next twenty-four hours. I heard them say they're pulling out tomorrow night for Estes Park so we don't have any time to waste. For now, let's all pile into the Mustang and blow this joint, while we…what is it you said, Dude? While we reconnoiter…"

"Leave our car here? What about THE BOX?"

"We'll go get it back right now. Just leave all your stuff here and you won't have to explain where you're going…"

Without getting to his feet, Pinto waddled over to whisper something to Papoose, then scooted back to his position against the wall.

"Damn! Pinto's right. Tomorrow's Sunday. We can't get to a bank 'til Monday morning…"

"So what's *that* mean?" Homer whined. "You want me and Orvie to stay here and wait for you?"

Papoose and Pinto exchanged knowing glances. Both of them shook their heads to indicate a veto of Homer's suggestion.

"My girlfriend, Maria Sanchez, works in a real estate office in Golden. Pinto and me could take the bonds with us and put 'em in her boss' safe..."

The words were barely out of Papoose's mouth before Orville and Homer practically shouted, "No way! We either take THE BOX along in the car with all four of us, or we leave it in the safe where it is now. Remember, Papoose, two of us have to sign for it at the same time..."

There was total silence in the room. After several minutes, each of the four men nodded in agreement. THE BOX would remain where it was until it was retrieved by Papoose and Orville together on Monday and in the meantime, they all stayed together.

CHAPTER 10

After Orville locked the trailer door, all of them struggled to get Homer into the back seat of the Mustang two-door sedan. The first attempt ended with him toppling forward to become wedged between the two bucket seats where his coat-tail hung up on the gear shift. Orville's tentative suggestion that it might be better for his brother to sit in front elicited such a scathing look from Pinto that the idea was quickly rejected. On the third try, they steered Homer into the car, butt first, with Orville guiding him backwards until he was finally settled next to his brother, whimpering softly.

The Stokes ate their chicken in silence for about thirty minutes, then Orville blurted, "You come up with anything yet, Papoose?"

No answer. Pinto leaned over and whispered something to him.

"Yeah," Papoose said, "we might pull off something like that."

"What? We could do *what*?" Orville realized he was getting shrill again.

"Well, Pinto knows I've got an apartment full of drugs, some modern ones plus a lot of stuff that's carried over from my days on the reservation. My great-grandfather was a medicine man and I learned how to put together all kinds of concoctions. One for any situation. With some of them, I could send a man to the moon without a rocket!"

"You talking about *poisons*?" Homer squeaked. "We ain't ever done nothing like that, have we, Orvie?"

Papoose shook his head. "Maybe we will. Maybe we won't. I've got a couple of ideas. Let's just drop it for now and talk about other things. Sometimes that helps clear my head so I can concentrate better."

"Sure. Whatever you say." Orville realized from now on they had to depend on Papoose to set the pace.

They travelled another fifteen or twenty miles in silence and Orville studied the interior of the car for the first time. The rear window on his side had been replaced by a piece of cardboard stamped THIS SIDE UP, and in the light from a passing car, he noticed there was something hanging from the rear-view mirror that was definitely not a raccoon's tail. He decided it was probably just a souvenir from a coyote Papoose had killed, maybe on the reservation. The snakeskin steering wheel cover and some kind of fake zebra fur on the seats added to the eerie sensation that this was a travelling zoo.

"Mind closing your window, Papoose?" Homer whined. "The wind's mussing up my hair…"

Pinto whispered something to Papoose, who relayed the message, "Pinto wants to know *how can you tell?*"

It became apparent that Homer was pouting about the comment, so Papoose directed the next question right to him in an obvious attempt to smooth things over. "Hey, Gopher. I been meaning to ask you, how come you wear them shades all the time? Even at night…"

Homer's pride in his Dagwood hairdo was always a touchy subject as was anything regarding his personal appearance. To protect his feelings, Orville answered the query himself.

"Ever since he was a little kid, Homer's eyes have been super sensitive. Any flashes of unexpected light and he goes plumb blind for a minute or two."

More silence.

Papoose seemed determined to ease the tension caused by his two attempts at casual conversation. "Tell me, Orville," he asked finally.

"What ever happened to your old lady? Weren't you married before you got sent to the joint?"

"Yeah, I was. Not any more, though." He wanted to avoid details of his breakup. It was still too embarrassing.

Homer started snickering and Orville had the uneasy feeling that those very details were about to be shared with the two men in the front seat.

"Want to know what happened, Papoose?" Homer giggled, the earlier slur already forgotten. "Orvie ain't gonna tell you but I will!"

"They don't want to hear about my family problems, Homer. Just drop it…"

"No. Go ahead, Gopher. Tell us."

"Well, right after all of us got out of Deer Lodge, Orvie and me went into Billings to find his wife, Maizy. He heard from a friend in the stir that she'd been fooling around while we was gone, so he didn't want her to know we was coming."

Orville began to squirm.

"Anyway, we found out she had a room in a three-story house at the edge of town and when we pulled in after dark, Orvie decided to spy on her before she found out we was there. From across the street we seen her and some guy in a service station uniform go through the front door together and when a light came on in a room on the top floor, she pulled the window shade down and we couldn't see if they was together or not."

"So what happened?" Papoose prompted. Apparently Homer was successful in distracting him from their current problems because he sounded eager to hear more. "Was the dude with her or not?"

By now, Homer was so caught up in his story that his words tumbled out one on top of the other. "The only way we could spy on Maizy was to climb up on the roof from an outside stairway. For some reason there was a small sky-light right over her room and I boosted Orvie up so's he could look in. I guess what he saw got him pretty upset because he began banging his head against the roof alongside the skylight, and with that red baseball cap of his, he looked so much like a woodpecker that I started laughing and let go of his legs. When he fell over on me, we both landed in a big elm tree and was hanging onto one of the top branches when Maizy and some naked joker looked out the window and seen us! She screamed at Orvie to get away from there and never come back. I sprained an ankle and Orvie broke his wrist when we dropped out of the tree and that pretty much ended his married life."

At the end of Homer's story, Papoose was nearly doubled over. Even Pinto's shoulders were shaking.

Orville decided it was worth his embarrassment just to see Homer enjoying himself for a change. When the laughter eventually subsided, all was quiet again as they rolled along the highway toward Denver.

Due to Homer's inability to bend his neck, Orville rolled his jacket into a makeshift pillow and placed it in his lap so his brother could get some rest. This presented a problem. When Homer tried to lie down, he tipped over sideways and his feet protruded into mid air. The only solution was for him to prop his legs on the head-rest of the seat in front of him and this resulted in several dirty looks from Pinto. By the time they reached Papoose's apartment, the tension within the group was at a noticeably high level.

On arrival at their destination, Orville needed help once again, this time to hoist Homer into an upright position. It was finally possible to extricate him in a reversal of the system they used at the beginning of the trip. Orville pushed from the rear and the other two men steered Homer through the door on the passenger's side while trying to prevent him from falling on his face before he could get his feet on the ground.

They piled out of the Mustang near the foot of a narrow wooden stairway at the top of which there appeared to be a small landing for entry into the top floor of a weather-beaten two-story house. Several other cars were parked randomly in the graveled area next to a vacant lot that was overgrown with tall sunflowers and tumbleweeds. Empty beer bottles, assorted fast-food containers and old newspapers afforded additional ground cover for this obviously neglected piece of property.

Papoose led the way with Pinto close behind.

Homer hesitated at the foot of the stairs. "Orvie," he whispered. "Hear the way them boards are creaking? I ain't sure them steps'll hold all of us at once!"

"You want to stay down here?"

"In this stinking place? No thanks…"

Orville elected to bring up the rear in case Homer lost his balance, as he had been prone to do since his accident.

"You go ahead, Homer. I'll be right here if anything goes wrong."

The other two men disappeared through a narrow doorway and by the time the Stokes reached the landing, Pinto's face appeared in a round curtainless window of what Orville assumed was the kitchen. As soon as all of them were inside an area that was actually a combination dining, sleeping and semi-kitchen room, Papoose moved toward the door as though to close it.

"That's okay. I'll get it in a few minutes," Orville told him." Because of the stench of rotten food, sour milk, mouse turds and what he assumed was part of the collection of *herbs and weeds,* he knew Homer would never survive if their supply of fresh air was cut off completely.

"I've got a swamp cooler in the back bedroom. Soon as I turn it on we'll get some breeze through here. The old lady that owns this house offered to come up here once a week and clean the place, but I don't want nobody snooping around my stuff so I tell her not to bother."

The floor covering consisted of cracked linoleum in the entry way and a strange conglomeration of unmatched tiles throughout the rest of the area that was visible from the kitchen. The curtains, such as they were, looked like they might dissolve into puffs of dust if anyone accidentally brushed past them too closely.

"You lived here long?" Homer's question came out in the form of a squeak. Because he was so finicky about everything, and for the moment seemed to be turning green, Orville hoped his brother could keep from throwing up until they found an excuse to go back outside. In the event this proved to be unavoidable, however, the result might go unnoticed if the rest of the place turned out to be anything like the kitchen.

"Naw, I don't really live here at all. I spend most of my time at Maria's house in Golden. Pinto stayed here a couple of times when I was out of town, but mostly we only come over if we need to use the lab for some reason."

Orville looked around at the unmade cast-iron bed in one corner and a wooden crate filled with Sears' catalogues. Through an open door in the opposite corner he could see another bed and a white three-drawer dresser, each drawer a different color. He steered Homer through the debris to the only available seating which happened to be lawn furniture that consisted of a dusty wooden bench with two matching chairs. Pinto squatted on his haunches against one of the paint-chipped walls, arms encircling his legs as usual. Above his head was a picture of five dogs playing poker, the only sign of decoration in the room.

Papoose came through a doorway that obviously led to the bathroom since the sound of a flushing toilet had caused screeching and thumping sounds generally caused by air in the water lines.

"Want to take a look at my lab before we go?"

Orville was so grateful for the word "go" that he jumped to his feet and pulled Homer with him. Homer even managed to keep from stumbling despite the quick movement.

When Papoose reached his grimy looking refrigerator, Orville's first thought was, *I hope to hell we ain't come all this way to watch him mix up a batch of spoiled food*! Just as he was expecting Papoose to open the door and display a stack of disgusting garbage, the refrigerator swung out of the way as though on a swivel and displayed a hidden room that was approximately eight feet long and four feet wide. The place had an antiseptic odor, definitely not in keeping with the rest of the apartment. The shelves on either side of a bare, spotless work bench, were neatly stacked with bottles, boxes and small leather pouches. Each item bore a label with small distinct lettering that reflected the contents. The room was so clean and sanitary-appearing, it could very well have been transported in its entirety from a medical clinic laboratory. On three shelves to the right there were assorted volumes with titles reflecting such information as pharmaceutical products, herbs, poisons and even two catalogues of explosive devices.

Papoose stepped aside to let his visitors absorb the full impact of the scene. He pushed his hat back and grinned at them, obviously enjoying their shocked expressions.

"Not quite what you expected, huh, Dude?" he asked.

Both Orville and Homer simply nodded. It was too much to absorb all at once.

"I only come back here to work. With this place looking the way it does, who'd ever suspect I could mix up just about any compound there is, right here is this little room?"

Orville finally found his voice. "You're not gonna do your mixing tonight, are you? We ain't even decided on what to do, so don't we have to talk things over first?"

"Sure, Dude. I just wanted to come by here to see if I needed any supplies." He slid the refrigerator back into its original position. "We'll head out for Maria's place, a nice little three-bedroom house where we can stay. Tomorrow morning we'll start making plans."

Homer looked so delighted that Orville thought he might actually survive.

"Sounds great." Orville could not keep the relief out of his voice. "We're ready when you are…"

They shut off the air conditioning, locked the windows and doors and started down the stairs ahead of Papoose.

"Don't worry about spies, Dude. There's no skylight in my ceiling!" Papoose nudged Orville playfully as they walked toward his car.

Much to Orville's surprise, Pinto allowed Homer to sit in the front seat, probably a concession prompted by the fiasco that took place earlier.

As they drove away, Orville asked, "How come you don't use one of your concoctions to kill off some of those roaches and stuff?"

Papoose answered solemnly, "All critters got a right to live…"

Homer was asleep again when they reached Maria Sanchez' home. It was too dark to see much of the outside of the two-story frame house but the aroma from a lilac bush near the driveway and the wooden porch swing reminded Orville of their grandmother's house in Nebraska. He rarely let himself think about the life he and Homer had before they decided small towns were not for them. After the first time the brothers were arrested, they were too ashamed to contact any members of their family. It was easier to let them believe the boys had gone on to bigger and better things just like they had vowed they would do.

"Come on in, Dude. I'll see if Maria's still awake." Papoose unlocked the front door and turned on a light in the downstairs hallway. "Go on through to the kitchen. I'll be right back."

Orville noticed that Pinto disappeared around the corner of the house when they first arrived. Papoose explained that his friend rented a small apartment over Maria's garage at the rear of the lot and they would see him the next morning. Although Pinto was not a person who aroused great concern for his welfare, Orville felt a certain relief that the man had someplace to live besides the grungy apartment they visited earlier.

Homer sat stiffly on one of the kitchen chairs and appeared on the verge of nodding off again. Orville moved closer so he could catch his brother if he fell asleep and toppled sideways, the only direction in which he was able to fall.

Papoose came back downstairs and offered to show them to their room on the second floor. Maria was asleep and they would meet her in the morning.

"We'll work on a plan tomorrow, right?" Orville asked.

"That's right, Dude. Everything's going to be okay."

CHAPTER 11

Orville slept so soundly it was difficult to remember where he was when Homer poked him in the back.

"Orvie, you gotta help me. I gotta pee and I can't get out of bed by myself."

By the time Orville managed to wrestle him into an upright position, Homer's bathroom needs surpassed his concern for modesty and he hurried down the hall wearing only dark glasses, baggy Superman undershorts and dingy white socks displaying Batman logos. It was an inopportune time for his first meeting with the lady of the house but he just grabbed his crotch, said, "Mornin' ma'am," and hurried past her to the bathroom.

Orville watched the encounter through the partially opened door of his room and he could hear the muffled laughter of Papoose and Maria when they descended the stairs. Homer was so embarrassed it was nearly impossible to convince him it was imperative that they join the others in the kitchen.

"Remember, Homer, if we don't get help from Papoose, we're as good as dead. Just go on downstairs and pretend nothing happened."

"Jeez, Orvie. Can't we wait awhile? Maybe she'll go off to work or something'..."

"Absolutely not. I'm going. You with me, or not?"

Reluctantly Homer followed him to the kitchen. He would have hung his head, had it been possible. As it was, he was forced to face the music head on.

Their hostess, Maria, was a pretty young woman who looked to be in her late twenties. She was dressed in a yellow linen suit with a white ruffled blouse, and wore very little makeup or jewelry. Her dark shoulder-length hair framed an attractive face with high cheekbones and dark eyes. Fortunately for all concerned, she had enough poise to pretend she had never seen Homer before their present encounter in the kitchen. The coffee was ready, having been brewed in a pre-programmed coffee machine.

There was a loud roar and a squeal of tires just before Pinto came through the back door and tossed a box of bakery bagels and a package of cream cheese onto the counter.

"Harley?" Orville asked.

For a moment, it appeared Pinto was going to answer but he just shrugged and Papoose said, "Honda."

Maria had an appointment to show some property that morning so she turned the place over to the odd assortment of men in her kitchen. Orville was somewhat surprised at the lack of frills throughout the house. Maybe he had expected something more like Grandma's place after the fleeting impression from the night before, but it stood to reason that a modern-day working woman required a place that was easier to care for.

Papoose waited until they finished eating before he cleared everything from the table and brought out a legal-sized tablet, two pencils and a ruler.

"Let's get at this, dudes. We've got a lot of thinking to do, and not much time to do it…"

"What'cha think, Papoose," Homer asked anxiously. "You figure a way to get rid of those two Hastings yokels before they turn us in to the law?"

Papoose used the ruler to draw a line down the middle of the top sheet of paper.

"The first thing we gotta do is decide what method of *elimination* will work best. We know they're headed for Estes Park tonight, and they're going through Nederland because I heard that Doug person say he wanted to stop over there and look for a saloon that was once owned by a friend of his. So that's the first item on the list."

"Is there any way we can fix it so they'd be in a car wreck?" Orville asked. "With them pulling a trailer, wouldn't that be a cinch to wipe them out if they tumbled down the side of the mountain?"

"Sure, Orvie! I could mess up their brakes so they'd lose control. I could do it, Orvie. I really could!"

Pinto leaned over and whispered something to Papoose.

"There's a couple of reasons that won't work, Gopher. For one thing, you can't crawl around under a car with that gizmo on your neck…we'd end up having to drag you out with a pulley when you got through. Besides, it'd have to be done at just the right spot in the road to be sure the accident was fatal.

On a second sheet of paper, Papoose made a rough drawing of the road between Bear Claw and Nederland. The highway appeared to have a few switchbacks but was otherwise fairly straight until it reached a point just south of Rollinsville and Nederland, where he drew in a zigzag stretch of road and marked it "Gamble Gulch…a good place to die."

"Ain't that a bit strong?" Orville asked. "There must be lots of cars travelling that road every day without nobody getting killed…"

"But not when some dude is asleep at the wheel!" He sat back and locked his hands behind his head. "All we gotta do is figure how to dope him so he'll pass out somewhere along that three mile stretch of switchbacks. No way they can come out of it alive!"

All of them were silent. The idea sounded possible, all right, but how could they pull it off? After a few minutes they began firing questions at

Papoose. He wrote QUESTIONS at the top of one column and ANSWERS in the other. At times they figured out their own answers but that was not indicated on paper.

Q: How do we get him to take any kind of drug?

A: I heard enough to know the guy is a lush. All we gotta do is put the knockout solution into something, probably a small bottle of beer. Maybe one of those with a screw-on top so it won't be obvious it was opened ahead of time.

Q: If we give it to him in Bear Claw, won't he pass out before they get to where the three miles of switchbacks start?

A: The secret is to find some way to stop them just before they start down the steep grade and get him to drink it at that point. The way he slops up the booze, it won't take him long to inhale enough to do the job. Even half a bottle would do it.

Q: What's going to cause them to stop right where we want them to?

A: How about we pretend to have car trouble and flag them down to help us? They might recognize the Chevy but we could use the Mustang, and after we get the car running again, we offer him a beer as thanks for giving us a hand. When he guzzles it down, he'll be out within two or three minutes. We'll stall that long before driving away to give the dose time to take hold.

Q: What kind of car trouble could you set up that can be taken care of in just a couple of minutes?

A: Maybe loose wires…

Q: Battery cable?

A: Yeah, that ought to do it.

Q: If Papoose and Pinto are the ones with car trouble, how will they know which car to flag down?

A: Orville and Gopher can follow them out of town and signal that they're coming.

Q: Signal *how*?

A: All we need is another cellular phone. With one in each car, it'd be simple to call ahead and say, "Here they come!" Maria has an extra cell we can use.

Q: Is it possible to fix his drink so it'll take a minute or so before he conks out? That way he has time to get back in the pickup and start on down the grade.

A: No problem. Like I said, he'll be out within two or three minutes. And remember, we've got a three-mile stretch of road to work with, so he can pass out any time on his way down that mountain and he's a goner…him and his son!

Papoose laid the pencil beside the yellow tablet and clapped his hands together, looking totally satisfied with their question and answer session.

"You really think it'll work, Papoose?" Orville asked. "It seems to me we're counting on a helluva lot of luck to make the timing come out right."

Papoose nodded. "It'll work, Dude. All we need to do now is figure out a few details like how much does he weigh, and stuff like that. The mixture I've got in mind will make him drowsy in a minute or so, then BANG, he's out. The drugs won't kill him. That'd look too suspicious when it's over with. I'll put in just enough chloral hydrate to be sure he passes out, then I'll add a touch of cyanogenic plants like Johnson grass and a little ground up apricot seeds to finish him off if the crash don't do it. I'm always careful of how much I mix in so's it won't be enough to leave the smell of almonds."

"Just in case the car wreck don't do him in, then what?"

Papoose clapped his hands together again. "Fact is, with an extra touch of loco weed added, he'd come out of it so ornery he'd be ready to fight the first person he saw. But there's no way he can keep from passing out. That's why it's so necessary to have the dosage match his exact size and weight to make it work. You're sure he's the one driving the rig?"

"Positive," Orville said. "Last I seen of either Hastings, the cowboy, Brad, couldn't even get into their camper without help, and the old man had to drive him back and forth to the arena to watch the rodeo. No way would he try to handle a truck with a horse trailer behind it."

"Then we're set. Gopher can clean up the kitchen while me and Orville straighten up our rooms. One thing Maria insists on is that we don't leave a mess."

"Excuse me," Homer asked, hesitantly. "What if somebody else stops to help you before our guys get there?"

All three of them looked at him, obviously surprised that he came up with a question they had not considered.

Papoose looked puzzled for a moment, then seemed satisfied. "We'll just have to wave them on and say we've got the problem solved…"

The first that Orville realized Pinto was gone was when he heard a door slam somewhere at the back of the house.

"He's got to clean up his place, too," Papoose explained.

Orville, on recalling the grungy condition of the "lab" apartment, found it hard to believe that these two mavericks were actually housebroken. Maybe Maria had also been the motivation behind the sterile condition of the lab. It was impossible to imagine she had ever actually been there but she may have furnished the disinfectants and scouring materials, with instruction as to their use.

Orville had just finished making the bed when he heard a gunshot.

In the hallway, Papoose shoved him aside and raced down the stairs. He had already disappeared through the back door by the time Orville reached the kitchen where Homer was struggling to bend over and pick up pieces of a broken cup. Orville brushed past him and almost collided with Papoose who stormed back into the house, pigtails flapping, and slammed the door behind him.

"What was it, Papoose? Anybody hurt?"

"Not yet, but he *will* be. I been telling that stupid bastard for months not to practice his quick draw with live ammo. He just shot the mirror in his room and if Maria finds out she'll kill all of us!"

Orville concluded that this was a good time to keep his mouth shut, so he returned to the kitchen.

"I didn't mean to break the cup, Orvie. Honest I didn't. That noise scared me, that's all."

"Don't worry about it. I'll help you clean up this mess and we can wait out front 'til Papoose is ready to leave." He could not admit that he had been looking for an excuse to try out the porch swing since he first saw it the night before.

"Orvie," Homer spoke so softly he was barely audible over the squeaking of the swing. "I can't go back into that awful apartment again. I just know I'll throw up all over the place and there's no telling what Papoose might do to me, the mood he's in…"

Orville heard footsteps coming toward the front entrance so he whispered, "Don't worry about it. You can stay outside while he's mixing up his magic potion, and I'll see if I can't clean up the place a little before we have to go over there the next time."

Papoose ignored both of them when he locked the front door of the house and headed for his car. "Let's go back to the lab and I'll stir up something that'll get the job done."

No mention was made of Pinto's absence and neither of the Stokes had any desire to bring up the subject. At least Homer had access to the front seat without any argument.

They were back at the Colfax Avenue turnoff before Papoose spoke again. "We need to be in Bear Claw before those dudes get ready to pull out tonight so you can tail them."

"Remember, we've got to pick up our car first," Orville offered quietly. He still was not sure how to handle Papoose's anger, even though it was not directed at him or Homer.

Papoose simply nodded. When they arrived at the apartment, he crawled out of the car without a word and climbed the stairs where he disappeared through the doorway.

Orville pushed the front seat forward and managed to crawl through the door on the driver's side so as not to cause Homer any undue discomfort.

"Orvie…" Homer whined.

"Not now, Homer. Not *now*! I'm doing the best I can and you'll just have to sit here for awhile and *shut the fuck up*!"

When Orville entered the apartment, he wondered for a moment if there was really anything he could do to the place short of burning it down. It was really not up to him to tackle this job, except for the fact that he had promised Homer he would. Besides, they might have to come back here again in the next day or so, and Homer could not sit in the car every time.

Much to his surprise Orville found assorted items of cleaning equipment in a hallway closet. After straightening the covers on the beds in the back room and the "living room," he scoured the kitchen area and threw away all of the debris from on top of the table and sink. Papoose had pulled the refrigerator around to the point where the lab area was nearly shut off from the rest of the room so Orville had the place pretty much to himself. There was nothing he could do about the rotting curtains. With a little more time he might have been able to clean the windows and cover them with tin foil or something, but for the moment that was not a critical issue. He used up what was left of a floral-scented aerosol spray by going over the place from top to bottom, and he had nearly finished sweeping the floor when Papoose emerged. At that moment, Orville took a swipe at a mouse that stuck its head out of a hole in the corner of the living room.

"Don't you *dare* touch him!" Papoose yelled. "That's my friend, Albert. He ain't hurting nothing! I told you once before, all critters got a right to live…"

Orville leaned on the broom and looked at this man who was both a friend and a stranger at the same time. Papoose, with his braided hair and beaded moccasins, was at times a modern man who used a cellular phone, talked like an educated druggist, and worked in a well-stocked laboratory that might well have been the envy of many legitimate pharmacists. At other times, like now, he was a native Indian who was concerned over the welfare of a small "critter" like a mouse. Of course, there were two ways to look at it. For one, possibly many of the containers in his lab were filled with potions he had garnered from his medicine-man ancestors. On the other hand, he was calmly plotting the death of two men while worrying about the fate of a tiny mouse, which might be explained if one considered the fact that Custer's horse was the sole survivor of a massacre by Indians!! This last tidbit Orville remembered from a recent television special.

Papoose took the broom from Orville and tossed it across the room. He had a small corked bottle in one hand and dug a set of keys from his vest pocket with the other. "Let's get out of here. We've still got a lot to do..."

As they pulled out of the parking lot, Orville couldn't resist asking, in light of the mouse episode, "What's that thing hanging on your mirror? You must of killed *something* to get that fuzzy tail."

"No way, Dude. That's just a fake coyote tail my nephew got at a toy store and gave it to me for my birthday!"

CHAPTER 12

Brad, as was his custom, awoke shortly after daybreak. His first impulse was to roll out of bed and hit the jogging trails but just the part about rolling out of bed immediately reminded him that he was in no condition to complete his daily routine. Actually, the soreness in his chest had already lessened a little, but the wide strips of tape that hampered his deep breathing convinced him that any strenuous activity was out of the question. Instead, he left the camper quietly so as not to disturb Doug, and rescued Smoky from the rear compartment of Tooley's van.

"Come on, partner. Let's go for a walk. *A nice leisurely walk….*"

They went through the foot-gate leading to the creek and traveled slowly along the bank for a mile or so before Brad sat down and leaned against the trunk of a willow tree. Smoky ran in circles for a few minutes in an obvious attempt to get Brad to play, then he finally gave up and lay down in the cool grass, only stirring occasionally when a fish jumped out of the water nearby.

Brad had not checked the time when he left the camper so he was unaware of how long he had been gone but he eventually rose and headed back toward the rodeo grounds. Smoky shook himself awake and followed.

The camping area was coming alive when he returned, with several cowboys leading their horses from the stable to the watering trough.

Some were grooming their mounts with curry comb and brush or checking hooves to see if they possibly needed to be reshod.

Brad decided to walk Skeeter around for awhile since Doug would no doubt stay asleep for another hour or so. He wished he were able to jump on, bareback, and lope around the race track but again decided this was not feasible. He was extremely frustrated at this enforced inactivity since this was the first time in quite a few years that anything or anyone had dictated what he could do. That, of course, did not include Cheryl, his almost-wife, with whom he split just weeks before their impending wedding. Her increased attempts to dominate him had really been the determining factor in the breakup and what had induced him to leave New Mexico on a one-year leave of absence.

"Hi, there, Son. Ready for a cup of coffee?" It was Tooley. He had just put the dogs in their *corral* and was sitting in the doorway of his van.

"Sounds like a winner. Wait'll I put Skeeter away and toss him some hay..."

They were on their second cup of "barefooted" coffee when Doug joined them. He brought along a box of doughnuts and his *fifth* of milk.

"I can get along without sugar, Tooley, but I gotta have some kind of cow juice to lighten up that black tar you call coffee!"

"You're sure picky for a man who hates to cook for hisself."

The two men exchanged good natured insults for awhile until Doug suggested he and Brad begin getting their things together in preparation for leaving town that evening. With only the one performance on Sunday from three o'clock until about six-thirty, the rodeo hands who were not local, went about "breaking camp" during the morning hours.

Doug returned from the horse trailer carrying Skeeter's bridle. "I need to go into town and pick up a box of rivets at the hardware store. I been patching this headstall long enough, and I guess it's time to repair it right. Want to go along, Bud?"

"Sure. Anything's better than just sitting around..."

"Ask Tooley if he needs anything."

Tooley, who apparently overheard the last part, called out from his doorway, "You might pick up some dog food. I forgot to get any last night."

In town, Doug parked in front of Smitty's Hardware Store just as Jerry Tandy climbed out of a Jeep Cherokee with New Mexico plates.

"Hi, there, Jerry T," Brad called out to him. "What are you up to this morning?"

"Just hunting a place to have breakfast. Join me?"

Doug was already out of the pickup and headed for the store.

"Why don't you two go ahead, Bud? I'm not hungry but I'll catch up with you in a few minutes for coffee. Okay?"

Jerry stepped around what appeared to be a permanent hitching post, and looked through the grimy front window of the Bar&Q, then suggested they go to the café around the corner. Brad was a little uneasy about leaving Doug in the vicinity of the pool-room/bar but shrugged it off once he and his friend Jerry T. settled into a booth and began reminiscing about New Mexico. He realized he couldn't keep his father on a short leash forever, but after the free-for-all Doug started a few weeks before at a little rodeo town in Arizona, Brad worried that the next time something like that happened, he might not be so fortunate as to get by without the law checking his past record. Doug served two years of his 3-5 sentence in Florence, Arizona, for killing a man in a drunken brawl, and he most likely would be sent back if he got into any more trouble during his probationary period.

"So how'd you do here, Jerry T? I didn't get to see any of your rides."

"I just barely managed to make the whistle on my last bull for second place in the day money. I won a first and a third so far in the bareback riding."

They both ordered steak and eggs before continuing their rodeo conversation.

"And what happened to you, Brad? I wasn't in the saddle bronc riding so I wasn't around to see your accident. You okay now?"

"Some bruised ribs and a horrendous headache. No big deal..."

"You weren't wearing a vest?"

"*Vest?*"

"I guess you *have* been away for awhile. Remember when our idea of protective gear was chaps and maybe a glove on our riding hand? And of course, our standard Durham bag of resin to slap against the palm of our glove so's we could hang on better. Since about '93 or '94, most of the cowboys wear either safety vests, mouthpieces, elbow braces or a combination of all three like I told you before."

"Where do they get all that gear?"

"A lot of it's made special. Vests are expensive, but they're damn well worth it. They're made out of the same stuff as they use in the space shuttles and they're supposed to absorb up to seventy-five percent of the shock. It sure beats the hell out of getting busted up all the time like we used to be when we first turned out. You sure could of used a mask that time the doggin' steer gouged your face, right?"

Brad rubbed his cheek and nodded. "It would have looked pretty silly in those days, but I guess you're right."

"I wish more people realized that professional cowboys are about the only free-enterprise athletes around who pay all their own expenses and only get what they win. But you know all that, Brad. A few of us who got hooked on rodeo competition in college never really figured to make a career out of it. I suppose you got into it on account of Doug. Right?"

"Yeah. Almost seven years. It was fun for awhile but I guess I'm too practical, like my mother, and need the security of a regular pay-check. If you're crippled up and can't perform well, or if you draw bad stock, you don't get paid. I decided to buy a small spread in New Mexico that bordered on our old place and I needed to make regular payments. It's just big enough to run fifty or so purebred cows and a few quarter-horses."

"You're a deputy sheriff, too, right?"

"On leave of absence right now, but when I go back I stand a good chance of being the next sheriff. The present one plans to retire soon. It's not very exciting, but it suits me just fine."

"Ever think about getting Doug to go back with you?"

There it was again. The veiled suggestion that maybe things were not going well for his father any more.

Brad did not refer to his accident again. It must have been obvious to Jerry T that he was ignorant about the use of the protective vests, but he was still reluctant to admit his total lack of recall regarding the bronc ride.

They were nearly through eating when Doug showed up. He smelled of booze but even if he had been drinking his usual boiler-makers, there had not been sufficient time for him to get out of control.

"How you two New Mexicaners getting' along?" His voice was a trifle shrill. "Order me a cup of joe, will you, Bud? I gotta go to the can…"

The three men chatted for awhile about upcoming rodeos, and although Brad, himself, had little to contribute to the conversation, he became increasingly aware that Doug's schedule sounded somewhat haphazard as compared to his usual well-planned itineraries in previous seasons. Again, he worried that his father's drinking might be forcing him out of the larger rodeos where the real prize money was available.

While Jerry T was paying the check, Brad left a tip for the waitress and asked directions to the town drug store. He had decided that morning to get rid of the annoying tape in the next day or so, and this was a good time to pick up a heavy duty Ace bandage to replace it. In the past, minor injuries such as bruised or cracked ribs had never required a "body cast," which was what he considered the armpit-to-waist tape job the local doctor had saddled him with. Always before, with no apparent ill effects, Brad had simply bandaged his own chest tightly without even seeing a doctor. No reason it shouldn't work this time.

On arrival at the rodeo grounds, Brad changed from his warmup and Nikes to levis and boots. He really wanted to bathe and was tempted to have Doug remove the tape for him right then, but the thought of a cold shower in their camper convinced him to wait until they reached a motel somewhere down the road that evening.

The afternoon performance proved to be fairly uneventful except for two of the chariots tipping over on their last lap around the track. Brad had parked Doug's pickup nearer to the bucking chutes this time so he could chat through the fence with a few old friends while they prepared for their events. Prior to the bronc riding, a couple of cowboys checked out the saddles on the ground in front of the chutes. They adjusted the length of the stirrup leathers and tested the flexibility of each one by swinging first one leg then the other in a spurring motion with their feet in the stirrups. Most of the local bronc riders used the gear offered by the rodeo committee, whereas the professionals generally brought their own. Doug was thinking again about the changes in equipment through the years and realized that the decision to build the bronc saddles without saddle-horns had been a real boon to the cowboys. Whatever had happened to him during his recent accident would obviously have been worse had he not used his own Association saddle with its smooth pommel. A saddle horn would have jammed into his stomach, possibly causing further injury.

Smoky remained at Brad's side during the early events so Brad was surprised, and concerned, when he headed back toward the pickup and realized his dog had disappeared. Only when he saw Tooley approaching the arena, did it occur to him that Smoky had gone to join his cousins. He hurried to the catch pens at the south end of the arena where Tooley was getting ready for his performance. As he suspected, Smoky was running in circles around the other dogs, trying to lure them into whatever game it is that dogs play when they are unencumbered by leashes or pens. The other three dogs wagged their tails but acted in a very professional manner by staying next to Tooley where they awaited the opening of their act.

"Wait 'til I get Smoky out of there," Brad called out. He'll mess up everything…"

"That's okay, Son. Let him stay. I never seen an Aussie sheepdog yet that didn't know how to handle a few woolies."

Tooley nodded to a man on the gate and the sheep were released into the arena. Brad leaned against the fence, his crossed forearms on the next to the top pole, chin resting on his clenched fists. He was not aware of holding his breath until he actually gasped for air. At the first gesture from Tooley, each of his dogs cut approximately one-third of the sheep away from the rest and herded them to separate areas. Smoky ran from one bunch to the next, wagging his tail and yipping softly as though trying to get them to play with him.

Brad hung his head and refused to watch but after two or three minutes, his curiosity got the better of him. When he looked up again, Smoky had settled down, and had obviously selected which herd he wanted to help isolate from the other two. In a very business-like manner, he assisted the dog already in charge of that group by quietly nipping at any animal that tried to stray.

"Well, I'll be damned!" Brad nudged a man who was standing next to him. "See that calico-colored sheep dog out there? That's *my* dog, Smoky!"

The man did not seem at all impressed. Brad decided the gunsel just didn't know a smart dog when he saw one, that's all.

When Tooley's act ended, he motioned to Brad that he was taking Smoky back to the van with him and his other dogs. Brad's return wave indicated his approval.

The next event was bulldogging and Brad was glad to see Tom Lizenbee throw his steer fast enough to ensure at least second place in the day money. This would give Doug a pretty good three-day total for hazing and might help to restore his failing reputation as a contestant.

Brad drove over to Doug's horse trailer. A cowboy who had just loaded his own horse helped direct him as he backed up to connect the trailer hitch to the pickup. The hydraulic lift adjusted the height of the hitch so even with his sore ribs Brad was able to complete the hookup and pull the trailer away from the fence before Doug arrived with Skeeter.

While Doug returned to the rodeo arena to wait for Tom to collect his money, Tooley came over to unsaddle Skeeter and help stow the gear in the front compartment of the horse trailer. He managed to do it in such a way that it did not imply that Brad was helpless, but instead was simply getting an assist from a friend.

"I hate to push you on this, Son, but I keep wondering if you remember anything yet about what happened."

"Not much, Tooley. Just flashes of things once in a while. What I don't understand is what would ever make me decide to ride broncs again after all this time."

"That's another thing that's strange. Why would you even bring along a bronc riding saddle if you weren't fixin' to use it? Seems to me actions speak louder than spilt milk..."

Brad frowned. "Yeah. I guess you're right."

It was already dark by the time Brad and Doug pulled around to Tooley's trailer to see if he wanted to have supper with them in town before they took off. He declined, saying goodbye to them and at the same time handing over the Olsen's phone number in Golden where he could be reached. "In case you need me," he said.

Brad felt the unspoken message was aimed at him and he nodded to his friend as they drove away.

CHAPTER 13

It was just barely twilight when Papoose pulled into the Cubs Den Motel and drove around to where the rented trailer was parked. Once inside, he told the Stokes to take a quick run out to the arena to be sure the Hastings were still there. He emphasized that they could not chance any slip-ups at this point.

With Homer driving, Orville took note of the few cars coming from the rodeo grounds, none of which looked like the Hastings rig. The continuing drone of the announcer's voice before they pulled off of the highway confirmed that the show was still in progress. They made a wide circle around the south end of the arena where they saw Doug's pickup parked near the fence and Brad chatting with one of the rodeo hands who was inside the arena. They were ready to go back into town when Orville suggested they make one more loop to check on Doug's location, and it was at this point that Brad drove the pickup back to the stables to hook up the trailer and load the roping horse with the help of the sheepdog man.

He reported back to Papoose and they began their final preparations.

There was a rough map of the area on another sheet of the legal pad and Papoose was pointing out various locations to Homer.

"Glad you're back, Dude. There's a few more things we need to settle before we take off. I'll stop and pick up some beer and ice it down in my Igloo cooler. We want to be sure he guzzles it right away while we're there to watch him."

"I meant to ask, why beer? Wouldn't something stronger hide the taste of the stuff you put in it?" Orville asked.

"Nope. For some reason, the malt and hops in beer mix better than anything else. I've used it a couple of times before and nobody ever caught on yet."

"Well, that part's up to you. Just show us what Homer and me have to do and we'll be all set to go."

Papoose explained the entire routine twice, just to be sure there was no question as to what everyone had to do. His attitude toward Pinto was still distant, even though Pinto had nodded in reply when asked whether the broken mirror had been replaced, after they picked him up at Maria's house. A time or two when he attempted to whisper something to Papoose, he was pushed away.

"You need to fall in behind them when they leave the rodeo grounds. There's a grove of trees right here on the north side of town," he pointed to the map. "That's where I'll park and wait for you to give me the go-ahead. I showed you how to use that cell phone, Orville, so all you have to do is tell me when they're leaving town and I'll take off ahead of them. It's set on quick-dial so you just turn it on, punch number one, and I'll answer."

"Sounds simple enough. What if they don't stop?" Homer asked, ever skeptical. "Then what happens?"

"They'll stop, all right. At exactly four-point-two miles from the edge of town, I'll get right out in the middle of the road and shine my camp light in their eyes and they won't have no choice. Besides, these cow-pokes are always good about helping people in trouble..."

"I thought you said it was *three* miles!" Orville interrupted. He wanted to be sure he had it straight in his mind.

"It's four-point-two to where we stop 'em, but there's *three miles* of switchbacks where they can pile up. Got it?" Papoose sounded impatient.

"So what do we do while you got them working on your car?" Orville asked.

"Just keep on driving. I'll keep 'em busy so they don't recognize the Chevy in case they seen it at the hospital or somewhere. But one thing you've got to remember, *don't go all the way into Nederland!*"

"Why not?"

"Once you're past Rollinsville, just watch for where Highway 72 turns off to the right. That's the road we take back to Maria's house, so you need to pull off to the side and wait for us there. Remember, if you're in Nederland, you've gone too far and I won't be able to find you."

"You can just give us directions…"

Pinto leaned over to whisper to Papoose, and this time he was not shoved away. Papoose nodded, and there was a knowing look exchanged by the two men.

"No, that's okay, Dude. For now it's best we all stick close together. We can't do nothing until the bank opens tomorrow, and we need to use the Chevy to come back up here. Maria wants the Mustang while her car's in the shop…"

Orville began to realize there was an undercurrent of distrust that had crept into the group. It had to be because of THE BOX. Maybe Papoose thought the Stokes were going to sneak back and try to get it for themselves. If they were thinking in those terms, it might also be a good idea to keep an eye on Papoose until the bonds were safely in the bank.

"Whatever you say, Papoose."

Pinto gathered the papers from the table and the two men prepared to leave. They glanced back from the doorway just as Orville dropped his right thumb onto his forefinger and fired an imaginary bullet at Papoose.

In retaliation, Papoose crouched behind the high-back chair, then stepped out into the open, pulled the bowstring back to touch his chin, aimed, and shot an invisible arrow at the devious white man.

All in fun, Orville thought. Or was it?

* * *

Doug pulled into the parking lot of a fried chicken drive-in/walk-in. "Let's pick up something to eat before we take off. Okay, Bud?"

"Sure. Turn on the overhead light while I'll dig out some cash."

"The bulb's burned out. Anyway, I've got this one. You get the next."

"Sure. I know that old ploy. The next one will be prime rib, right?"

"Would I do that to you?" Doug stepped out of the pickup and quickly closed the door to keep Smoky from jumping out. Most of the time the dog appeared content in his space between the two men, but he was always on the alert for a chance to escape and go for a run. Brad grabbed his collar and held him back when Doug returned.

"Want some of this now, Bud, or later on?"

"There's no great hurry, but the way Smoky's sniffing at that sack of food, I doubt if we can keep it away from him for very long. I hope you got something he can eat..."

"That'd be just about anything, right?"

A large sliding window behind the front seat opened into the front of the camper so Brad tossed a handful of chicken tenders through the window and Smoky scrambled after them.

"That's a good place for him. He gets pretty restless just sitting up here with us. You want a chicken leg for now, Doug?"

"Might as well. Let's head on down the road..."

* * *

Orville flipped the cellular phone open and punched number one as instructed, but he still had doubts as to whether the tiny black thing would work. "Papoose. You there?"

"Yeah, Dude. What's happening?"

"They're just leaving the chicken place now on their way out of town."

"We got tired of waiting in that grove of trees so we been sittin' here inside the Taco Bell waitin' for your call. We're done eatin', so we'll take off right now and wait for you at the four-point-two mile mark. That's *four-point-two*, got it? You remember what to do?"

Orville was getting tired of Papoose implying he and Homer were unable to follow instructions. "Of course I know. Just *you* be ready when I give you a call."

Orville had watched enough PI movies on TV to know he should not stay directly behind Doug's horse trailer all of the time, so he varied his speed by dropping back to second or third place until they pulled out of town. He figured once they were on the highway, Doug would be too busy handling his rig to pay any attention to who else was on the road. Besides, he had no reason to suspect that he was being followed.

From the very beginning there were a lot of switchbacks but the road was not too steep, just enough to force the cars to travel at a moderate pace. Also, the locals returning home from the rodeo caused a slight buildup in the amount of traffic and when Orville noticed a sign on the right side of the road that pictured a truck on a steep downhill slant, he assumed they were near the area where Papoose would be waiting. A glance at the odometer showed they had travelled 4.0 miles from the edge of town and apparently Homer was also aware of the mileage because he began excitedly stomping his feet.

"Stop that, Homer! I gotta call Papoose right now and I can't hear him if you keep that up…"

Papoose answered on the first ring. "They coming?"

"Yeah! Right behind that white van. He's going pretty slow so you oughta be able to stop him."

"I see them! After they pull over, you just go right on past us and do like I told you."

Orville could see a light beam ahead, swinging back and forth in a low arc like a railroad signal. Doug, just ahead of him, slowed down and for a moment it appeared he was going to drive on by. Homer stomped his feet again.

"Relax, Homer. This'll work. It *has* to…"

"There. Look Orvie. They did it. They stopped!"

He was right. The pickup and horse trailer slowly eased over to the side of the road. Doug stepped out after quickly closing the door behind him.

Orville would have liked to hang around and watch the action being played out but he knew Papoose was right when he insisted they drive on past and leave the operation to him.

"It's working, Orvie! It's working…"

* * *

Brad had just started on a large piece of white meat when he saw someone in the middle of the road, with a flashlight, trying to hail them down. Another man peered around the raised hood of their Mustang, then ducked back out of sight.

Doug slowly pulled over and stopped.

"You know him, Doug? He doesn't look like a rodeo hand."

"Appears to be Indian. I met a few when I was messing with that Blackfoot squaw a couple of summers ago. Don't think her old man would've been following me all this time, though, so I guess it's safe to see what he wants."

"I remember seeing him someplace," Brad said, "or maybe just some garb like he's wearing. Probably at the rodeo…"

Doug stepped out of the pickup and Brad exited from his side after tossing the rest of his piece of chicken to Smoky and telling him to stay in the camper.

"Sure could use some help if either of you dudes know anything about a car," the Indian said.

"I'm afraid I can't do much for you," Doug told him as he walked around to the front of the Mustang, "but my son, here, might know something. His pickup is always quitting on him…"

The Indian handed his flashlight to Doug who aimed the beam at different areas of the motor when Brad pointed to specific locations.

"I can't figure why it wouldn't start again. The car handled like there was a low front tire and I stopped to take a look. When we got back in, the damned engine wouldn't even turn over!"

"It was working okay up to that time?" Brad asked. "That happens to me sometimes when the battery connections are loose. Did you check the cables?"

The Indian said he had not, and the tall man who had ducked out of sight when they first approached shook his head to indicate he had not examined the wires either.

"Move the light over here, Doug." Brad jiggled the battery cables, then removed them and with his Swiss army knife he scraped each post and the inside of its corresponding connection. After replacing each cable and tapping it in place with the handle of the knife, he told the Indian to see if the car would start.

A grinding sound, followed by a loud purring noise, indicated the problem had been solved. Brad felt relieved that the solution proved to be simple because his mechanical talents were definitely limited, and the short time he spent leaning over the engine caused considerable discomfort in his chest.

The Indian motioned for his friend to get into the car and keep the motor running while he stepped back out and shook hands with Brad.

"Sure do appreciate your help, Dude. Can I offer you a couple of cold beers? It's the least I can do."

Doug hesitated, looking toward Brad.

"Sounds like a winner. Go ahead, Doug. Have one."

The Indian opened a small cooler in the back seat of the Mustang and when he came around to the front where Brad was preparing to close the hood, he had already removed the top of the first beer and handed it to Doug.

"Just leave the lid on mine," Brad said. "I'll drink it on the way."

Doug gulped several swallows of beer, followed by a loud satisfied belch.

The Indian shook hands with both Doug and Brad but his companion stayed in the car, saying nothing. Brad noticed that the Mustang did not pull out immediately and secretly hoped there was no more trouble. He wanted to get going.

Doug opened the door on his side of the pickup, and paused to take another drink. Just as he was seated, Smoky lunged past him out of the darkened interior and ran across the road. This had been his first chance to escape and he took full advantage of it.

"Dammit, Bud. That hound of yours spilled my beer. Ain't you ever taught him that a man's drink is sacred?"

"Never fear, Doug. Here's mine. I didn't really want it anyway. I have to catch Smoky before he gets run over…"

Smoky ran up an embankment and under a barbed wire fence, trying to entice Brad to chase him. After several minutes of this, with no response from his master, Smoky lifted his leg at a couple of pine trees and reluctantly returned to the truck.

While Brad held the door open for Smoky on the passenger's side, he noticed Doug was leaning forward with his forehead resting on the steering wheel.

"You look kind of bushed, Doug. Why not let me drive on in to Nederland? We could both use a good night's sleep in real beds."

He went around to the other side to try and move Doug. It was no easy job to lift his father's legs over the gear shift and scoot him to the far side of the cab, especially with Smoky in the way. He gestured toward the sliding window and his dog obediently disappeared into the camper. Even with Smoky out of there, Doug's legs were sprawled out so much it was difficult to shift gears.

"Good thing you didn't drink my beer, too," Brad mumbled as he started the engine. "Guess you're more tired than you realized…"

CHAPTER 14

Orville and Homer reached the point where CO-72 merged with CO-119. "What was we supposed to do when we got to this place?"

Homer shrugged as much as the restraint would allow. "He said something about Nederland. but I can't remember *what*. There's lights up ahead so that must be it. Maybe he said he'd meet us there. I need to eat, anyway, before too long. You shoulda got me some food back there in Bear Claw …"

"How the hell was I supposed to know you was hungry? There's always *something* wrong with you, so how can you expect me to know what it is if you don't tell me?"

"Jeez, Orvie, I'm sorry. It's just that we got so busy there toward the end trying to keep an eye on that horse trailer, I forgot."

"Okay. Okay. We'll drive through town and see if we can spot a place to eat. I could sure use a drink, too, while we're at it."

"There's a bar, and the sign says EATS. Let's just wait there for Papoose. He'll see our car when he gets here, and maybe by then there'll be some news about the accident. Think so, Orvie? Think so?"

"I sure hope we hear something before long. I can't stand the 'spense."

Orville parked the car without causing a single dent in another vehicle. He had begun to feel quite competent behind the wheel in the past few days.

They entered the Main Street Bar & Grill to find themselves in the midst of a crowd of noisy drunks. There were a few scattered tables and a row of booths along the left side of the room, and on the right a bar extended from the front window all the way to the swinging doors to what must be a kitchen.

Orville ushered Homer to a booth with instructions for him to stay put. "I'll get us a couple of beers and a menu."

"You'll be right back, won't you Orvie? I gotta pee…"

"Come on, I'll help you find the mens'can."

The restrooms were in a narrow hallway just past the end of the booths and Orville noticed an EXIT sign over the last door. He always liked to be aware of an escape route no matter where he was.

"Go back to the booth when you get through. I'll be there in a couple of minutes."

On his way to the bar, two or three of the revelers elbowed Orville aside so they could reach their own tables, but he took no offense because they just seemed to be having a good time. Besides, most of them were pretty big.

Orville and Homer both ordered cheeseburgers with fries and baked beans. It was kind of a do-it-yourself setup where you picked up your own order when the number was called, but the food was so good that there were few complaints. Orville carried both of their orders on a tray. He felt safer doing it himself.

They were through with the sandwiches and were nibbling at the few remaining fries when they saw Papoose charging through the front door. His pigtails were flapping from one side to the other. This was not a good sign.

"Just what the fuck are you two doing here? I told you to wait at the Highway 72 turnoff and *not to come into Nederland*! Here I am working my ass off to try and help you two, and you can't follow even the simplest orders…"

Orville got to his feet but managed to stay within the protection of the high-walled booth. "We just weren't sure what you said to do about that intersection, so we came on in here to get a bite to eat."

"Jeez, Papoose," Homer whimpered, "we didn't do nothing wrong. You found us, didn't you, so it can't be too bad. So tell us. Did it go okay?"

Papoose appeared to calm down slightly and dragged an empty chair over to their table. Apparently, by sitting in the aisle, he indicated that they were not entirely forgiven, but he was now close enough to relate his encounter with the Hastings. Pinto quietly slid into the booth next to Homer.

"So what happened?" Orville prodded.

"Just like clock-work. Doug took a big swig out of the bottle as soon as I gave it to him and was just starting to drink some more when he got behind the wheel. There wasn't no dome light in the cab so I couldn't tell for sure, but knowing what a lush he is, I'm convinced he drank it all before he even started the engine."

Orville and Homer exchanged "high-fives" and offered to buy drinks for the other two men. Papoose seemed to have accepted the fact that no real harm was done by the Stokes not following orders, and he agreed to have a shot of Jack Daniels to settle his nerves.

"Any news yet about a wreck?" he asked. "I suppose not. They might not even be found 'til tomorrow…"

* * *

Brad continued to be uncomfortable in his "body cast," especially when driving the steep few miles of hairpin curves from the top of the grade to the outskirts of Rollinsville. Once they rolled past the sparsely scattered buildings of the town, it was only a few more miles to Nederland.

There was a small strip mall on the right at the edge of town where he thought about stopping to ask information regarding Goldie Cameron's old bar and also inquire about a motel where he might be able to park the horse trailer for the night. Someone was locking the front door of the only store that still had its lights on, a bakery, so he drove on into town. Several blocks further on, at the Mountain View Motel, he parked across the street where the rig would be out of the way while he checked in. Dogs were not allowed at some places where they had stopped in the past, such as one small motel in Phoenix, but Brad always insisted that Smoky actually *tiptoed* past their front office when they went from his pickup to their room.

This time there was no problem regarding Smoky or the horse trailer. There was even a small yard at the rear where they could hobble Skeeter and let him graze during the night.

Once Brad had signed the register and picked up the keys to a double room at the far end of the building, he returned to the pickup to tell Doug they were all set for the night. There was only one problem. No Doug.

With Smoky at his heels, Brad searched the immediate area, calling his dad's name. "He must of gotten out to take a leak, huh, Smoky? He can't be too far away…"

* * *

Papoose produced a rough drawing that designated which roads they would take on their return to Maria's house in Golden.

"Just in case we get too far ahead of you on the way back," he explained. He had actually loosened up enough to propose a toast to their success. "What'll we call ourselves, Dudes? Every gang has to have a name!"

"How about what you called us before? How about *Pros and Cons*?" Homer beamed with pride when the other three looked at him with obvious admiration for a change. He was the only one actually facing the front entrance so he had no time to bask in his fleeting glory. Before any of them heard the commotion, he reached across the table and grabbed Orville's arm.

"Aw *shit*, Orvie. Look what's comin' in…"

They all turned in time to see the front door swing inward. Doug stumbled against the door jamb and padded along in his stocking feet (with his right big toe protruding through a hole in his sock), hair disheveled, and shirt unbuttoned down to his navel.

"I can whip any sonnabitch in this crummy joint!" he yelled. "Any takers?"

The *Pros and Cons* were stunned into complete silence.

There was so much noise in the place that most of the drunks were unaware of a challenger in their midst.

"Fact is, I can whip any sonnabitch in this whole two-bit town!"

Two or three men at the bar turned toward Doug but still ignored him. By then, he had staggered into to a table where two couples were eating dinner, and he nearly knocked over the chair of one of the women. Her companion jumped to his feet.

This time Doug threw his shoulders back and tried to shove his way to the bar. "I can even out-fight any sonnabitch in the *whole damned state of Colorado…*"

At that point, the woman's companion hit Doug with a hard left to the jaw and knocked him flat on his back.

Brad and Smoky pushed through the entrance just as Doug slumped to the floor, signalling a "T" for time out. He look up at Brad and grinned, "Guess I just took in too much territory, huh, Bud?"

In the Stokes' booth, they were all in a state of shock.

"What happened, Papoose?" Orville finally managed to whisper hoarsely. "What the fuck they doin' *alive?*"

Papoose pulled his hat down with the brim touching the bridge of his nose. He shook his head and looked at the others with total disbelief. "I have no idea! I *saw* him drink about a third of the bottle when I first gave it to him, and like I said, he was about to finish it off when I last saw him get into his truck."

Orville was the first to come out of his trance. "We got to get the hell out of here without them seein' us! I sure hope they didn't spot our cars out there on the street. They might recognize the Chevy from the hospital." He helped Homer out of his chair and pushed him into the aisle. "There's a back door…"

Papoose was already gathering his money off of the table, his drink forgotten. Since he, and Homer with his neck brace, were more apt to be recognized than the other two, he followed closely behind the Stokes to the rear of the building. "Main thing is to ditch this place and get outta town. Right now!"

The *Pros and Cons* did not look much like victors when they sneaked down a narrow hallway to exit into the alley that reeked of garbage and urine.

"Get your car before they come back out onto the street. Then follow me out of town. Do it. *Now!*" Papoose ordered. "We'll talk later at Maria's place."

"Don't drive too fast. Even with that map, I maybe can't find the right house." Orville realized he was whining again and it made him furious to know he sounded more and more like Homer.

* * *

Brad helped Doug to his feet and steered him toward the front door. "How'd you get drunk so fast? You have a flask hid in your pickup?"

Doug leaned against Brad for support. "Hell, no, Bud. All I had was a few swallows of beer. You seen it, Smoky spilled the rest."

Brad wanted to believe his father but he knew from past experience that Doug was not averse to lying if it meant keeping himself out of trouble. There must have been some booze in the camper.

They crossed the street, arm in arm, with Smoky trailing behind. At the next corner, Brad steered Doug over to their rig and loaded him into the pickup until he could park at the end of the motel lot and unload Skeeter. When everything was taken care of for the night, he practically carried his father into their room and put him to bed.

Brad was so tired by then he even decided to forego the tape removal and hot shower until the next morning. He undressed and fell into the other bed, exhausted.

CHAPTER 15

Homer wanted to drive when they left Nederland but Orville was concerned about his state of mind and refused the request. Homer reacted by pounding his fists on his knees for the first fifteen minutes of the trip. Orville conceded that, at the very least, this tantrum was less noisy than the usual foot stomping.

When Homer's temper subsided, they began to discuss their situation. Both men were concerned about Papoose' ability, or lack of same, in carrying out their plans.

"Maybe we shoulda just put a bomb in their truck and not messed with Papoose and his *concoction*," Homer suggested.

"Considering what happened the last time we tried it by ourselves, maybe not."

"You never forget nothing', do you? One little mistake…"

"All I'm saying is, if Papoose don't have no ideas that'll really work, we maybe could suggest a car bomb to get rid of the Hastings at Estes Park. It won't hurt to listen to what he says. We'll sure need help if that's the way we decide to go."

"Is that the Mustang ahead of us, Orvie? Can you still see him? We sure don't want to get lost out here in these mountains."

"Yeah, that's him. We must be getting close to Maria's house. I'm ready to hit the sack and try to forget this whole mess until morning."

"As pissed as Papoose was, I just hope he'll let it ride until morning…"

Lost in their own thoughts for the next few miles, both men sighed with relief when they arrived at their destination. Papoose stepped out of the Mustang, slammed the door and stomped into the house without a word. Pinto disappeared around the corner, silent as usual.

"Suppose it's okay for us to go in, Orvie? I ain't sure we oughta be here…"

"Only one way to find out." Orville hoped he sounded more confident than he felt. He looked longingly at the porch swing and wished they could just sit out there all night without having to face another verbal assault. He took Homer by the arm and together they tiptoed through the front door and quietly slipped upstairs to their room, fearing any second they might be ordered into the kitchen for further discussion. With relief, they closed the bedroom door and retired, after a hectic and disappointing day.

"Tommorow'll be better, Homer. I promise…"

The Stokes were the first ones downstairs the next morning. They helped themselves to coffee and day-old bagels while harboring mixed feelings about Papoose's impending arrival. They were anxious to make new plans and yet both of them knew it was quite possible he might refuse to help them any more at all. They agreed that the failure of the Nederland thing was not really their fault, it was just one of those things. All they did wrong was to drive on into the town and how did that hurt? Maybe Papoose was just mad because their scheme had failed.

When Maria darted in and out of the kitchen, grabbing a mug of coffee on her way, Orville was relieved to be spared making small talk while they waited. Pinto was noticeably absent, and it was nearly thirty minutes before Papoose came downstairs, drank two cups of coffee and read the morning paper without acknowledging their presence. Rarely was he seen without his sheepskin vest and black flat-crowned hat, so Orville was somewhat surprised at how much younger he looked in a burnt orange polo shirt, chinos, brown loafers, and his hair in a pony tail instead of the usual braids. At the age of twenty-seven he could have passed for twenty-one. Although he was small in stature, the short sleeved shirt revealed a wide chest, large wrists and muscular arms not evident in his Indian garb.

The Stokes exchanged anxious glances, with Homer squirming more and more as the silence continued.

"Papoose, we got something to suggest," Homer blurted, finally. "If you can't help us, maybe you know somebody who can."

"If I can't help you? Is that what you said, if I *can't* help you? Listen to me, Gopher, there's nothing I can't do if I set my mind to it…"

"Homer didn't mean nothin'. Honest. It's just that we talked about it last night and decided maybe the best way to get rid of the Hastings before they talk to the FBI is to bomb their pickup truck."

"And you want me to build you a bomb? Right?" Papoose shook his head in disbelief. "You mean you can't even put together a simple pipe bomb?"

"It's not that, so much," Homer began, "it's just that the fed we killed only had three fingers on his right hand and we figure he musta been messing with explosives. If somebody that savvy gets blowed up, maybe we oughtn't try it ourselves."

"Last time we tried…" Orville began.

"No need to talk about that, Orvie…"

"What happened, Dude?"

Orville avoided looking at Homer.

"Well, we located the man who turned us in, that time we got sent up for three-to-five in Montana, and we wanted to get even with him."

"And?"

"And we bought a book about bombs at a spy-supply store and rigged a package to send to him that would explode when he opened it."

"And?"

"Aw, Orvie…"

"Dammit, Homer. He's got a right to know why we need his help."

Homer pushed away from the table and disappeared through the front door.

"You were saying…?"

"Well, when Homer mailed it to him, he didn't put enough postage on the package. Even that wouldn't have been so bad, but he put *our return address* on it! When it was delivered back to us, I caught Homer just as he was about to open it *hisself*. Another couple of seconds and he would have been blown all to hell!"

For the first time in twenty-four hours Papoose smiled. "For the life of me, I can't believe you two have lived this long. I guess it's up to me to save your asses, you sure as hell can't do it alone. I'll brew us another pot of coffee and we'll try to figure out something."

Homer apparently had been hovering just outside the door because the jovial tone in Papoose's voice seemed to give him the courage to return to the kitchen.

Pinto also joined them a short time later when they were already well into one of their discussions where a yellow legal pad was used to document an assortment of ideas.

"Can we put a bomb in the motor," Orville asked, "so it'll blow up when they turn the key? Like they do on TV?"

"Who'd hook it up, Dude? You don't know nothing about cars and I can just see Gopher trying to raise the hood and reach over far enough to hook some wires to the ignition. He'd probably topple over and you'd have to drag him out of there before he blew himself up!"

"So what kind do you have in mind?"

"I figure a pipe bomb's the best way to go. Gopher can break into the pickup easy enough, and all he's got to do is place the bomb under the seat so's it'll roll out and explode the first time they go over a hard bump or slam on the brakes real quick." Papoose leaned back and locked his hands behind his head. "Sure would like to do this before they're out on the highway. Be a shame to kill that horse."

"Better him than us," Orville grumbled.

Papoose shrugged as though it might be difficult for him to make such a choice. He reminded them that their first priority was getting the bonds into a safety deposit box, and the bomb thing could be done any time in the next two days. The Hastings would already have arrived in Estes Park, and since Brad's FBI friend wasn't due to arrive in Denver until the coming weekend, all the Stokes needed to do was blow up their pickup, with them in it, sometime before Thursday.

"How d'you know all that stuff about the feebee?" Orville asked. "I don't remember nothing about when he was supposed to be here..."

"Sure you do! I told you what I heard that night at the eatin' joint. The dude's name is Laredo. Guess it's a nickname of some kind, but anyway, him and the cowboy have worked on some cases together. The Hastings also mentioned going back to the lake for a few days, after Estes Park, so we might even get a couple of whacks at them if need be." Papoose glared at the two brothers and added, "But we don't need *two* chances. *Right, boys*?"

Orville nodded. "When you suppose we can do it?"

"That's just a small two-day rodeo for some kind of local celebration so if you missed them at Estes Park, they'd be back to the lake about Thursday *if they was still alive and kicking...*"

"Jeez, Orvie! What if the cowboy gets back to the lake and starts 'membering what happened to the guy we iced? What if that happens, huh, Orvie?"

"Don't worry. We'll get him before that, won't we Papoose?"

"Damned right!" He leaned toward the table again and wrote a few more entries on the yellow pad. "Most of the supplies I need are at the apartment, but I'm not going to mess with putting a bomb together 'til tomorrow, anyway. We'll take care of the business at the bank, then pick up a couple of things from a dude I know. After that, you two are on your own 'til Maria and I get back to the house this evening."

"A night on the town, huh?" Orville asked.

"You got it, Dude. Big night for us. The Rolling Stones are playing in Denver and I got us two tickets…"

"Terrific!" Homer leaned forward, excited. "What's the point spread? I'd like to get a bet down if you can fix it for me!"

The other three looked at him without commenting.

Papoose pushed away from the table. "All set? Let's go pick up that famous box and stash it in a safe place. Tomorrow I'll start looking for a fence but it might take a few days to get the kinda deal we want."

Just hearing those words brightened the day for the *Pros and Cons*. When they approached the Chevy, Papoose looked it over before climbing into the back seat beside Pinto.

"First car I ever seen that leaves *moccasin tracks*! Ain't an ounce of tread on any of them tires…"

* * *

Doug moaned and put the bed pillow over his face.

"What kind of truck ran over me last night, Bud?" His voice was muffled through the pillow. With an obvious effort he sat on the edge of the bed. "I've never had nothing hit me like that beer did. You suppose it was a bad batch, Bud?"

"You still insist you didn't drink anything else?"

"I swear to it. I might stretch the truth from time to time, but as Smoky is my witness, I'm not lying to you now."

Smoky jumped from the other bed where he had been stretched out next to Brad, and came over to Doug wagging his tail.

"See, Bud? He knows the truth when he hears it…"

"Well, I'll take your word for it, but I do know if I hadn't found you when I did, your ass would have been in the local hoosegow by this morning. For now, let's toss out that other bottle and stick to coffee for the next few days. Okay?"

"Sounds good to me. I'm glad the Estes Park rodeo only lasts for two days. The way I feel right now, I'd never make it for a whole week…"

"I meant to ask you, how come this middle-of-the-week schedule? Kind of strange, isn't it?"

"Yeah. It's some kind of anniversary thing to celebrate when the town was first organized, or something like that. Just a small show that doesn't put up enough prize money to attract the top hands. If I can get to feeling better by tomorrow, I ought to be able to make a few bucks…"

Doug removed Brad's "body cast" so he could take a shower and then helped wrap his chest with the six-inch-wide Ace bandage before they both dressed and walked down the street for breakfast.

Of the people they questioned, only one grizzled character, who was sitting on a bench at the Exxon station, had any information about Goldie Cameron. He recalled that she had owned several bars throughout the years, and toward the end of her life she ran a place called the "Branding Iron" that was later known as the Green Lantern. The local folks always referred to that place as "Goldie's Corral."

"Guess that's all the info we're going to get, Bud, so let's *head 'em up and move 'em out!*"

"'Rawhide' reruns, right?"

"Beats the hell out of all them *spook shows…*"

Smoky was sulking because they had left him tied to a tree near where Skeeter was grazing, but once they were ready to travel he appeared happy to settle into his spot between the two men. Brad said he might as well drive for awhile and Doug seemed relieved at the suggestion.

"Map shows just over forty miles to Estes Park, Bud. I'll take the wheel soon as I feel better…"

Between Ward and Allenspark, CO-7 from Lyons intersected CO-72 and the sparsely located road signs indicated CO-7 only, for the rest of the way to Estes Park. Doug stirred just once and that was when they reached the outskirts of Estes Park and the signs indicated they were now on a street called St. Vrain.

"Watch for a big lumbar yard, Bud. You'll see a sign telling you where to hang a right."

"Okay, Doug. I was here a couple of times before, but as I remember, we came into town from the east on CO-36 and turned left to get to the arena."

"It's only a few blocks from the center of town either way. What say we park the trailer, put Skeeter in one of the horse barns, and find someplace to chow down?"

"Sounds like a winner…"

As they approached the town, Brad was aware of how much the area resembled Sedona, Arizona. There were no red rock cliffs but other than that, the same old-west theme was predominant. Motels on either side of the road (all of which had flashing signs to indicate NO VACANCIES), were rustic-western in appearance, but off in the distance, north of town, the multiple complexes of apartments and/or condominiums covering the hillsides appeared to be a mixture of modern-looking buildings or chalet-like structures.

Brad turned to the right at the sign: STANLEY PARK FAIRGROUNDS, HOME OF THE ROOF TOP RODEO, HORSE CAPITAL OF THE NATION. About one mile down the road, on the left, the arena was visible as were several large barns, one of which was labeled LIVESTOCK, and another BLACKSMITH. A pole fence encircled the entire fairgrounds area. On each side of the entrance there was a "double-decker" log cabin that appeared to be about eight-foot-square. No doubt these served as ticket booths whenever a local event took place. Off to the east another log structure, somewhat larger, was designated as the RODEO HEADQUARTERS.

The usual pre-rodeo activities were evident with contestants unloading their horses, parking trailers along the west end of the grounds, and either putting their horses in one of the barns or saddling them for a short workout in the arena. There did not appear to be a designated area for camping such as the one available at the Bear Claw rodeo, but Brad felt confident that Doug would be informed of accommodations when he checked in at the rodeo office. He slowed down at the entrance and was waved through by a small gray-haired man with a long white beard who looked like an off-season Santa.

"Wanna drop me off at the headquarters, Bud? You can pull over next to the stables and as soon as I get signed up, we'll unload Skeeter and take off. Sometimes the rodeo committee has a job for any cowboy who's laid up, and even if you don't wanna work around the chutes, you could handle the stop watch and whistle in the riding events. They generally need somebody extra to time the roping and dogging, too. Want me to ask? Give you a chance to pick up a few bucks if you'd like…"

"No, I don't think so, Doug, but thanks anyway. I'd just as soon not be tied down to any kind of schedule. You go ahead and get signed up and I'll let Smoky run around while we wait for you. Do you already have a team roping partner?"

"Yeah. A good *header* from Idaho named Rex Sandford. Don't think you know him, but he gets a loop on a steer's head as fast as anybody I ever worked with. We've won a few bucks together the last couple of years. Also, there's a chance somebody might need a hazer…"

It was fortunate Brad had already planned to let Smoky run for awhile because the instant the door was opened on the passenger's side, his dog jumped through the camper window and scrambled over the top of Doug, managing somehow to get out first.

Brad watched his father climb out of the pickup and head for the rodeo office. He wished they had taken the time to clean up a little before coming to the fairgrounds. Even though most of the contestants signed in prior to doing anything else when they arrived in a rodeo town, Brad felt his father's future in the business was a bit more precarious than the majority of cowboys and his overall image was especially important at this stage of his declining career.

Smoky ran alongside the pickup until Brad parked and unloaded Skeeter from the trailer. He felt pleased that the simple factor of removing the *body cast* had provided him with a much broader range of pain-free activity and although he still felt a few twinges when doing something like lowering the end-gate of the trailer, these were minimal when compared to a few days ago. For some reason, he experienced more discomfort when attempting such a simple movement as throwing the Frisbee for Smoky. No doubt, he decided, the cross-over effort required to hurl something "back-handed" produced the pain.

There goes my tennis career! he thought wryly. *Might as well count my blessings that I'm able to do as much as I can at this point.*

CHAPTER 16

After about thirty minutes, Doug came over to the horse barn. Brad was thankful for the interruption of his Frisbee activity and listened with interest when Doug explained that Rex had already signed up both of them for the team roping. Brad had a feeling that Doug was relieved to know that he definitely had a partner and wondered how many times in recent months he might have been disappointed by other people dumping him at the last minute. As Doug had known beforehand, Tom Lizenbee went to another rodeo after Bear Claw, but two other bulldoggers asked him to haze for them so he was assured of working in that event, also. Brad knew that there had been a time in the past when his father had hazed for as many as eight or ten different cowboys at the same show.

"You find out where we can park for the night, Doug? Looks like there's no chance to get a motel room…"

"Yeah. Millie Jacobs is handling the rodeo entries and she gave me directions to a campground east of here where we can stay. They got showers, laundry facilities, telephones and even a small market where we can pick up supplies. Might as well stake out a spot before it gets too crowded, then we can drive through town and have a look-see."

Doug drove this time and they turned north for several blocks after leaving the arena. He turned right on CO-34, toward Loveland, and pulled into the Pine Cone Campground about two miles down the road. Each campsite had its own water and sewer hookup and they selected one at the south end as far from the highway noise as possible. Although they did not take advantage of the hookups, they unfurled a mini-awning from the side of the camper and set out a couple of lawn chairs with a small table where they relaxed for awhile after getting cleaned up at the shower facility. Brad said he would wash some of their clothes later that night after the other campers retired.

"I been meaning to ask you, Bud," Doug said as he settled back to sip on a Coke and smoke a cigarette, "about that box you left in the horse trailer. You must have tossed it into the manger when we loaded our gear to go into town. I figured it was your old boots so I put it in the front compartment with our saddles. You take it outta there?"

For the first time in almost twenty-four hours Brad was reminded of his memory loss. How many days now? He had no idea what box his dad referred to, but he still felt uncomfortable discussing it. The hand-made boots he had ordered from Hummel's Bootery in Reno couldn't possibly be finished yet and he was still wearing the 'ropers' that he had when he left New Mexico several weeks ago.

"I guess it's around someplace, Doug. Maybe with my laptop?" He seized this opportunity to ask about his computer because he was sure he would not have left it in his pickup truck but had been reluctant to ask.

"No, it ain't there. That *gadget* of yours is in the front compartment of my camper, right above the sofa where you sleep. Fact is, I been won-dering' why you ain't had it out looking at that bunch of maps you bring up on the screen to locate where we're headed!"

"Just had a lot else on my mind, I guess."

"Suppose so…"

Remembering his trip to Reno where he met Valerie Hummel at her late father's bootery, Brad realized he wanted to hear her voice again. Was it possible he had already called her sometime in the past week? It would be embarrassing if he had, and failed to remember. Still, he needed to phone her, as promised, and figure out from the conversation if they had been in contact. After Reno, he had hoped to get to know her better.

Doug interrupted his thoughts with the suggestion that they drive into town and get something to eat. They rolled up the awning but left the chairs and table to indicate they were "homesteading" that particular campsite.

As they drove through the town, Brad was reminded again of Sedona. Everything was geared for tourism with most of the shops displaying either western garb or Indian artefacts and jewelry. Signs indicated local tours to ski areas, fishing and hunting sites, and rides on the Aerial Tramway one block south of the postoffice. The sidewalks were packed with people elbowing their way from store to store like a bunch of women at an "after Christmas" sale.

It was impossible to park on the main drag so Doug drove through the town, then headed back again before spotting a Mexican restaurant with customer parking on one of the side streets.

Brad and Doug shared one pitcher of draft beer while they ate their Chimichangas, but there was no request from either of them for a refill. Smoky, who remained in the camper, would have to settle for canned dog food since Mexican cuisine was not exactly his doggie bag favorite.

After they returned to Pine Cone, Brad gathered a bag of their dirty clothes and headed for the laundromat. Doug said later that he had taken this opportunity to browse through the magazines at the small market where he picked up copies of USA Today and The Western Horseman before returning to their campsite. He also mentioned stopping to chat with a few rodeo hands whose rigs were parked nearby. Before they turned in for the night he sounded pleased when he reported to Brad that he had picked up two more hazing jobs.

"Almost like the old days, huh, Bud?"

"Almost…"

* * *

Orville backed the Chevy out of Maria's driveway. He looked over his left shoulder to be sure he avoided a large cottonwood tree near the street, but in the process, the right rear wheel ran over the lilac bush on the far side.

"Jeez, Orvie, look what you done now!"

Papoose simply moaned and shook his head. Orville was afraid to look straight at him but he was aware of flapping pigtails and he knew what that meant.

"I'm sorry, Papoose. Honest I am." He stepped out of the car and looked across at the mangled bush. "Ain't there something we can do?"

"Just get in the fucking car and drive, if that's *possible*! Maria's going to kill me anyway, but first we got to get those bonds to the bank. After that we'll worry about what you just done…"

There was complete silence for most of the drive to Bear Claw. When directions were needed, Papoose simply leaned forward and pointed left or right. Orville flinched each time the arm came past his shoulder but there was no physical contact. He conceded that Papoose was showing a great deal of self-control and hoped it would last until the critical issue of the bonds was resolved. He dared not let himself think any further ahead than that.

At the Cub's Den Motel, after both signatures were verified and the grumpy manager retrieved the shoe box from his safe, there was a brief interlude where it appeared there might actually be a fight about who would hold it until they arrived at the bank in Denver. Since they were all riding in the same car, Orville felt the overall tension among them had more to do with the situation than with who was awarded temporary custody.

Following Papoose's directions again, Orville drove cautiously through the deep canyons and switchbacks leading into Denver. In one of the few conversations they had, Papoose explained that they were not returning through Golden because this was a shorter route to the Wells Fargo Bank he had in mind.

Orville was somewhat surprised at what a simple procedure it was for them to rent a safety-deposit box. Again, it was set up so that both his and Papoose's signatures were required for either of them to have access to the box. Homer pouted for awhile until it was explained to him that adding more signatures would simply complicate things, and besides, this way both sides were represented equally so nobody could get hurt.

They stopped at the apartment to check on what supplies were needed to construct the pipe bomb. Papoose made a phone call from there and ordered a landscaper in Golden to replace the lilac bush in Maria's yard "with something as nearly like the previous one as possible."

"This is a matter of life and death, Burt. Mine. So please do the best you can…" He snapped his cell phone closed and glared at Orville. "You dudes are a real pain in the ass, you know that?"

Orville and Homer both nodded, silently.

Papoose went into his lab, then came out and pawed through several drawers under the sink, writing on a yellow pad as he searched.

Pinto whispered something to Papoose who nodded and pointed toward the back bedroom. When Pinto emerged again, he was carrying a small packet the size of a Bull Durham sack and he tucked it into the pocket of his denim vest.

"Whatcha got, Pinto?" Homer asked curiously.

"Mary Jane," Papoose answered. "Just a little something to help us get through the day…"

"Mary Jane?"

Orville nudged him in the ribs and muttered softly, "Marijuana. That's another name for it."

"Jeez, Orvie. I thought marijuana was some kind of a big leaf that they just rolled up and smoked!"

Papoose heard their discussion and explained to Homer how he had started raising his own supply after he took over this apartment from its former owner, a man he met in the penitentiary.

He walked over to the window and pointed to the vacant lot next to where the Chevy was parked.

"See them tall sunflowers? You'd never guess what's growing out there, would you? That's right. Enough M.J. for me to make a fair living right here in Denver and even have a little left over for my own use!"

"Don't it grow real tall?" Orville asked. "In the pictures I seen, it looked more like a tree?"

"That was before growers from all over the world started producing it scientifically. This dude that lived here, Dago Joe, was really into that stuff. A friend of his went to a big seminar they have in Amsterdam every year on Thanksgiving weekend, and he got so involved with the stuff he decided to stay over there. This friend sends back all kinds of info on how to grow these small hybrid plants that can produce more buds in a shorter time and can be raised indoors or out in the open. When winter comes, I just move everything inside. Joe has me sort his mail, and any letters from his friend I keep here in a file for him."

"Where's this guy Joe now?"

"Back in the pen. He got picked up for robbing some damned penny-ante food market and was scared the law'd find out about this place and really throw the book at him. He turned it over to me to run until he serves out his *deuce,* and anything I make off the grass in those two years is all mine. We'll partner-up when he comes back."

"How'd you happen to come to Denver to start with?" Orville asked. It felt good to have Papoose talking to them again and he wanted to take advantage of the situation.

"Funny thing. You been out to the new airport here? From the air, the thing looks like an Indian village with about forty tepees! I was headed for Nevada and when we came in for a landing, the place looked so much like home I decided to stay. That's when I run into Joe again."

Papoose finally made one last tour. He pushed the refrigerator back in place and headed for the door, apparently satisfied that his shopping list was complete. At the foot of the stairs he retrieved a letter out of a small wooden crate that served as a mailbox. The Stokes and Pinto followed obediently.

It had started to sprinkle when they first arrived at the apartment and by now there was a full-fledged rain storm. Homer offered to drive and no-one protested.

"You can't be any worse..." Papoose grumbled.

Papoose read some excerpts from the letter. "These new hybrids look like marijuana bonsai trees," his pronunciation was bon-zay-ee, "and are no larger than a patio tomato plant but are fully mature. A skillful gardener can foreshorten the life cycle of a marijuana plant to the point where it will produce a heavy crop of flowers in less that two months on a plant no bigger than a table lamp. Several dozen such plants can be grown in an area the size of a pool table."

"Wow!" Orville exclaimed. "If you got hold of a few of them babies, you'd be a millionaire in no time..."

"That's the big reason I need my share of the money from the bonds. If I have a big stake to work with in two years, no telling how far Joe and me can go. Right now I ain't in the same class as them gardeners in Amsterdam, but I keep reading up on this stuff and eventually I'll know what I'm doing." He continued to read from the letter, "With all of the new techniques, the potency and quality of the *Cannabis indica* has improved one-hundred percent!"

Papoose folded the letter and tucked it into the hip pocket of his chinos and directed Homer to several stores where he dashed inside while the others remained in the car. The Stokes were enjoying their introduction to marijuana and Orville decided it was a relief to hear Homer giggling, for a change, instead of whining. As for himself, he felt like he was just slightly drunk, maybe a bit silly and mildly happy. There was no noticeable change in Pinto. By the time they made their last stop, Papoose and Orville were both talking loudly at the same time; Homer complained about the pungent odor in the car but continued to giggle; Orville glanced at Pinto, whose shoulders shook from time to time in an apparent effort to suppress any sign that he was enjoying himself.

Papoose gave Homer directions to return to the apartment.

"Orvie, I think we just blew a tire!" He pulled the car over to the curb. "We gotta put on the spare…"

Papoose kicked the back of Orville's seat so hard it threw him forward against the dashboard. "I shoulda guessed something like this would happen. I never been hooked up with a couple of jinxes like you two in my whole life! Get that goddam tire changed and get me back home. Now! I gotta date tonight and the only thing keeping me from getting killed on sight is a landscaper in Golden and two tickets to the Rolling Stones. *Do it now!*"

"Jeez, Orvie. I can't change a tire with this thing on my neck! You gotta do it for me…"

"I don't know how to change a fucking tire! Besides, it's pouring down rain!"

Papoose leaned forward between the two brothers and grabbed each of them by the shoulder in an iron grip. "We're going to change that tire, and we'll do it now, or you two'll never live to see daylight tomorrow!"

Pinto pulled Papoose back and whispered to him.

"Okay. That'll do it. Since it's raining so damned hard, each of us, except Gopher, will do our share and nobody has to be outside for very long at one time. Orville, you jack up the wheel and get the spare out of the back. Pinto'll take this wheel off and I'll put the new one on. Okay?"

Homer meekly handed the keys to Orville who jumped out of the car, unlocked the trunk, took out the jack and the spare tire and jacked up the right rear wheel before getting back into the car. Pinto disappeared into the rain and could be heard loosening the lug nuts and removing the wheel before he climbed back into the rear seat. Papoose slammed the door on his way out to put on the spare, and quickly returned after closing the trunk.

"Now let's get out of here before something else happens!" Papoose shouted.

Homer started the car, shifted the gears and started down the street. All of them could hear the thump! thump! thump!

"*Now, what?*" Papoose's voice was almost a squeal as he leaned forward and gripped the back of the seat between the two Stokes.

Homer no longer giggled. "Orvie, we *still* got a flat tire," he croaked. "The flat was on the right front wheel. Which one did you jack up?"

No-one took a breath while they waited for the answer.

Orville whispered, "The first one I come to…the *back wheel* on my side…"

Papoose grabbed Orville by the throat and started to choke him. "That's it! That's the last time you're gettin' a chance to fuck things up for me. I oughta strangle you right now and put all of us out of our misery!"

Homer turned to the right as far as possible, and tried to pry Papoose's hands loose. Even Pinto attempted to pull the Indian away, but it was like trying to stop a starving coyote from its attack on a stray lamb. When he finally released the gasping Orville, he slumped against the door on his side and continued to shake with anger.

"You two assholes do what you want," Papoose finally panted. "I'm calling a cab to take me to the apartment and Maria can pick me up from there." He gathered his packages and crawled out into the downpour.

Before the door closed, and just as Pinto was climbing out of his side of the car, Homer said, hesitantly, "We could still change the flat…"

Papoose glared at him, slammed the door and walked away, talking into his cellular phone.

"…or *not!*" Homer concluded.

The Stokes sat silently for some time. Orville was the first to speak. "What now, little brother? No way I can change that tire by myself. Any ideas?"

Homer's voice revealed a touch of pride that the decision had been left up to him. He would have thrown his shoulders back, but in his current condition, that was already pretty much standard everyday posture.

"What say we just dump this heap? I can pick up another one in ten minutes right along this street, and that beats the shit out of messing with this car. Okay?"

Orville's main concern, at the moment, was Papoose. They not only needed him to construct a bomb for them, but the double signature at the bank made it imperative that they patch up the conflict between them in order to sell the bonds.

"Huh, Orvie? Sound okay to you?"

"Yeah, sure. Go ahead. I'll gather up our duffle bags and wait for you here."

Homer collected his gloves along with his notebook-sized set of tools that included a Slim Jim to unlock the "target" car, and stepped out into the rain.

"How about getting' the license plate off this car for me, Orvie?" he asked, handing Orville a screw-driver before he closed the door. "We been using this same one since California and it ain't been traced so far."

"We actually *owned* that one. Remember?"

"Yeah. I forgot."

In what seemed to be even less than ten minutes, Homer pulled alongside the Chevy and honked the horn of a white Isuzu two-door. Orville had already made an effort to smudge whatever fingerprints any of them might have left before he grabbed their two duffle bags, made one last survey of the interior, and stepped out into the rain.

"You still got them maps, Orvie? And don't forget the license plate."

"Yeah, I'll get it now. And about them maps, we sure can't go near Papoose too soon. We'll just check in at that Days Inn Motel we seen on Colfax and try to reconnoiter…"

CHAPTER 17

Brad and Smoky went for a run through the trees bordering Pine Cone. A jogging trail, that he judged to be about three miles long, wound back and forth through the pines to the top of the hill and circled back down to come out at the far end of the campground. Doug was stepping down out of the camper, yawning, when he returned.

"How you down', Doug? You up for all day?"

"Weird. That's what it is…"

"What's weird?"

"Waking up without a hangover! I'm not sure if it's an improvement or not. Seems like I'm more aware of how old I really am when I can feel these creakin' bones. Maybe it's better to be *numb*!"

Brad smiled. "You'll get used to it after a while. You'd be surprised at how much you actually miss when you're half-soused most of the time."

"Could be. One thing I discovered, though, is that the guys I was hanging out with ain't nearly as funny as I thought they were. That, in itself, is a real let-down."

"Well, let's take advantage of the hot showers while we can. After we bathe and shave, how about taking care of Skeeter and then having some breakfast in town. Okay, Doug?"

"Sounds good to me…"

Brad was pleased to see that his father managed to eat his first complete meal in a week. At least for the few days that he could recall.

Anyway, it was an indication that the healing process was taking place and he hoped to be able to keep his father moderately sober for awhile.

"You worried about something, Bud? You're rubbing that scar on your cheek again."

"Nope. Everything's fine…"

When they returned to the fair grounds, Brad saddled Skeeter and loped him around for thirty minutes or so to get him used to the rodeo arena. He was familiar with a few of the contestants, but at this small show there was more local talent than professional. No doubt the majority of these entries only competed in a three-state area near home.

Brad recalled discussing with his cousin Gary, at the rodeo in Phoenix, about how many of the young cowboys were from various cities around the country instead of from rural areas. Gary told him about the number of rodeo "schools" that had come into existence in the years since they had both dropped out of the business. There were so few working ranches any more where someone could learn how to ride broncs or rope cattle, city dwellers now attended these rodeo schools to learn a lot of things, not just about riding techniques but safety, also. It was possible to save themselves several years of bumming around the country, taking a good many unnecessary hard knocks, when they could be trained by experts in bull riding, bronc riding, roping and bulldogging. They learned these events in the safest, most effective way possible. Even the wannabe bull-fighting clowns had schools where they could be trained.

Since this was only a two-day rodeo, with no facilities for night shows, and since there were more entries in roping and bulldogging than in the other events, the first go-rounds started at ten o'clock in the morning. Two of the men Doug was hazing for were up in the early rounds so he was kept *on tap* nearly all day. He and Rex were just two seconds short of first place in the team roping for the day, and three of the four men he hazed for were in the day money: first, second and fourth.

In the team roping event, the contestants backed their horses into the "wings" on either side of the chute in which the steer was held. This was the same as with the bulldogging only in this case it was the "header" who was required to be on the left side of the steer and the "heeler" on the right as they faced the arena. Brad never ceased to feel proud of the talent his father displayed in whipping his loop under the belly of the steer already roped by the header. He did it in such a way that the open noose stood on end, waiting for the steer to be pulled forward by the header. It was a rare occasion when he only caught one leg. A two-leg catch with the steer stretched out between the two ropers was the signal for the field judge to drop his flag. This designated the "time" they received as their score, but the horses must be facing the animal with their front feet on the ground; the steer must be standing, and the ropers, still mounted, were required to dally the rope around their saddle horn after a catch. Very few of the spectators were aware of how exacting the requirements were for a team to make a qualified "catch." Any contestant over fifty years of age was allowed to tie the rope "hard and fast" to his saddle horn as opposed to dallying (taking quick wraps around the horn), but even though Doug qualified for this privilege, he never took advantage of that rule. Brad always felt it was a matter of pride that his father still roped and dallied as fast as the younger men.

Brad caught himself chuckling when he remembered the time in New Mexico when Doug was tending bar at a local saloon and Brad's mother, Edna, sent her son over there with a plate of fried chicken because Doug was working a double shift. When Brad came in the front door, the place was empty and Doug was throwing loops at a bar stool in the center of the room. The noose stood on end perfectly in front of the legs of the stool and Doug yelled at his son, "Jerk him into the loop, boy…we got him nailed!"

Smoky had been following Brad around the outside of the arena and now he nudged Brad's leg for attention.

"Getting bored, are we? How about some tennis?"

With this cue, Smoky headed for the camper where it was parked near the horse barn. He arrived first and ran in circles until Brad got a well worn tennis ball out of the front compartment and began throwing it for Smoky to chase down and return. After ten or fifteen minutes of this, Brad could see the dog was tireless so the only way to end their game was to just call it quits.

"Enough's enough, you mangy mutt! I'm going back to the arena." Smoky hung his head briefly, then followed at his master's heels.

Brad enjoyed watching the wild horse race, as always. It was one of the rare events seen only at smaller shows, where the wild broncs were all released at the same time to teams of three men per horse. With only a halter and twenty feet of rope already on each bronc, the team was required to saddle the horse for one of them to mount and ride it to the far end of the arena before any of the other entries. Sometimes it was necessary for a member of the team to "ear down" the horse, which consisted of grabbing the animal by both ears, in order to accomplish this feat. Because these broncs were always straight off of the open range and had never been handled before, it was an excitingly unpredictable event that promoted a great deal of laughter and applause from the audience.

Two of the girls who were in the barrel racing at Bear Claw, had the best times for the day with one of them only two-tenths of a second ahead of the other. The remaining contestants, probably all local girls, were much slower in completing the go-round.

When the saddle-bronc riding began, Brad was standing just outside of the arena fence near the bucking chutes. He had an eerie feeling when the rider started to climb down into the chute only fifteen feet away. It was like watching a replay of a previous event. His stomach muscles tightened. Breathing became rapid. Mouth dry. He, himself, was settling into the saddle. Just briefly he experienced what had happened to him at Bear Claw, then the chute flew open, the rider was thrown, and Brad's temporary recall ended.

"Jesus!" he said to himself. "I almost remembered…"

Doug walked up beside him. "You say something, Bud?"

"Nope. Just thinking out loud. That bronc was pretty tough for a small show like this…"

"Yeah, they have some good livestock here. See the size of the dogging' steers? Glad I'm just hazing." Doug rubbed Smoky's ears and headed toward the camper. "Skeeter's put away for the night. We could pick up an order of fast food, if you want, and head for the campground. Maybe a six-pack of Coors?" he asked hopefully.

"Sure, Doug. That sounds like a winner."

"Or even play a few racks of nine-ball?"

"I think I should warn you, I'm tougher to beat than I was the last time we played! There's not much else to do in Los Gatos. Just play pool and arrest an occasional drunk. Most of them are off of the Mescalero Indian Reservation…"

"We'll see. We'll see. I picked up a few pointers myself watching the pros play on ESPN. How about loser buys the beer?"

"You sound like Angie when she's hustling up a game. Remember when Tooley sent me to find her in Reno when you were in jail in Mesquite, Arizona? She was playing eight-ball against a bunch of locals when I finally caught up with her, and she was already a couple of hundred bucks ahead." He thought about what her dad said a few days before. "Tooley sounds like he sure misses her now that she and Chip are in protective custody."

"Your friend Laredo said it was the only way he could be sure they'd be safe. You say he's coming to Denver?"

"Yeah, next weekend. You've never met him, but you two'll really get along great. He had a ranch near Laredo, Texas before he got into law enforcement. He's retired now, sort of. Keeps his hand in when there's something interesting in the works…"

"You're stalling, Bud. Let's find a pool hall so I can get myself some free beer!"

* * *

When the Stokes checked in at Days Inn, they drove around the corner from the office and parked near the doorway to the building where their room was located. After checking a chart of the layout, Orville had requested a room on the first floor so they would be near the swimming pool and Jacuzzi. He explained that his brother needed easy access to both.

Homer did not attempt to swim, but he did, in fact, remove his cervical collar when he reached the jacuzzi and he soaked in the hot bubbling water while Orville swam laps in the pool. They both ordered chicken-fried steak and apple pie from room service and Homer went to sleep almost immediately after eating. Orville watched television the rest of the evening and even went to sleep with the set turned on. He awoke a couple of times during the night and watched parts of old movies before dozing again.

It was nearly eight o'clock the next morning when Homer stirred. They discussed what would be the best way to approach Papoose after what happened the night before. The motel address on Colfax was not too far from the apartment so they decided to drive over there and just park outside until Papoose arrived and they would let him make the first move.

"Hope he's not packing a pistol when he makes that move!" Orville said.

"Or a tomahawk…"

The continental breakfast was still available so they grabbed a couple of doughnuts, some juice and coffee before taking off. Orville picked up a Colorado map at the service station across the street when they gassed up the Isuzu, so he suggested Homer drive while he looked over their possible routes to Estes Park. On arrival at Papoose's apartment they saw the Mustang parked near the foot of the outside stairway.

"We ain't going' up there, are we, Orvie? No telling what he might do."

"Nope. Let's just sit here for awhile and see what happens."

They opened the car doors to allow some breeze to blow through and after about thirty minutes they agreed to take a look at Papoose's marijuana crop. Both were astounded at how many plants were growing in the small area hidden among the sunflowers. On their way back to the car they saw Pinto descending the stairway. He was about half-way down when he seemed to spot them and returned to enter the apartment. In a moment, Papoose stepped out onto the landing and motioned for them to come upstairs.

"He's gonna kill us, ain't he, Orvie?"

"Damned if I know. He's the only game in town so all we can do is take a deep breath and hope for the best…"

They approached the apartment as quietly as possible with each of them trying to shove the other through the doorway first.

Papoose leaned against the sink, arms crossed over his chest. He made no mention of the fact that they were now driving an Isuzu in place of the Chevy. The reasons must have been obvious. His hat was tipped forward touching the bridge of his nose, and he remained silent for several minutes, then with a sweep of one arm he indicated they should sit down. Orville pulled a wooden lawn chair to the center of the room and Homer plopped onto the matching bench facing Papoose. Pinto was already on his haunches against the wall.

"Before I show you what we've been puttin' together," Papoose began, "we need to get one thing straight." He paused and glared at Orville, then Homer. "Maria reminded me how important it is for me to get my share of the bond money. She says to make that happen, I've got to help you assholes whether I like it or not. Agreed?"

They nodded.

"So I'll show you the pipe bomb I built and tell you how to carry it in the "cradle" Pinto built. Then it's up to you to take care of the easy part: put the damned thing under the seat of Hasting's pickup truck and get the hell out of there before they move it. Okay?"

They nodded again.

Pinto slid to an upright position and followed Papoose into the lab.

"Sometimes Doug and the cowboy sleep in the camper, Orvie. We gotta plant the bomb while the rodeo's going' on, right?"

"We'll see when we get there. Shhh! They're coming back…"

Papoose came to the table carrying an eight-inch piece of pipe that appeared to be about two-inches in diameter. Both ends were capped off and there was a small hole drilled in the top near one end. He handled it as though it were pure nitro. Pinto followed and placed a handmade wooden cradle onto the table. Papoose carefully laid the pipe lengthwise in this holder. The sides were just high enough to prevent the pipe from rolling out unless there was a moderately severe jarring motion to the structure in which it had been placed. Papoose explained to them something about eighty percent potassium permanganate, twenty percent sugar mixture, and the top hole filled with sulfuric acid. He said a membrane glued in place kept the mixtures apart and when the pipe was dislodged from its cradle, the membrane would burst allowing the sulfuric acid to come into contact with the mixture and it would explode violently. Sounded like he was quoting from one of his books.

"So how do we haul it sixty miles away?" Orville's voice quivered.

"See this roll of duct tape? Just wrap the tape around the pipe and the cradle at both ends and don't remove it *until the bomb is placed under the seat of the pickup.*" He looked from one to the other, uncertainly. "Tape both ends securely. *Got it?*"

Orville thought there must be an easier way to do this, but he knew they had no choice. He looked at Homer's pale face and reached over to pat him on the shoulder. "We can do it, can't we, little brother?"

"Sure, Orvie," he squeaked. "No problem…"

Papoose carefully retrieved the bomb and headed for the door. Pinto followed, carrying the cradle.

"Orville, you get a couple of towels from the bathroom, and Gopher can grab that roll of tape, then open the trunk of your car. Once we've placed this in the trunk, in the rack, with towels all around it, you can head north. But above all, *don't forget to tape it in place.* Okay?"

With the trunk open, the bomb was delicately placed in the cradle before Papoose and Pinto backed away.

"I picked up a map this morning, Papoose. Want to show me the best way for us to go?"

"Sure. Come over here by the steps and I'll mark it for you."

Pinto headed toward the "garden," which was no doubt where he had been going when he first spotted the Stokes from the stairway earlier.

"You all set, Gopher?" Papoose asked when he walked back toward the car with Orville.

Homer's small tool kit had already been moved to the front seat of the car to make room for the bomb and Orville now watched while Homer finished surrounding the cradle with several towels, tucking them around the sides and over the top of the bomb. A buffer area was also created using their duffle bags and a bedroll from the back seat of the car.

"All set!" Homer's voice sounded less tentative now that the bomb was secure. Papoose jumped forward just as he started to slam the trunk.

"Hold it, Gopher! No sense jarring that thing even if it is tied down…" He eased the trunk lid to close it and stepped away from the car.

Orville settled himself on the passenger's side, still holding the folded section of map with its red pencil markings to indicate their route. Once Homer was situated in the driver's seat, he let go of the large roll of duct tape he had been clutching to his chest and placed it on the front seat next to his tool kit and gloves. They both closed their car doors softly before waving goodbye.

"Wow! Sure a good thing Papoose knows what he's doing, huh, Orvie? That'd scare the shit out of me to try and build something like that!"

They pulled back out onto Colfax and turned left toward Denver. "We stay on this street until we get to Wadsworth, then go north on Colorado 121 where we hit I-36. That takes us through Boulder to Estes Park. We should make it easy before the afternoon performance is over. You okay, Homer? You looked a little scared there for awhile."

"Naw, I'm all right now. It shook me up at first when Papoose started talking about how touchy that thing is, but I ain't afraid no more."

They drove in silence with Orville watching first for Wadsworth, then checking the map constantly to seen how far they were from I-36. About five miles before that intersection, Homer asked if he could stop at a strip mall and pick up something cold to drink. He was driving through a parking area where there were several speed bumps ahead of them when Orville noticed the roll of duct tape on the front seat.

"You taped that pipe down real good, didn't you Homer?"

Homer gripped the steering wheel and stared straight ahead. Orville sensed the eyes behind the dark glasses were almost popping out of Homer's head. "They said to tape the pipe *after I put it in his truck,* right?"

Just as Orville screamed, "Oh, *FUCK!*" Homer slammed on the brakes and the entire back end of the Isuzu, rear axle and all, was blasted across the parking lot into someone's back yard. What was left of the car was filled with smoke and was still vibrating from the shock when both men jumped out and ran for nearly a block before stopping.

When they felt they were a safe distance away from the blast, Homer sat on the curb and began to whimper. Orville was so shaken by what had happened that he made no attempt to console his brother. Instead, he just collapsed beside him, and put his head in his hands.

CHAPTER 18

Brad rolled out of bed and dressed quietly to avoid waking Doug. In warmups and Nikes, he left for his morning run with Smoky, and decided to jog over to the arena to take care of Skeeter before coming back to follow the trail through the trees. He wanted to shower without returning to the camper at the end of his run, so he tied a towel around his waist over the top of a fanny pack containing soap, toothbrush and razor.

On returning to the camper, he put the contents of last night's doggie bag into a dish for Smoky, gave him a bowl of water, and retrieved his laptop computer.

The first document he brought up on the screen was the rodeo schedule he updated annually to tell where Doug might go from week to week. With so many shows left on the list for this year, he had the sinking feeling that it would be virtually impossible to talk Doug into going back to New Mexico with him in a couple of months. As for himself, he realized this life no longer interested him like it did when he was younger. He wanted to get back to his job and his small spread, all of which would no doubt sound dull to his father, but might also be his salvation if only Brad could make him see it that way.

When Brad switched over to *DIARY*, he noted that the pages were blank following the day of his accident. Prior to that, there was one brief statement that he "might try riding saddle broncs *at this little show*." It was understandable that everything stopped there, but he had really hoped he might have typed something during his blackout phase that would help him to remember. Nothing. Earlier entries depicted their trip from the rodeo in Mesquite, Arizona, to Phoenix, and on to Colorado Springs where they stopped over so Doug could show off the headquarters of the Professional Rodeo Cowboys Association and their museum. Although it had not been that many years since he dropped out, Brad was very impressed at the advances made in the organization as a whole. Doug showed him a copy of the current bylaws and rules which Brad skimmed through, commenting on the precision with which the events and the livestock were handled. What he did not mention to his father was that it seemed to him that all of these new rules and regulations, while improving the quality of the performances, seemed likely to take the *fun* out of it for the contestants. Right out of high school he and Gary had done everything spontaneously, going from rodeo to rodeo on a whim with no particular schedule (no longer possible), and travelling with first one group and then another (no longer feasible with some cowboys working as many as three or four shows on the same weekend, and flying back and forth from one to the other to compete.) And it was no longer permissible to just hang around the chutes and shoot the breeze with other contestants if your own stock was not ready for you to mount. He wondered if this "new breed" ever headed for a pool hall or local bar, *just for the fun of it*, after the show was over.

As he shut off the computer and replaced it in the case, he thought to himself that there were definitely reasons for the advancements made in the rodeo profession, but it was sad that something had been lost in the process. He also felt let down because nothing in *DIARY* depicted their arrival in Bear Claw or time spent at Little Bear Lake.

Doug appeared in the doorway of the camper.

"Hi, Bud? See you found that gadget of yours. Can you get it to tell you how much money I'm going to win here?"

"I'm afraid not. Maybe someone will come up with a program named 'Virtual ESP' that flashes tarot cards onto the screen and tells your fortune, but right now it won't be a hell of a lot of help!"

"Well, in that case, if you can't give me any kind of an edge in the roping, why don't you make yourself useful and pick up a couple of cups of coffee and some breakfast rolls at that little market?"

"I don't mind brewing a pot of coffee here in the camper, and fixing some French toast if you'd actually eat something. They have eggs and bread…"

"Don't push, Bud. If you're hungry, we can drive into town later and you can grab a bite to eat at that Denny's we saw, but as for me, I'm just trying to get through one more day of this *soberness* you've inflicted on me. So don't push!"

Brad nodded, and with Smoky trailing along, he headed for the market.

They did, in fact, drive into town after Doug showered and shaved. While Doug looked on, almost disapprovingly, Brad consumed a large order of pancakes with a side of bacon and eggs. They browsed through a few stores so Brad could check their prices but he soon cancelled his shopping when he saw how much a plain western shirt would cost. He had intended to buy two or three when they came through Denver (and when *was* that, he wondered?), but on checking his luggage yesterday, he found no evidence of having done so.

They pulled onto the rodeo grounds and Doug parked near the horse barn shortly after noon. With the first go-round of the roping and bull-dogging out of the way, there was no longer a need to have anyone compete before the actual performance time of two o'clock.

"I picked up a copy of the local newspaper this morning," Brad said, "and I noticed that Jerry T was entered here. I didn't watch the barebacks yesterday and we left before the bull-riding, so I missed seeing him. Unless you want me for something, I think I'll track him down now…"

"Sure. I'll walk over with you."

As they passed by a small cluster of people, obviously family and friends of a young cowboy who turned around to show off the contestant's number on his back, Brad heard one of the men say, "We seen the damnedest thing just before we left home a couple of hours ago."

"What was that, Uncle Joe?"

"You know that little market across the street from my house in Boulder? A white two-door sedan, one of them Japanese cars, pulled into the parking lot and just flat blew apart! Billy Boy says it was an Isuzu…he knows all them foreign cars…"

Brad and Doug were both compelled to slow their pace, curious to hear the rest of what "Uncle Joe" had to say.

"Anybody killed?" one of the women asked.

"Nope. Funny thing, though. The whole back end of the car blew plumb off and landed in Scotty Gilbert's back yard. The driver and passenger simply climbed out and run down the street, like they was headed for Denver on foot!"

"You ever hear who they were, Joe?" someone else inquired.

"Nope, but just as all of us were piling into the car to come up here, I seen them sauntering back like this was nothing out of the ordinary for them. One man reached into the front seat, which of course was the only seat left, and took out what looked like a tool box. The one with a brace on his neck went over into Scotty's yard and walked off with a small piece of the car that still had the license plate attached."

"You think he hurt his neck in the explosion?"

"I doubt it. There hadn't been enough time for him to see a doctor. Anyway, they just took off down the road carrying the tool kit and the license plate, and never looked back."

"Any police on the scene, Joe?"

"Not before we left. I can't wait to get home tonight and find out from Scotty what happened…"

Doug stopped in his tracks when he first heard mention of "a man with a brace on his neck". He looked at Brad, who had also paused to catch the rest of the man's story. "You don't suppose…?"

"Can't be. They were driving an old grey Chevy at the hospital. Anyway, there's got to be hundreds of people with neck braces."

"Too bad it wasn't them, Bud. That gunsel deserves to get blowed up!"

They walked on toward the arena. Jerry Tandy was talking to several riders while he braided a bull-riding rope. The honda end, where the braiding began, was fastened to the pole fence with a leather strap and as he backed away, he continued weaving the three thick strands into a tight flat surface that would be tied off when he reached the end.

"Hey, there, Jerry T!" Brad slapped his friend on the back. "Building yourself a winning rig, are you?"

Jerry looked up and smiled. "I wouldn't go so far as to make any predictions, but I do know my old rope was almost shot." He turned to Doug. "You're doing okay, here, huh?"

Doug stood a little straighter. "Yeah. So far. Three of my men already won some dogging money."

"We missed your rides yesterday, Jerry T," Brad leaned against the fence as he spoke. "How'd you do?"

"Second in the bareback go-round. Bucked off my bull. About average, I guess you'd say…" He looked toward Brad. "You see that screwy horse race last night?"

"No. In fact we left right after the dogging. What kind of race was it?" Brad asked.

"Somebody on the rodeo committee is from Australia and he insisted they run around the track *clockwise* like they do where he used to live. Ever see race horses run the wrong way, Doug?"

"Sure have. Every horse I bet on does just that!"

Brad straightened, and moved away from the fence. He was more tired than he realized from the extra running that morning.

"Doug, I think I'll go back to the camper for awhile. You want any help before your team roping?"

"No. But thanks, anyway, Bud. You go ahead, and I'll see you later."

Smoky ran in circles, trying to encourage Brad to play with him, but he soon gave up and by the time they reached the camper, they were walking slowly, side by side.

Brad slept for nearly two hours and when he returned to the arena, the bull-riding was about to begin. He knew this was the final event of the day so he thought he would see if Doug planned to leave town that evening or wait until the next day.

Brad saw Jerry T standing just outside of the arena. He was talking to a bull-fighting clown who called himself "Poncho Villa," and they were discussing the bull Jerry T was to ride that afternoon.

After introducing the two men, Jerry T continued, "That bull called Pikes Peak, is he pretty tough?"

"Not really," Poncho replied. "He don't buck too hard, just spins to the left, into your riding arm, as soon as he leaves the chute. But when you *do* get off of him, get the hell out of there! He's a *mean mother* once you're on the ground…"

Jerry T laughed, but it was a nervous laugh. "Where'll you be, Poncho? Isn't that what they hire you for?"

"Me? Probably in my barrel. I'll make a couple of swipes at him, just enough to look like I'm earning my wages, then I'll take a dive. I'll protect you the best I can, but you'd better hit the ground running and haul ass to the nearest fence!"

Brad interrupted at that point. "Poncho, I've always wondered something, aren't you guys ever afraid of getting killed by the bulls?"

The clown makeup was in the form of a permanent smile, but Poncho's eyes were serious when he replied, "To tell you the truth, a man's more apt to get killed making them long drives from show to show than he is here in the arena. Folks think it's the horns we have to worry about but it's really their feet. A one-ton bull stompin' on you can put quite a dent in your carcass, and if the ground's a little wet, it's hard to get your footin'. Mostly, we just play around with them enough to make a good show and try to keep the cowboys out of trouble."

Brad decided to watch Jerry T's ride before looking for Doug. He noticed that Smoky ducked behind him and lay down as soon as the first Brahma came out of the chute. He stayed there during all of the rides. Smart dog.

Jerry T's ride was the fifth one, and as predicted, Pikes Peak spun to the left and gave a showy performance but was not tough enough to throw its rider before the whistle. Then the fun began. The instant Jerry T's feet hit the ground, the bull took out after him, swinging his head as he charged. At times, the horns barely missed the target, who was zigzagging his way toward the fence, with Poncho trying desperately to distract the bull by running alongside and swiping at him with a bright orange straw hat. Jerry T was cut off from his escape route to the fence and before anyone realized what was happening, the bull had maneuvered both the rider and the clown into the position where their only shelter was inside the barrel. Poncho reached it first and jumped in, followed immediately by Jerry T who landed on top of the clown.

"Get off'n me, you moron!" Poncho's voice was muffled because of his position at the bottom of the barrel. "There ain't room in here for both of us!"

"By damn, there'd *better* be!"

Pikes Peak hit the barrel just then and sent it rolling. Somehow the two occupants held onto the inside straps that were placed there for just that purpose, and every time the bull thumped them again, they cursed each other loudly.

Since Poncho was the only bull-fighter hired for such a small rodeo, it was up to the other cowboys to try and distract Pikes Peak before he "rolled them to death," as one rider put it. He was waving his chaps in front of the charging animal at the time, without any success. The entire episode only lasted a matter of three or four minutes before the bull was herded out of the arena, but to the two men who crawled out of the open-ended barrel, it must have seemed like an eternity.

The audience obviously thought the *entertainment* was hilarious. Horns honked, people cheered, and the two bedraggled "stars" took a bow to acknowledge the applause.

Brad met Jerry T at the gate when he left the arena.

"Are you having fun, yet?" he asked. "See why I never took up bull-riding?"

Jerry T just shook his head and walked toward the catch-pens to retrieve his loose-rope. Brad could hear him mumbling, "A man's gotta be nuts to do this for a living…"

Doug rode over to where Brad was standing. "What d'ya think, Bud? Want to take off tonight or stay over? Makes no never-mind to me…"

"Tell you what I'd really like to do, Doug, is see if any vacancies have opened up now that the show's over, and check into a motel for one night where I can soak in a tub of hot water. What would be even more perfect would be to find a place with a jacuzzi."

"Sounds good to me. Let's put Skeeter away and see what we can find…"

CHAPTER 19

Orville settled back, watching for the Colfax intersection. They had continued travelling south on Wadsworth after Homer *recruited* another vehicle. This time it was a 1989 red Ford pickup. Orville would have preferred something less conspicuous but he was so glad to be riding instead of walking that he offered no criticism. The California plate should give them a slight edge, and with a can of spray paint, they could stencil a logo of some business or other on the doors. It had worked before.

"You know where we're going, Orvie?"

"Right now I'm just trying to get back to familiar ground. I lost the map Papoose wrote his directions on, but I've still got the small one he drew for us showing how to get to the apartment and to Maria's house. I kept that drawing in the crown of my baseball cap."

"Ain't you scared to see Papoose again? I sure as hell am! There's no telling what he might do this time. Do we *have* to tell him the truth, Orvie? He ain't too crazy about me as it is…"

"If I could think of even one good excuse about why this deal got fucked up, I'd tell it to him myself, but you know how you are about lying…"

Homer whimpered, "I can't help it if I get the *hiccup*s when I try to lie. You know I been that way since we was kids."

"There's Colfax at the next light. Turn right at that signal and we'll stop some place before we get to the apartment. We need to reconnoiter."

The Stokes were definitely in no hurry for a confrontation with Papoose so they spent the next few hours having something to eat, picking up supplies from a hobby store, and completing the camouflage job on the Ford in a vacant lot behind what appeared to have been a lumbar yard before it closed down. They realized by now that at least two of the stolen credit cards they traded for had never been cancelled so they were not completely broke. Maybe the former owner was now an unidentified corpse somewhere in the Mohave Desert. In any event, this was about the only thing that had gone right for them in quite awhile.

"Well, as the saying goes, I guess it's now or never, Homer. Either Papoose kills us or the cowboy turns us in for murder. Either way, we're at the end of our rope."

"They're going to *hang* us? Jeez, Orvie. Ain't there some other way outta this mess?"

"All I know is, we got to find him, tell him the truth, and see what happens."

Homer's words were barely audible. "Whatever you say, Orvie."

They pulled off of Colfax and made one loop through the parking area at the apartment. Since neither the Mustang nor Maria's car was there, they continued on toward Golden. At the outskirts of town, Homer began driving slower and slower until Orville reminded him that they might as well get it over with, no matter what the outcome.

Homer drove to Maria's house and parked along the curb. This made for a faster getaway in the event they needed to escape in a hurry. Orville pointed at the new lilac bush as they walked along the empty driveway.

"Looks as good as the other one, huh, Homer? Things have a way of working out."

"If you say so, Orvie."

They were sitting on the porch swing when the Mustang pulled into the driveway. To avoid any chance of further discord, Orville insisted they not move back and forth for fear the squeaking noise might irritate Papoose even more.

Papoose came around the back of his car and looked at the red Ford at the curb, the one with AMERICAN PLUMBING SUPPLIES, Oceanside, California, in bold black lettering on the door.

"What the...?" He sounded irritated and puzzled at the same time. Then he peered through the semi-darkness and suddenly seemed to recognize the two men sitting there, woodenly, staring back at him.

Pinto ducked around the front of the car and quickly disappeared into the darkness.

Orville realized neither he nor his brother was breathing. He nudged Homer and whispered, "Go ahead. Take a breath. No sense dying before we know what's about to happen."

Papoose approached, still straining to positively identify the two men on the porch. Or maybe he simply hoped he was wrong. When his expression disclosed the fact that his fears were confirmed, he slumped onto the top step and leaned against the stair rail, moaning softly like Indians do during a funeral ritual for a member of their tribe.

Neither of the Stokes wanted to be the first to speak so they simply sat there, not moving, breathing as shallowly as possible to avoid a confrontation until it was forced on them.

Eventually the moaning stopped. Papoose looked up at the two men. "Why am I not surprised? Funny thing, I actually expect something to go wrong when it involves you two, but you know what? I'm a stubborn bastard, and ever since I was a kid I've tried to hang in there 'til I got the job done. Once when I was about seven, I went to a Saturday movie where John Wayne and some soldiers wiped out a whole Indian village. Know what I did? I sat there through three more performances, 'til my older brother came to drag me home. I was still waitin' for the Indians to win at least once!" He took off his hat and wiped his forehead with a bandanna handkerchief. "Maybe that's what I'm doing now. I'm hanging in there in hopes you two will do something right, in spite of your past record. The odds are about the same as they were for that tribe of Sioux."

Homer was the first to speak. In spite of his attempt to sound confident, there was a telltale quiver in his voice. "It wasn't our fault. *Hiccup.* Papoose. Honest. *Hiccup.* A big semi rammed us. *Hiccup.* And the car just exploded…"

"That right, Orville?" Papoose asked. "That what happened?"

Homer's *hiccups* were louder now and he showed signs of having a panic attack.

"That's right, Papoose. Just like he told you."

"*Hiccup. Hiccup. Hiccup…*"

"Can I get Homer a drink of water? Sometimes he passes out when he has these spasms."

Papoose seemed reluctant to let the Stokes into the house but when he headed for the kitchen, they followed right behind him.

Since lack of water had nothing to do with Homer's problem, his *hiccups* continued until Papoose's demeanor indicated that he bought their story. At that point, the attack subsided.

They were almost able to convince Papoose that they were in no immediate danger because of the stolen pickup truck, but their track record kept him from buying the theory completely.

Without being invited, Orville and Homer seated themselves at the kitchen table. It would be more awkward for Papoose to throw them out if they acted like invited guests. There was still a strained silence while the three of them sat and stared at each other.

Finally, Papoose spoke. "So tell me, what wild scheme have you two decided on now? You've only got a couple of days left if you're going to get rid of those two turkeys and I'm not at all sure there's any way for me to save your asses this time. Two ideas that seemed fool proof have blown up in our faces. Literally. So outside of buying a couple of uzis and blowing them away, I don't know what to tell you."

Silence again.

"Orvie," Homer began, tentatively, almost in a whisper. "Could we try poison again? Only this time, we figure some way to put it into their *food* so they'd both kick the bucket for sure…"

Silence.

It was Papoose who spoke next. "There just might be a chance to pull off something like that, but I'd have to know more about the setup there at that lake. Do they stay in their camper? In a tent? In a cabin?"

"Cabin." Orville wanted to speak as little as possible. He was so relieved that Papoose had again taken the reins, he dared not risk saying the wrong thing.

"Any chance you could get inside, like maybe while they're fishin' or something, and put poison in the food in their ice box, or cooler, or whatever the hell they use for keepin' their meat fresh…?"

Silence.

Orville cleared his throat and spoke a little more confidently this time. "The cabin we were in, the one belonging to the boss man from L.A., had electric lights and a small fridge. I could hear a motor running someplace out behind the place, so I guess probably all of them have the same equipment. The cabins are about a mile apart and look like they've all been built by the same person. Probably sold them off to different people."

"What kind of locks did they have on the front door?"

"Padlocks."

Papoose looked worried. "That'll be tough. You two don't know nothing about locks. Right?"

Homer sounded excited. When he actually had something to contribute to their plans, he was always eager for their approval. "Remember that bathroom window, Orvie? It didn't even have a lock on it!"

"You're right. I suppose all those places are pretty much alike, but the windows weren't very big."

"I could do it, Orvie! I could crawl through there and unlock that *ar-kay-dee* door for you. And I'd wear my gloves. I really could do it, Orvie!"

Papoose shook his head and frowned. "Think about it, Gopher. Remember what we went through just getting you in and out of the Mustang? You'd likely fall head first into the toilet if you tried a stunt like that."

Homer looked crushed.

Orville spoke quickly, as much to spare Homer's feelings as anything, but mainly to keep the ball rolling while Papoose was in the mood to help them again.

"I think maybe I could do it, though, Papoose. The windows are about three feet wide and I'm sure I could squeeze through…"

Papoose got to his feet and stared at first one, then the other. "You can stay here tonight, and tomorrow we'll go back to the apartment and I'll brew up something that'll knock off both of the Hastings, pronto. I got an idea now about how much the two of them weigh, total, and I'll give you something to stir in or sprinkle on, so there's no reason it won't do the job this time. Right?"

Afraid of breaking the spell, the two Stokes simply nodded. They stood, then followed Papoose quietly upstairs.

"Maria's at some kind of a real estate meetin' but she'll be home pretty soon, and we gotta scram before she gets up in the morning. She's still a little hot about her lilac bush, and I'd rather she don't see you two at all."

Orville said, meekly, "Me, too…"

Papoose added, before closing his bedroom door, "And don't forget to make your bed!"

CHAPTER 20

Doug awoke early, for a change, and was anxious for them to be on their way. Brad made one last trip to the jacuzzi before getting dressed, and he was almost tempted to leave the Ace bandage off, but decided not to press his luck. Outside of a sharp pain once in a while when he lifted Doug's saddle, he felt very few after-effects from the accident. Of course, there was the blow to his head which still caused occasional throbbing.

"You all set, Bud?" Doug appeared in the bathroom doorway where Brad had just finished shaving. "I checked us out at the front desk and picked up Skeeter and the trailer while you was in that bubble thing. I suppose you want food, but we can get something further on down the road."

"Sounds like a winner. Smoky with you?"

"Yeah. He's already in the camper. The only thing holding us up is you."

"Like you said once before, let's *round 'em up and head 'em out!*"

Doug was still pretty "antsy" from so many days of forced sobriety and he was already behind the wheel when Brad joined him. They stopped for coffee and doughnuts at a Circle-K and were on their way. It was obvious to Brad that they were not going to eat breakfast any time soon, so he decided to ride in the camper where he could make a few entries in his laptop. Smoky rode back there with him until Doug finally stopped and they crawled out to find themselves in Nederland.

After breakfast, during which Doug actually ate one fried egg and a single hotcake, Brad was recruited to drive. He felt reluctant to bring up the fact that he had no idea how to get to Little Bear Lake and he could only hope that Doug might realize this and save him the embarrassment of asking.

When they came to the city limits (if the beginning of a five block area could be referred to as such), Doug suggested they pick up some supplies before going to the lake.

"I don't doubt we'll catch enough fish to keep us going," he said with a smile, "but it won't hurt to have some extra grub just in case. I'll get us some charcoal so we can barbecue a couple of steaks tonight." He paused, looking surprised. "I can't believe I'm actually thinking about food!"

"That sounds good to me. Maybe we can eat three meals a day now, instead of the infrequent occasions when your stomach gives its permission…"

Doug did not respond to the last remark, which had been offered in a joking tone of voice. When he loaded the boxes into the camper he made no attempt to hide the fact that his purchases included two six-packs of Coors, and a small bottle of wine.

Brad made no comment. His father was trying so hard to please him, it would not be fair to make him feel guilty about having a small amount of liquor to drink in the evening. In fact, it was Brad who felt guilty about putting so much pressure on Doug to stay sober, but it was all part of his plan to encourage his father to return to New Mexico in the fall.

Doug agreed to drive on out to the lake after Brad mentioned that his ribs still bothered him a little bit when he was driving their rig off of the highway and he would rather his dad take over. He had no way of knowing whether Doug accepted this excuse, since he made no comment.

Doug had said something about a barbecue at the Gorman cabin as though Brad should be familiar with the facilities there, but he still had no recollection of the place. Maybe when they arrived, something would jog his memory and at least bring him up to date as to what happened immediately *prior* to his accident.

Doug drove south out of town for about three miles before turning right onto a graveled road. They were already into timber country with tall pine trees blocking their view in every direction. This utter seclusion from the outside world made the view appear even more spectacular when a narrow trail branched off to their right and an immense circular bowl of pine trees with an oval-shaped lake in its center suddenly appeared. Rays of fading sunlight glistened on the ripples trailing behind a small motor boat.

They passed a small log building that displayed various signs advertising groceries, ice, bait, tackle, and boat rentals. Doug geared down to drive slowly along Little Bear Drive, the narrow road that encircled the lake. It gave Brad a chance to absorb the beauty of the cottonwood trees, pines and aspens growing along the shore line and the narrow grassy meadow that spread out toward a wooded pine forest on the edge of which were two-story A-line cabins spaced about a mile apart all around the lake. From a distance, they appeared to be identical, with each cabin a little over three hundred yards from the water where small piers were scattered at intervals suggesting one to every four cabins. As far as he could tell, either a canoe, a rubber raft or a small row-boat was tied up at each pier, and as they passed the first one, a man climbed out of a ten-footer followed by a small boy proudly carrying a string of five or six fish.

At the end of the fourth driveway, Doug pulled around to the side of the log cabin. Brad noticed a redwood sign above the doorway that indicated this was "Gorman's Hideaway".

"Well, Bud. Here we are again. This place is still as peaceful as ever." After he stepped out of the pickup, he turned to stare back toward the lake. "If you had something like this in New Mexico, I might even be persuaded to go back home with you…"

Brad and Smoky were already out of the truck and were standing on the front steps when Doug joined them and began searching under various planters on the window sill.

"Key oughta be here someplace. That's where I left it last week."

A station wagon pulled into the driveway just then, and slowly approached the cabin. A small bespectacled man with a receding hairline, skinny arms and legs and a long nose, all of which made him look like a *roadrunner*, stepped out of the car and approached them tentatively. He wore knee-length khaki shorts and a thin yellow tee shirt which may have been the reason he was shivering, considering the distinct drop in temperature at this altitude. Of course, the possibility of an unaccustomed confrontation with strangers could have brought on the same reaction.

"Anything I can do for you?" he asked suspiciously. The others remained in the station wagon, peeking through the windows.

Doug turned. "No, that's okay. Fred Gorman let us stay here for a few days before the Bear Claw rodeo and we just came back to pick up my son's truck. That's it in the carport."

Relief flooded the man's face. "Oh, well. That's fine. That's just fine. I guess you're looking for this, right?"

He dug a key out of his pocket then turned toward the remaining occupants of the station wagon and motioned for them to join the trio at the front door.

Introductions all around confirmed that the two couples were also friends of the Gormans and had borrowed the cabin for a few days. They said they were leaving the following morning, but if the Hastings had planned to stay overnight, there was plenty of room for them in the loft.

Brad and Doug assured them it was not necessary because they had sufficient sleeping quarters in their campers.

"My dog and I sleep in the back of my truck all the time, so we'll be fine…"

"If it's okay with you, though," Doug interrupted, "I'd sure like to unload my horse and picket him out in back of the cabin. We'll pull down by the lake to camp for the night and there's not really any place for a horse."

While Doug and the roadrunner, whose name was Phil, took care of Skeeter and unhooked the horse trailer, the two wives went on into the house and the second man, Arnold, watched Brad pull his truck around to the front of the cabin. Smoky had planted himself on the front seat and gave no indication that he would move until he was assured that Brad had taken permanent possession of *their* pickup.

Arnold seemed fascinated by what Brad referred to as his calico truck. It was spotted with various layers of orange, white, red and black paint plus patches of gray primer, to say nothing of an aluminum camper shell. As he had mentioned in his conversation with Gary, all four replacement fenders were a different color.

"Sure a colorful rig you have there, mister," Arnold said. "Any particular reason for the way it's decorated?"

Brad had to laugh at his diplomacy. Doug generally called the vehicle "a patched-up pile of junk."

"Nothing really planned, I guess. I keep threatening to get it painted all one color, but I get kind of a kick out of having a truck with a dog to match!"

Doug and Phil came back around to the front entrance. They were discussing a problem with the generator that supplied electricity to the cabin. This had left them without a refrigerator but since the cook stove and two Coleman lanterns were fueled by propane, the addition of an ice chest enabled them to get by.

"We just now got back from town," Phil was saying. "They told me at Smitty's Hardware that the part we need comes from Denver and won't be in until tomorrow. I need to bring it back out here and get the thing running before we leave…"

"I need to go back into town again, anyway, to buy up a few things I forgot. If it'd help you out, I could pick up that part for the motor and bring it back with me. Brad and me will probably hang around for a few days and do some fishing so we might as well bunk here. That is, if you was leaving, anyway."

"Great! I really need to be in Omaha by tomorrow night so that would sure save us some time." He turned to Brad. "Your dad says you know a little bit about motors. If you'll come outside with me, I'll show you where the replacement part goes."

Before Doug and Brad pulled away from the cabin to find a camping spot for the night, Phil called to them from the doorway.

"You might want to pick up some ice tomorrow, either in town or at the bait shop. Just a precaution in case the generator still won't work." He waved and closed the door.

Doug drove toward the lake and parked under a large cottonwood tree near one of the small piers. He climbed out and directed Brad to pull in parallel to his rig at a distance of about fifteen feet. Smoky literally *flew* out of the pickup when Brad opened the door.

"What say we dig through these boxes, Bud, and see if we can find something for supper? Okay?"

"What about the steaks?"

"Let's wait 'til tomorrow night. Meat cooked on that outdoor barbecue grill at Gorman's always tastes a heap better than it does off'n my propane stove."

"Sounds like a winner." While Brad was sorting through the boxes, he asked why Doug had told Phil he needed to go back to Bear Claw the next day.

"I thought if we took care of the generator they'd be out of here sooner, and we could move into the cabin soon as they're outa sight."

Doug hung the fluorescent camping lantern on the right rear-view mirror, unrolled the awning and set out the folding table and chairs while Brad took charge of the food. The resulting baloney and cheese sandwiches with Coors' *chasers* tasted as good to both of them as an "uptown meal".

What'll we do about the meat, Doug? Think I should go get some ice at that little store?"

"No need to. Cool as it gets up here at night, we'll just rig up a cowpuncher's feedbag like I used to do when I was herding cows in Montana. We wrap the steaks in foil, put 'em in a bag and tie the whole thing to a tree branch high enough off the ground so critters can't reach it." He sat down at the table and opened two more cans of beer. "Once we've et, I'll show you how to *hang 'em high* as Eastwood would say..."

CHAPTER 21

Before going to sleep at Maria's house, Orville and Homer discussed the chances of success with the new poisoned-food project.

"Think Papoose knows what he's down', Orvie? His last try, at Nederland, sure as hell didn't work out."

"We'll just have to trust him, Homer. Like I said before, he's our only chance so we gotta play along. For now, let's get some shut-eye and we'll talk about it tomorrow…"

It seemed to Orville that he barely closed his eyes before Papoose tapped on their door and whispered for them to get dressed and meet him outside. He reminded them to be quiet.

There was no easy way to get Homer dressed but Orville managed to get the job done as quickly as possible. They were afraid to use the bathroom for fear of disturbing Maria, so they made the bed, tiptoed down the stairs and stepped out onto the porch where Papoose waited for them.

"Where's Pinto?" Homer asked.

"He's staying here to take messages for me. About orders.."

Orville wondered about Pinto's secretarial abilities, considering the fact that they had never heard the man say a single word out loud. Maybe he was simply shy. Somehow that description was not consistent with his appearance, but then how could you tell?

Homer drove the Ford pickup and followed Papoose into Denver. Orville had done such a good job of cleaning the place that Homer no longer protested when they climbed the stairs and entered the apartment.

Papoose motioned for them to be seated and he disappeared into his lab, coming out twice with a bandanna tied over his face to pore over pages of two large books laying open on the table. On the last trip he nodded, silently, then turned to the refrigerator where he retrieved two small vials before returning to the lab.

On one of the times when Papoose appeared, Homer spoke tentatively, "Think it'll work this time?"

Papoose paused and turned to glare at him, his black eyes shooting sparks. Then he walked away. In a minute or so he reappeared and stomped over to where Homer was seated. He bent down with their noses only inches apart and lifted the bandanna so he could speak.

"The dude either threw up before the dose took hold, or he didn't drink enough to do the job. Understand?"

Homer nodded.

"Just keep in mind that I'm not the one who's been fuckin' up everything we try to do. *Agreed*?"

Homer nodded. When Papoose returned to the lab, Homer took a deep breath.

"You're sure hell bent on committin' suicide, ain't you, Homer? Don't ever pull a dumb stunt like that again. Hear me?"

Homer nodded.

Papoose emerged after about forty-five minutes and placed two small capped vials on top of the table. He removed the bandanna and tossed it into the garbage can, then replaced his black hat.

"There it is, you two dudes. Just enough chloral hydrate to knock 'em out before they know what hit 'em." There was pride in his voice when he itemized the contents of the vials. "I added a mixture of cyanogenic stuff like ground up apricot kernels, Christmas berries, and some Johnson grass to finish them off. A couple of the poisons I really like to use are not deadly when the food's cooked, so I left 'em out."

"Why the bandanna?" Orville asked tentatively.

"Some of the cyanide fumes might get to me in that small lab. You dudes need to be careful not to inhale it, either."

"Anything else?"

"Don't think so, as far as this project goes.. It's the same basic mixture as before, but it's strong enough to kill 'em outright this time." He laid his hand on one of the opened books and continued, "The Lily of the Valley causes hallucinations along with the touch of marijuana and loco weed tossed in for good measure. Grandpa used to say 'loco weed won't kill 'em by itself, but give 'em *enough* of it and they don't give a shit whether they're poisoned or not!' Like him, I use young plants…lots more poisonous. The bodies'll still smell of almonds when they're found, but by then, who cares?"

Orville was hesitant to ask questions but felt he had to know more. "You sure this is strong enough for two men their size?"

Papoose leaned against the sink, arms crossed over his chest, and stared at them with his eyes half closed. At first it seemed he would not reply, then he said softly, almost too softly, "*Of course it is.* I spent three years in the stir learning all this pharmacy shit, besides what grandpa taught me. Any one body or combination of bodies up to three-hundred-fifty pounds will get zapped as soon as this crap gets inside of 'em, but give it to a horse and he'd just go nuts, kicking and stomping. You ain't feeding it to no horse, though, are you?"

From his expression, Papoose looked as though even that might somehow be within the realm of possibilities, considering how they'd handled things so far.

"So how d'we use it?" Homer asked. "Mixed in their food, or what?"

"Either way. This stuff's so strong you can stir it right into hamburger or chili, anything like that, or you can sprinkle it all over solid stuff like steak or ribs. Either way, it'll get 'em!"

Orville reached for the two vials and just as he picked them up, Papoose stepped forward and reached across the table to grab each of them by the throat, glaring at both brothers alternately.

"There's just one thing we're gonna do before I turn this stuff over to you. Guess what that is?"

Their motions were restricted but both shook their heads, implying a negative answer..

"We're gonna make *one more stop* before I turn this stuff over to you. Wanna *guess*?"

They shook their heads again.

"We're going to the bank and get those goddammed bonds!"

Papoose loosened his hold but did not release them completely.

"But…" they both began sputtering, then looked at the wild expression in Papoose's eyes and mumbled, "Guess you're right…"

"And remember one other thing, you two. If this don't work, or you fuck it up some way, just *stay away from me!* Understand?"

Orville nodded. Homer gurgled.

"In fact, if you don't kill off those two cowboys this time, I might turn you over to the sheriff myself! I've got a deal workin' with a fence to handle the bonds, and much as I wanted my thirty percent, I'd rather have forgot it than repeat what I been through this past week with you two. But seein' as how you might never come back, anyway, I'm gonna hold onto those bonds *myself* to make damned sure I don't get screwed out of my share. Is that *clear*?"

Orville's knees had begun to buckle, and when Papoose released the vise-like grip on his throat, he sunk deeper into his chair and gasped for breath. Homer looked like he was about to cry.

Papoose tossed a piece of paper at Orville that looked like another map, but he was too weak to reach for it.

"After we leave the bank, you take the roads I marked for you and stay away from Golden. Maria finds out I'm still helpin' you, she'll kick my ass outta her house, and maybe outta the whole state of Colorado."

He pointed toward the exit, still glaring.

Homer helped Orville to his feet, picked up the vials and the piece of paper and they headed for the door.

Once outside, Homer whined, "Where'd he come up with that thirty percent shit? All we ever 'greed to was twenty percent!"

At the bottom of the stairs, Orville turned and looked at his brother. "So who's going to bring up the subject? You? I sure as hell ain't. Right now we're about to lose the whole damned thing if we mess up again!"

Homer climbed in behind the wheel and sulked in silence. They followed Papoose to the bank and after reluctantly turning over the bonds to Papoose, they headed out of town.

With Orville as his co-pilot, Homer simply followed instructions and decided to not worry about the money split until after there was actually something to divide. About a mile from the intersection where they were to get onto Interstate 70 going south, they pulled into a service station across the street.

Orville filled the pickup with gas while Homer struggled to add one quart of oil and clean the windows. On his way inside to pay the cashier, Orville showed one of the mechanics the piece of paper Papoose had given him and asked if that was really the best route to take to Bear Claw.

"You could go that way," the mechanic said, "but it's a lot shorter if you take US-6 over to CO-119." He spread a map out on the counter and pointed to the different routes as he spoke. "The way your friend marked it, I-70 makes a big loop south and ends up at the same place, but you save maybe ten-twelve miles by getting off on US-6 just south of here."

Orville was thinking about Papoose's warning when he asked, tentatively, "We don't have to go through Golden, do we?"

"Sort of, but it just skirts 'round the west side and don't really go through town at all. Why? That a problem?"

Orville felt a little foolish, so he just waved away the objection and said, "No, that's okay. Looks like your way's the best."

He paid for the gas and oil with one of his "special" credit cards, and had them add the price of a map to the total. The small scrap of paper from Papoose might simply serve to confuse them, rather than help.

He looked around for Homer. "Anybody see my brother?"

A young woman with purple lipstick and a long blonde ponytail, pointed across the street. "He went over there while you finished gassin' up. Looks like he's on his way back right now."

Homer emerged from a store named "Eye-Spy/Do You?" He was waving a package over his head and yelling across the street, "Wait'll you see what I got, Orvie! Wait'll you see…"

Screeching brakes, honking horns and shouted curses accompanied his dash back to the service station, completely oblivious to the chaos he caused.

Orville grabbed him by the shoulders and shook him.

"Don't ever pull a stunt like that again! Hear me?"

Homer's head snapped back and forth, making a popping sound each time his chin hit the neck brace. When Orville realized what he was doing, he apologized and hugged his brother before shoving him toward the truck.

"Wanna see what I got?" Homer was still too excited to see how much he had frightened and angered his brother.

"I'll move us outta the way and you can show me."

As soon as they were parked near a cluster of pay phones, Homer pulled a small box out of a plastic bag and began tearing it open. The package said "Nite-Brite: Bright as day in black of night. Reduces peripheral vision and depth perception." Homer unwrapped a pair of goggles that resembled stubby two-inch binoculars and held them up to his face after removing his own dark glasses."

"See, Orvie? See what I found? Ain't they great?"

"For what? To get you a job spying for the CIA? That oughta be a cinch, right after the FBI tags us for murdering one of their men."

"Jeez, Orvie. I thought you'd be as tickled as I am. I can use these tonight when we sneak up to that cabin, and the next time we go *burglaring* I won't even need a flashlight!"

"Sure, I'm happy for you, but for now, you'd better drive so I can watch for all the turnoffs this joker just told me about."

They pulled out on to Colfax but traffic was too heavy for them to cross back to the far side so they turned right and circled around the block before heading west again. One mile later they were on I-70.

US-6 took them along the west rim of Golden, just as the mechanic had said. Orville avoided telling Homer where they were since any mention of Papoose at this point might upset him again. If something as trivial as "spy goggles" made his brother happy, there was no need to bring up unpleasant subjects and spoil his mood.

It was soon evident that their chosen route was not the one to take if you were in a hurry. US-6 twists through Clear Creek Canyon, a precipitous gorge that slices through the lower Front Range escarpment. The main benefit of such a slow trip through the deep winding canyon was that it offered Orville a chance to look at the scenery, which he rarely took the time to do when they travelled. The canyon walls varied from tree covered slopes to solid rock cliffs that looked, in some places, like the carved monuments of presidents' faces he remembered from the Black Hills when he was a kid.

From Golden, most of the road through the canyon was one long "no-passing zone." Every four or five miles there would be a short stretch that was straight enough to allow vehicles to go by, but in general, the cars were one behind the other for at least one mile with their speed limited to how fast the lead car could travel. Orville began to understand why Papoose had told them to stay on I-70. It may have been a few miles further but it sure would have been faster.

Homer remained quiet, obviously tense from the strain of being restricted, first by the very nature of the highway, and then by the burden of complying with the strict regulations that governed each winding stretch of road. At one scenic viewpoint where the signs indicated that you were to "pull out if you are in a slow-moving vehicle," a man was selling tickets to something or other out of his van. Homer insisted on stopping to rest and stretch his legs. They looked back at as much of the canyon as they could see from there, and Orville was surprised that they had not really dropped to a much lower altitude than where they began. The road dipped and turned for awhile, then climbed and turned, so the change was not as evident as he expected. The man in the van told Orville that they would reach an elevation of nine thousand feet at Central City, not too many miles from where they were now standing.

Orville took over the driving at this point and Homer surprised him by pointing out various types of bushes and flowers along the way. He mentioned columbines, willow thickets, dwarf birch, pines trees and cedar.

"Where'd you learn all that crap? About the names of all them bushes?"

"Remember when we hung out in the prison library? While you was workin' on new money-making schemes, I was readin' all kinds'a books about flora. That's what they call the bushes and flowers and stuff. I mostly looked at pictures and tried to remember the names..."

Orville was pleased that his brother showed an interest in something practical and wanted to encourage him at every opportunity. "So what about the bright colored flowers along the sidehill? Know what they are?"

Homer's pride was evident in his voice when he answered, "Pink ones on the right are prob'ly Rocky Mountain shootin' stars, and the blue ones are monkshood mixed in with tall larkspurs."

Before long, Orville was almost sorry he had given his brother an opening to go on and on and on about the plants. It was a relief when Homer's attention switched to the three tunnels they passed through, and he questioned how people could blast their way through solid rock without causing the entire hillside to collapse.

Not to be overshadowed by Homer's knowledge of plant life, Orville explained in detail how the ceiling and side walls in all three had been reinforced with concrete. After all, he had his own image to protect.

When they reached the intersection of CO-119, Orville felt greatly relieved. "This is the highway that runs right through Bear Claw. Remember? I kinda feel like I finally know where we're headed!"

"A sign back there says it's only seven miles to Central City. Can we stop there, Orvie? I really need to eat something."

"Might as well. We've lost so much time now, another hour won't make much difference."

As soon as they pulled off of CO-119 they found themselves in the unique ex-mining town where signs indicated it had been dubbed "the richest square mile on earth" by early prospectors. Both of them were surprised to note that nearly every building housed a gambling casino of some sort. Orville drove slowly uphill through the town, then made a U-turn at the top where the commercial area ended and returned down the hill. In the middle of town he came to a side street that offered assorted dining, drinking and gambling in places with names like Bronco Billy's, Lily Belle's Casino, Fire House Casino, and Golden Rose. Each one boasted of having "slots, poker, and blackjack." A modern Harvey's Hotel appeared slightly out of place even though it had been built with the new part of the structure squeezed in between two old buildings that may have been mine entrances at one time.

They stopped at a place called Red Dolly's for lunch. In the small parking area there was a black limousine with a uniformed chauffeur leaning against the front fender smoking a cigar.

"When we get our money outta them bonds, you think we could hire some *dandy* like that to drive us around, Orvie?"

"Not sure I'd want to even if we could afford it. I'd hate to have some-body that spiffy hanging around all the time. Just make us look bad. Strange, though. Looked like he was packing a rod. Funny thing for a driver…"

"Think maybe his boss holds him responsible for the limo?"

"I suppose..."

They played a few hands of blackjack while they waited for their food to be prepared. All gambling was low-limit and the table they played on allowed only two-dollar bets. Homer tried to palm a card to avoid having his hand total more than twenty-one but Orville kicked him so hard under the table that he not only dropped the card but also knocked over the few chips he had in front of him. When they returned to their table, Orville reminded him of how stupid it was to take such a chance for a measly two-dollar bet.

"Sure be smart to get yourself tossed in jail right now, wouldn't it? Don't you think we got enough trouble as it is?"

The limo was gone when they returned to their truck. They each drank two beers with their meal and it was soon obvious that altitude really did make a difference in a person's ability to handle liquor. Apparently Bear Claw and Nederland were at a lower altitude because Orville did not recall any such reaction from the few drinks they had in those two towns. Homer quickly dozed off as soon as they left Central City, and Orville, although not really sleepy, was light-headed for the rest of their trip.

When they reached the turn-off to Little Bear Lake, Orville switched on the headlights. He had not needed them until he entered the dense forest area, but the dusk of evening provided very little light once he left the main highway.

Homer awoke when they pulled off the graveled road and arrived at the open area surrounding the lake. In the darkening twilight, the headlights were of little help so Orville dimmed them at first, then finally switched them off entirely, so they would not be spotted approaching the cabin. At dusk, they could still find their way.

"Which road goes to the cabin where they stayed?" Orville asked. "Was it the fourth one or the fifth?"

Homer, still groggy after his nap, replied, "Jeez, Orvie, I don't 'member. Fourth one, I think. You ain't gonna drive right up there, anyway, are you? We gotta be careful."

"Just need to locate it. We passed number four a minute ago and the lights are on, so we know they're here. We'll just go on up to the boss man's cabin and leave the Ford there."

Orville drove almost to the mobster's cabin before he realized there were also lights inside that house and a black limo was parked out in front.

"Damn! He must of loaned out the place to some of his hot shot friends. Wonder if that's the same limo we seen before? We'd better steer clear for now."

"Jeez, Orvie. Suppose it's somebody who knows about us? They might be mad about the lost bonds…"

Orville backed down to Little Bear Drive instead of trying to turn around. Tracks in the tall grass the next morning might arouse suspicion.

"I'll just park down there near the lake. I can kind of pull it in among the trees close to shore and we'll walk up to the cabin where the cowboys are. We passed two campers back there a ways so we have to keep out of their sight, too. You got them two vials with you?"

"They're in the front compartment. You want 'em now?"

"Yeah. We might not have time to come back."

Homer put on his spy goggles but since it was not quite dark enough for them to be effective, he kept tripping over twigs and stepping in gopher holes until he finally removed them. At the cabin, Orville motioned for Homer to circle around to the right side of the house and indicated that he would go to the left. At the kitchen window he stopped abruptly. Two women that he had never seen before were clearing food from the table and washing dishes.

"What the…?" He returned to where Homer was standing, open-mouthed, staring into the living room at two men playing cards by the light of a Coleman lantern. He put his hand over Homer's mouth to keep him quiet, and pulled him away until they were out of earshot.

"We got the wrong place, Orvie? Them jokers sure ain't the Hastings!"

"This is the right cabin. Sign on the front says 'Gorman's'. My guess is they ain't come back from Estes Park yet. Let's go sit down some place where I can figure out what to do. We gotta reconnoiter. We might even have to go into town and come back tomorrow."

"Sure can't stay at Bossman's place..."

A car was approaching on Little Bear Drive. They squatted down as low as possible to avoid the headlight beams. When they stood up again, they were slightly disoriented and walked further down the road than they intended. Before they realized what they had done, they were already past the campsite that Orville saw earlier. He noted that their Ford pickup was now off in the distance on the far side of the vehicles parked by the lake. He collapsed onto a fallen log and put his head in his hands. Coyotes were howling some place in the distance, not far enough away to suit him. *They don't attack people anyway, do they? Only sheep and small animals like that.* He was startled when Homer grabbed him by the arm and pointed toward the campers.

"It's them, Orvie!" he was trying to keep his voice low, but it was more of a squeaking sound when he pounded on Orville's chest and pointed to the nearby campsite. "I see 'em plain as day, just like the pamphlet says!"

"See who? What the hell you babbling about?"

"There. Right there." Homer removed his goggles and held them up to Orville's face.

"I'll be a sonofabitch! It really is them. What d'ya know?"

"I told you them goggles would help, didn't I, Orvie?"

"You sure did. Only thing is, now that we found 'em, what'd we do about it? We can't sneak into a pickup camper in the middle of the night, that's for sure. Best we come back tomorrow and maybe break in while they're fishing."

"Let's creep up on 'em right now, Orvie. Sneak along the shore and listen in. Maybe they'll mention their plans for the next couple of days. Won't that work, Orvie? Huh?"

"Sure won't hurt. Let's give it a try…"

CHAPTER 22

Doug tossed the left-over ham to Smoky and dumped their used paper plates into a garbage bag.

"Want more pork and beans, Bud, 'fore I toss the can away? No use trying to save stuff 'til we get a block of ice for my camper fridge."

"I'm full for now, but we might need that loaf of bread to make toast for breakfast."

Brad leaned back in his chair and propped his feet on top of a folding foot stool. He was intensely aware of the pungent odor of pine needles, decaying leaves and water-soaked logs along the shore. He heard Smoky chasing a rabbit through the trees along the lake.

"When you going to show me that famous 'cowpuncher's feedbag' you mentioned?"

"What's wrong with right now? I got a gunny sack here someplace that's left over from a bag of oats I bought for Skeeter. I can cut it down to size and we'll be all set."

Doug disappeared into his camper and returned after a few minutes carrying a lariat rope, some wax paper, the gunny sack and scissors. And, of course, the steaks.

"Thought I had some foil to wrap this meat in, Bud. Seals in the smell better'n this wax paper, but we'll make do." He began cutting the top half off of the gunny sack after he handed the package of steaks to

Brad. "Here. Make yourself useful. Wrap each of these separate, then cover all four of them with one more layer of wax paper."

"Isn't there a chance some bear will smell the meat, anyway?"

"Won't do him no good, Bud. We find a tree branch just thick enough to hold the bag of meat up in the air, but not stout enough for a critter to crawl out there and swat it loose. Works every time."

By the time Brad had wrapped the steaks as instructed, Doug was ready with the bag and rope.

"Come on, Bud. Bring that lantern and let's find us a feedbag-hanging tree!"

They checked a couple of cottonwoods nearby and Doug okayed the second one they examined.

"You hear something, Bud?" he asked. "That noise over there by the water?"

"Just Smoky chasing a rabbit."

"I guess." Doug walked slowly around the tree two or three times before selecting a medium-sized limb and tossing one end of his lariat over the top of it. He had already placed the steaks inside the gunny sack and tied a knot in the bag to keep it closed. He then took the noose of the lariat and pulled it tight just below that knot and tugged on the loose end of the rope until the bag was halfway between the top of his head and the branch of the tree.

"Here you go, Bud. I'll hold this in place while you take the rope and loop it around the bottom of the tree. Better take a couple of wraps before you tie it off. We don't want it slipping down."

Once they completed the job, Doug stood back and checked their handiwork, smiling.

"Your old man a genius, or what?"

"Never a doubt in my mind, Doug. Never a doubt."

* * *

Orville and Homer crouched in the bushes and watched, fascinated, while the Hastings put together the package of meat and tied it to a tree branch. The cowboy's sheep dog stopped once and sniffed at them, then continued chasing a rabbit after Homer threw a rock at him. They were afraid of being discovered and moved further away when they heard Doug commenting on the noise, but once they felt it was safe again, they crept closer and squatted behind a willow tree to watch what was happening. When at last the sack had been hoisted into the air and the rope tied to the base of the tree, Orville put one hand over Homer's mouth to keep him from squealing with delight, and gave him a high-five with the other hand.

They retreated back to their fallen log where they felt it was safe to talk.

"We finally got a break, huh, Orvie? They practically put the meat right in our hands!"

"It's about time. Now all we gotta do is wait here 'til them two cowboys go to sleep and we doctor up their meat and head for the hills. I mean *out of the hills*. Right?"

"We gonna drive all the way back to Denver when we get through, Orvie, or stay over in Bear Claw?"

"It'll be so late, I don't want to start out tonight. When we do go, we'll take that I-70 freeway on the way back like Papoose told us. No use going through that canyon again."

Homer was getting restless after a few minutes so he wandered down the road and back a couple of times. He was still wearing his goggles and he could hardly contain himself when he spotted a deer in the grassy area between him and the nearest cabin. Each time he returned to the log he had another story to tell Orville.

When at last they decided it was safe to go back to the cottonwood tree, Orville checked to reassure himself that Homer still had their precious vials.

"Got 'em right here in my shirt pocket, Orvie. Ain't let 'em out of my sight. Not for a minute."

Since they had watched Doug's entire procedure, they were able to release the rope from where Brad had tied it to the base of the tree, and in a matter of ten or fifteen minutes they had opened the bag, unwrapped the steaks and smothered them with the contents of the two vials. They both used the wax paper to spread the poison so as not to get it on their hands but Homer wore his gloves anyway. After rewrapping, Orville held one of the steaks up to his nose and then put it in front of Homer's face.

"Think they'll notice any odor? All I smell is a chunk of beef. How about you?"

Homer refused to remove his goggles and since it slightly impaired his distance vision, he was startled when the package of meat touched his nose. "What the hell's that, Orvie? What'd you put on my face?"

"Guess if you can't smell nothing wrong, we're okay."

They repeated each step that they had observed earlier, including rewrapping the package the way it was originally, and when it came time to hoist the bag into the air, Homer complained that he was unable to lift anything above his head so he would have to be the one to tie the rope to the bottom of the tree. He diligently took two wraps then tied it off and stepped back to admire his work. Through the goggles it appeared to be nothing short of amazing.

Orville grabbed him by the arm. "We'd better get back to the Ford and get out of here, but first I got to figure out where we left it…"

"I'll find it, Orvie! Just give me a couple of minutes to look around with my spy glasses and I'll locate it for you." No need to check the lake on his right so he scanned the area behind them, then looked to his left toward the nearest cabin, and finally straight ahead. "There, Orvie. Straight ahead of us down the road a ways. Oh, shit, Orvie! There's something' else, and it ain't our truck!"

"What? What d'you see?"

Homer pointed just past the Hastings vehicles and grabbed Orville's arm. "It's a bear, Orvie. *It's a fucking bear!*"

Orville was so sure his brother's imagination was simply out of control, that he removed the goggles from Homer and held them up to his face. He immediately handed them back and pulled Homer behind the nearest aspen tree.

"You're right! *It's a fuckin' bear!*"

"Now what d'we do, Orvie? Will he kill us?"

"For one thing, let's duck back over there by the lake so's we can wash off the smell of meat. Then all we got to do is hide 'til he goes on by…"

"How do bears feel about water, Orvie? Maybe we can just wade out there a ways and wait for him to leave."

"Damned if I know. I hear that cats hate the water but I don't know about bears. He'll be gone in a couple of minutes, anyhow, so don't worry."

The water was so cold that Orville was glad they had not decided to walk out into the lake. In a matter of three or four minutes they came back and peeked through the bushes to check on the predator. At first it seemed that he was gone, then Homer, with his goggles on again, grabbed Orville by the shoulders and pointed him toward the "meat tree."

The bear was standing on his hind legs, pawing with his front feet in an attempt to reach the bag of steaks!

"Think we can sneak past him now, Orvie?"

"I ain't moving 'til he's hell and gone out of here!"

They retreated to their log and sat, hypnotized, while they watched the bear's struggle.

"What's happening, Orvie? Take a look through my goggles. Seems like he's getting' closer and closer to the bag!"

"It ain't that, Homer. The bag's just getting closer and closer to the bear. The rope's coming loose! You tie that sonofabitch to the tree or didn't you?" Orville could barely keep his voice down. At that point, there was little danger from the bear, but he didn't want to rouse anyone else, especially the Hastings.

"I did, Orvie. Honest I did," Homer whimpered. "It was kind of awkward with my gloves and my spy glasses, but I tied it best I could."

Orville dragged his brother back to their fallen log where they sat, side by side, trying to decide what to do. They were afraid to make a run for it to the mobster's cabin. Strangers were in Gorman's cabin. Their truck was a mile down the road on the other side of a hungry bear!

"Maybe if he gets into that sack, he'll eat enough to knock him out and we can sneak by."

"What about the cowboys? What d'we do about them, Orvie?"

Before Orville could answer, he saw that the bag of meat was now within reach of the bear who grabbed it in his teeth and shook it like a cat with a mouse.

"Damned if I know, Homer. Damned if I know. We'll worry about that later, if we ever get out of here without getting eat up by that bear."

They watched, hypnotized, while the bear tore into the sack of meat, scattering packages of steak and sheets of wrapping paper. He then lay on his stomach and began gnawing at first one piece of meat and then another.

After fifteen or twenty minutes Homer became restless. He made a move to stand up but Orville pulled him back. "Stay put for now. Give that poison time to work and we can make a run for it."

"Remember what Papoose said, Orvie? About using that stuff on a horse? That bear ain't big as a horse, but he sure weighs more than them two cowboys. What if the stuff don't kill him outright? Maybe just make him crazy?"

"Shhh! Just sit still a little longer. Let me see those spy glasses of yours again." He held the goggles up to his face and studied the bear more closely. "I think he's gone to sleep, Homer! Take a look…"

"You're right, Orvie! His head's resting on his front paws. Looks like he's either asleep or maybe even *dead*. Let's get out of here. Fast!"

They stood and slowly circled past the Hastings' trucks, trying to be as quiet as possible. Homer, again wearing his goggles, stumbled over a fallen tree branch and was only able to stay on his feet due to the fact that Orville had a grip on his arm.

"Watch where you're going! Sure don't want to wake up them cowboys at this point."

Homer had been pulled around to face the "meat tree" when he stumbled and now he shoved Orville toward their pickup truck.

"What's *that* for? I'm just trying to help you."

"It's the bear, Orvie. He's back on his feet again! Look..."

Orville peered into the darkness, but without the goggles he was unable to clearly distinguish what the bear was doing until all of a sudden the lumbering hulk began to gain on them and was only about thirty feet away, stumbling, growling, shaking its head and frothing at the mouth.

"Run, Homer, *run!*"

They reached the pickup a few steps ahead of the bear, due mainly to the unsteady gait of the slobbering animal. Homer closed his door just as the bear slammed against it. The truck teetered sideways and Orville thought it was going to tip over.

"Get us out of here, Homer. And don't panic!"

"*Why not?*"

"Good question..."

Homer was so scared he flooded the motor in his anxiety to get it started. When it finally caught, he slammed the gearshift into low and took off, spinning the wheels and shooting dirt and gravel at the bear who still gave chase for the first half-mile.

As they raced along Little Bear Drive, Orville was aware of an approaching vehicle that was almost on top of them before the glaring panel of flood lights on top of a pickup cab seemed to explode in their faces. Homer, wearing his night goggles, must have been blinded completely because he whipped the steering wheel hard to the right and drove the Ford between two cottonwood trees straight into the lake. The last thing Orville heard, as the water level reached half-way to the top of his window, was loud singing and the clank of empty cans hitting the cab of their Ford pickup. Homer had jumped out as soon as the truck hit the water and grabbed his tool box out of the back when he waded past. The back wheels were still on dry ground but the entire vehicle was slowly slipping into the lake when Orville escaped into the icy water and floundered toward shore. He slumped to the ground and looked back.

"What the fuck you doing?," he yelled.

Homer was following the truck into the lake in an attempt to retrieve the license plate before the Ford became completely submerged.

Orville scrambled to his feet and pulled on Homer's shirt tail. "Let it go, Homer! It ain't worth it. Let's get out of here…"

"I can't, Orvie. That's all I got left!"

Orville gave one final yank and managed to drag his brother out of the water where they both fell backwards with their legs still submerged.

Homer's goggles were on top of his head and for once he seemed unconcerned about his hair-do. He struggled to sit upright and triumphantly waved his precious license plate in the air. "I done it, Orvie. I really done it!"

The Stokes rested for awhile beside the lake. They continued to check behind them in case the bear continued its pursuit, but once they were partially dried off and felt reasonably safe, they plodded along Little Bear Drive in the direction of Gumpy's Bait Shop. Neither of them spoke until the lights went off in the small store when they were still about two hundred yards away.

"What now, Orvie? Even if we used that phone next to the store, who the hell could we call?"

"Not Papoose, that's for sure. No way can we tell him what happened tonight. Our best bet is to get back into town somehow, where we can reconnoiter…"

They circled quietly, searching for a car. Whatever transportation Gumpy had was locked in a garage attached to the store. The only vehicle in sight was a small John Deere tractor parked at the timberline where someone had been building a fence around the store owner's property.

Homer nudged Orville. "What about that thing with the big drill on the back? Bet I could get it started easy enough, if it wasn't too damned noisy."

"That's a post-hole digger. Cousin Maynard had one at his place in North Dakota, remember? Tractor made a lot of racket, though, so we might need to push it a ways before you start up the engine. Wanna give it a try?"

"Don't know how much help I'll be when it comes to pushing, but I'll do the best I can…"

Homer placed his tool kit and license plate on a tiny platform next to the seat and tried to steer the tractor toward the road as he walked alongside, but most of the pushing was done by Orville. Fortunately the keys had not been removed so when they reached what they considered to be a safe distance from Gumpy's shop, Orville boosted him onto the tractor and he immediately started the engine.

"There ain't but one seat, Homer. Where do I ride?"

"You got to straddle that post-hole digger and face back down the road." He tittered. "Might be a little rough on your 'private parts', as grandma would say, but at least you can watch out for bears!"

Orville's next words were choppy, due to the rough ride, but he tried to avoid sounding bitter about how their latest "project" had turned out. He knew Homer had screwed up his part of the job at the tree, but there was no sense brooding about it now. *Maybe once we're safe, I can laugh, too…*

CHAPTER 23

In the camper shell of Brad's pickup, he was awakened at dawn by what he referred to as his "Smoky alarm." The dog had nudged him off of the narrow inflatable mattress in an apparent effort to keep warm and Brad decided he might as well get up and cover the animal with his sleeping bag. The mountain air was brisk but so clear and clean that he found himself taking one deep breath after another while he sat on the tailgate and laced up his Nikes. During his pre-jog stretching, he looked around for signs of other early risers and saw only one small row boat leaving the dock on what was no doubt a mission to snag a few hungry trout.

Doug would remain asleep for awhile so Brad began trotting slowly along Little Bear Drive then veered toward the edge of the lake where he found a well worn trail among the trees. He had only jogged about fifty yards from camp when Smoky caught up with him and ran alongside without his usual tail-wagging early morning greeting.

"Hey, there, mutt! You pouting 'cause I left you behind?"

No response.

Brad was surprised that he was short of breath before going only one-third of the way around the lake. He knew he should not be this much out of shape when he was forced to slow to a walk and even leaned against a willow tree briefly to catch his wind.

"Must be the altitude, huh, Smoky?" The dog returned from chasing a gopher into its hole, and finally condescended by wagging his tail in forgiveness for being deserted earlier.

As Brad looked around, he saw two people in a boat who appeared to be anchored near the center of the lake. No doubt it was simply a favorite fishing spot for the pair, but the scene was so familiar to him that he continued to glance in their direction even after he resumed his jogging along the trail. On the far side of the lake he had a better view of the occupants of the boat and recognized the man and boy he had seen on his arrival the night before. No doubt that explained the deja vu, but it still bothered him.

Brad picked up speed on the final leg of his jaunt and was brought up short when he approached their camp. Doug was standing in front of his camper, hands on his hips, nodding his head as though carrying on a heated discussion with someone. This scene was reminiscent of the few times in Brad's childhood when his father was really angry at something the boy had done. The occasions were rare, but were to be avoided whenever possible.

"Morning, Doug," Brad began cautiously. "Thought you'd still be asleep…"

Without looking at his son, Doug pointed with both hands in the direction of the tree where they had suspended their steaks on a tree limb.

"Look at that! Just *look* at that! What the hell kinda knot did you tie in that rope? Any goddam gunsel knows a granny knot won't hold nothing. How could you do something so damned stupid?"

Brad was too shocked to reply. To begin with, he had no idea what had incited Doug's tirade until he looked toward the tree and realized the bag was no longer suspended in midair but instead was lying on the ground, torn to shreds.

Brad sensed that the main reason for Doug's anger was having to accept the failure of his big project, but he had no intention of letting himself be blamed if he were not at fault. He walked over to the tree and looked at the end of the lariat and pointed to where it encircled the tree trunk.

"For Chris sakes, Doug. Take a good look. You think I'd ever tie off a rope that way after all these years? You know better than that…"

Doug still bristled, but he calmed down a little when he joined Brad at the tree.

"Then how…?"

"I don't know. All I'm sure of is that's not the way I left it, and when you cool off a little, you'll realize it, too."

Doug pointed to the scraps of paper and remaining bones.

"A couple of coyotes come by a few minutes ago but I scared 'em away. Whatever et our meat sure did a job of it." He rubbed his hands across the top of his head as though trying to find an answer to the puzzle, then he turned toward Brad and said, apologetically, "You know what? I got up once to go to the can, and this pickup full of drunks drove by with them panel lights across the top of the cab like hunters use when they're out prowling around at night. They was singing and carrying on, with two or three of them standing in the truck bed and leaning over the top of the lights. Maybe them knot-heads come back and pulled this off as some kind of prank!"

"That's possible. Kind of a stupid prank, but whoever did it *meant* for the rope to come loose. If they're dumb enough to hunt coyotes, or anything else, with flood lights, they're apt to pull anything. Some game warden'll have their asses if he ever catches them."

Doug, finally satisfied that the mystery had been solved, turned back toward his camper.

"Aw, what the hell," he mumbled, "no real harm done. We'll pick up our five-day fishing permits and maybe we won't need any steaks. Right? And bring in my lariat, will you, Bud?"

"Sure, Doug," Brad grinned, relieved that the tension had subsided. "We could always get a few more steaks when we go into town, just in case…"

* * *

Orville lay in bed staring at the triangular area of chipped paint in one corner of the ceiling. The events of the previous day kept going through his mind and this time he conceded total defeat. On arrival at the edge of town they had ditched the tractor behind some trees and walked the few blocks to the Cubs Den Motel. The manager had been his usual grumpy self at being wakened in the middle of the night but the flashing VACANCY sign must have reminded him of the occupancy deficit since the end of the rodeo, and he became almost congenial by the time he zapped their credit card through the machine. He shoved the register toward Orville and traded a room key for his signature.

"Checkout time's still noon," he mumbled. "Gotta know by then if you're staying over. Where's your car?"

Orville smiled, recalling Homer's reply, "Broke down, *hiccup*, just outside of town. *Hiccup*. Havin' it towed in the morning."

Orville mulled over the meager options they had left. He decided their best bet might be to try and steal back their share of the bonds and head for L.A. before trying to unload them. Then again, this would no doubt be a life-threatening project and even if it worked, L.A. was probably the worst possible choice since they had to avoid the mob members who staked them to the cash to begin with. Better yet, maybe if they dared to ask Papoose about his *fence*, they might just be able to sell their share outright! They could tell him they'd killed the two cowboys so he wouldn't be mad at them, and by the time he found out different, they'd be long gone...

Orville said they didn't really need a lot of cash, in case Papoose refused them their share. They could simply find an island someplace to hide and have a bunch of pretty babes serve them fancy drinks with flowers sticking out the top. With even part of the loot in hand, another option would be Mexico. Neither he nor Homer had ever been south of the border but he remembered hearing how you could live there on almost no cash at all, and if they only ended up with thirty or forty thou, they'd be set for life. Forget about the Hastings. Homer could simply pick up another car, they'd take whatever the cash they came up with and they'd head south. But what about the FBI? When it came out about them killing one of the feebees, there'd be no place to hide. No place.

Homer began to stir. He had finally learned how to roll over on his side and push up onto his elbow to get out of bed by himself.

"'Morning, Orvie. You figure out what we're gonna do?"

"I've got two or three ideas but I ain't too sure any one of 'em will work. We'll talk things over while we get dressed and have some breakfast."

"Jeez, Orvie. We ain't even got a change of clothes any more. Think we could pick up a few things, and maybe a new pair of shoes? Mine are still soggy from that dip in the lake…"

"Long as these two credit cards hold out, we might as well."

They avoided any questions from the manager by not returning the key to the front desk and just as they started to cross the street to the Come-N-Get-It Café, a dilapidated pickup stopped in the middle of the street and intercepted them.

The driver stuck his head out of the window and said, "Hey, there, you two. Glad I finally caught up with you. We've got something to settle…"

It was Brad Hastings!

"Holy shit, Orvie! Run!" Without looking back, Homer darted around the back of the pickup and headed for the restaurant. The pickup moved on down the street without stopping or turning around.

Homer reached the doorway first and slammed through the entrance to shove his way past the customers waiting to be seated. He rushed over and peeked between the slats of the Venetian blinds.

"He gone?" Orville joined him at the window. "Maybe he just wants to talk about your accident at the rodeo…"

"Jeez, Orvie. What's gotta happen 'fore you realize he's got us by the balls? He *knows*! Might as well face it. We gotta forget the bonds and everything else and get the hell out of here while we can!"

Just before he turned away from the window, Homer pointed across the street.

"There's another of them damned black limos. How come everybody else has one and we can't even hang on to one measly car for more than a day or two?"

Without waiting for a waitress to seat them, Orville pulled him over to a booth and forced him to sit down.

"The yokel never came back so he's no threat for now. Remember, Papoose said the FBI friend wouldn't be in Denver 'til the end of this week and we'll be gone by then."

"We will? *Honest*? You gotta promise, Orvie…"

"I promise. We'll catch a bus into Denver and see about splittin' our take with Papoose. Soon as you get us some wheels, we're heading for Mexico. How's that sound?"

"I could grab us a car right now…"

"Dangerous. Town's too small."

Homer slumped into the corner of the booth, banging his head in the process. He removed his dark glasses and wiped his eyes with a paper napkin.

"I ain't hungry no more, Orvie. You grab yourself a bite to eat and let's hit the road. I seen a Greyhound bus stop at that service station on the corner so we can maybe hide over there 'til it's time to go."

Three men in dark suits, white shirts, striped ties and shiny black shoes entered the café and came straight over to the booth where the Stokes were seated. Orville had not yet had a chance to order.

"You Stokes?" A dark-complexioned barrel-chested man with a deep scar that extended from his right ear to his chin looked at the two men.

Orville nodded. Homer tried to move further away but he was already against the wall so he attempted to slither under the table.

"You with the thing on your neck. Sit up straight where I can see yez!"

One of "scar-face's" companions, a tall black man with enormous hands, grabbed Orville by the neck and pulled him out of the booth.

The third man, whose only distinguishing feature was the fact that he had none, reached across and dragged Homer to his feet, hauling him toward the front door.

The only sound out of either of the Stokes was the whimpering noise from Homer after he was shoved into the limo. He nearly toppled over when he was dumped onto one of the narrow jump-seats facing toward the rear.

"Hey, take it easy," Orville said, more as a plea than an order. "Can't you see he's hurt?"

The chauffeur held the door and shoved him into the seat next to Homer while the three muscle-heads watched.

"See that driver, Orvie?" Homer whispered. "That's the same one we seen at Central City."

"I know," Orville hissed. "Just shut up 'til we see what they're after…"

Scar-face and the black man, who by now had been identified as "Morty", climbed into the back seat. The third man sat in front with the driver. No one spoke. *Morty*, facing them, glared at Homer, then Orville, alternately. To add to Orville's discomfort, he remembered their local mortician in Nebraska had shared the black man's nickname and the tie-in with corpses was unsettling. After what seemed like an eternity to the Stokes, Scar-face told the chauffeur to drive out to the edge of town.

When they arrived at a roadside park with picnic tables and rest-rooms, Scar-face removed his suit coat and loosened his tie. When he rolled up his shirt sleeves, Homer began to whimper again.

"So let's get down to facts, fellas. Yez want to explain what happened to the bonds you come here to buy?"

Homer and Orville looked at each other. Before Orville had a chance to say anything, his brother blurted, "Like we told Mr. Bossman, *hiccup*, two cowboys stole 'em. *Hiccup*. That's right, ain't it, Orvie? *Hiccup*. Took 'em right out of our cabin, *hiccup*, the same night we bought 'em off the men from Denver. *Hiccup*."

"So where are they now?"

Orville kicked Homer on the shins to shut him up.

"Homer's right! Him and me was here in town getting the car gassed up to leave the next day, and when we got back to the cabin we found out we'd been robbed. From the tracks around the place, we figured the two men from the next cabin, that's Gorman's place, had been there and gone..."

"And *now*?"

"One of them had an accident and we been tailing them ever since, trying to find out where they hid the box."

Scar-face leaned forward and jerked Homer's dark glasses from his face. "Take them damned things off. I wanna see yer eyes when I talk to yez..."

Morty spoke for the first time. "What about Three-fingered Joe? Nobody ain't heard from him since the day he left L.A."

The Stokes looked at each other. Homer squinted and shaded his eyes with one hand.

"Who?" Orville asked.

"Big guy. Two fingers chopped off in a knife fight. He was sent here to keep an eye on you two and he ain't been heard from since..."

Homer began gasping for breath. Orville pounded on his back and shook him until he toppled to one side. Morty shoved him back into an upright position and asked, "What the hell's wrong with him now?"

Orville tried to control his own voice and absorb this new bombshell at the same time. *Holy shit! The man we murdered wasn't FBI...he was sent by the mob!*

"Can't we get out for a minute and get some air? My brother just got out of the hospital..."

Homer was starting to turn blue so the two men from the front seat jumped out and opened the rear doors, pulling Homer through one and Orville through the other. Arm-in-arm they staggered over to a willow tree where Homer leaned against it and began to throw up. The low-hanging branches and narrow leaves that covered his face caused him to sneeze, and that, combined with the vomiting, forced Orville to step around to the far side of the tree to avoid getting sick, also.

Orville was glad for a chance to rethink the situation and with his back still turned, he whispered to Homer hoarsely, "Papoose said we was in deep shit before, I wonder what he'd think about the spot we're in now!"

Homer reached around the trunk of the tree and grabbed at Orville's arm for support but lost his grip and slid to the ground. "They're gonna kill us for sure, ain't they, Orvie?"

"Sure possible…"

"Hey, you two. Get back over here. We gotta talk."

Orville helped Homer get to his feet and removed a bandanna from his own hip pocket to try and clean him up a little. When Homer attempted to hide behind the willow tree, Orville grabbed a rear belt loop of his pants and pulled him back.

"Might as well face 'em now, Homer. Just keep your mouth shut and let me do the talking…"

Back in the limo, the intense grilling began. As the questions were being hurled at them about the two men from Gorman's cabin, and what the Stokes had done so far to retrieve the bonds, Orville's thoughts were racing on some way to stall for enough time to plan an escape.

At the point where the two men facing the Stokes in the back seat suggested they all confront the cowpokes immediately and "settle this thing one way or the other," Orville leaned toward Scar-face and grabbed him by the arm.

"We can't do that! There's a chance they might not have the bonds after all."

"But yez said…"

"I know what we said," Orville pleaded, "but the fact is, a con we know who has *connections* in Denver, thinks we might've been mistaken about who stole them in the first place. If what he heard in Denver is right, him and his men'll have the loot back to us by nightfall. He thinks the men we bought the goods off of in the first place sent a couple of pals back to rip us off! We was supposed to call him right after breakfast today and see what he found out."

Scar-face looked down at his arm, then frowned at Orville who released his grip and settled back, apologetically.

"So let's haul-ass and see this con right now," Morty said. His menacing look suggested this was a done deal, not to be questioned.

"But we can't…" Homer began. Orville kicked him on the leg one more time but he could not be silenced. "If anybody but me and Orvie show up, it'll blow the whole deal! *Hiccup*. We had to promise them twenty percent, *hiccup*, and even then they warned us not to bring anyone else in on the deal. *Hiccup*. Ain't that right, Orvie?"

Scar-face and Morty stepped out of the limo and were joined at the rear of the car by the driver and the man Orville thought of simply as Number Three. Orville was unable to hear any part of their conversation but it was obvious they disagreed heatedly about how the situation should be handled. From their facial expressions, it seemed the others were not amenable to Scar-face's final decision but it seemed he was the main man. When they climbed back into the limo, only Scar-face spoke.

"Okay, we'll give yez 'til tonight, but if yez ain't back at the cabin by dark, we'll find yez! Unnerstand?"

Orville nodded. Homer bobbed his head as much as possible.

Scar-face continued, "In case yez plan to run out on us, the only way the two of yez will leave here will be in body bags…"

"Right," Orville said, weakly. "Never gave it a thought."

A wave of Scar-face's arm signaled the driver to go back into town. With a simple knife-across-the-throat gesture from Scar-face, the Stokes were released in front of the café where they were first accosted. Silently they exited the limo and tried not to run when the doors closed behind them.

CHAPTER 24

Brad spotted Doug's pickup near the boat dock so he stopped there instead of going to the cabin. His father was sitting at the end of the pier, casting a line out into the lake.

"Any luck?" Brad asked.

"Just started. Really need one of them small boats but I waited 'til you got here. Get the part for the generator?"

"Not yet. The bus from Denver already came and went but no package for Smitty's Hardware. They said there's another one at four-thirty and told me to check with them this evening." Smoky raced over to greet him and together they joined Doug. "Crazy thing happened, though. You know those two weird ducks from the hospital?"

"Yeah. What about 'em?"

"Well, I ran into them in town and was going to tell that one with the brace on his neck that there were no hard feelings, but when I tried to talk to him he high-tailed it out of there like I'd pulled a gun on him or something!"

Doug laughed. "Maybe somebody told him how I felt about the whole deal! Anyway, you pick up a bag of ice and some steaks?"

"Yeah, which reminds me, I'd better get this stuff into your cooler. I brought some sandwiches, too. Want one now?"

"What say we fish an hour or so before the sun gets any higher, then we can relax and eat?"

"Sounds like a winner…"

They managed to catch three trout that were "keepers," but the rest were too small and they threw them back. Smoky rode in their rental boat for awhile but he became restless and nearly tipped them over several times until Brad finally tossed him overboard and motioned for him to swim to shore, which he did. Brad mentioned that he had called Gary while he was in town since his cell phone was still recharging. His cousin said to be on the lookout for Laredo who flew into Denver a couple of days early to do some fishing with the Hastings before his weekend meeting.

"Be good to see the old reprobate again. Guess I've told you before, he's really an ex-FBI agent named Kevin Collins. He always reminds me of a huge teddy-bear, and with his cowpuncher garb and husky south-Texas drawl, he sure isn't your typical fed. His irreverence toward the Bureau's *rules and regs*, as he calls them, eventually caused him to retire. He's semi-active, though, and works with them occasionally."

"When you think he'll be here?"

"Gary didn't know but he told Laredo to get directions in Bear Claw. He'll spot my old pickup when he arrives."

Later, at Gorman's cabin, Brad cleaned the fish after they unloaded their gear from both pickups, and while Doug stretched out on a hammock between two cottonwood trees, Brad went for a ride around the lake with Smoky running alongside. Because of the twinges of pain he felt in his chest when saddling Skeeter, it took him several attempts before he was successful. He had rejected Doug's offer of help originally, so he silently struggled to accomplish the job alone.

Half-way around the lake Brad veered away from the trail and followed a path into the woods, one that he had observed while jogging. He travelled at a leisurely pace through the trees with Smoky disappearing from time to time, giving chase to a rabbit first, then a tree squirrel. The trail led him over the top of a small hill where the timber ended and a wide grassy meadow spread out ahead of him. A few Hereford cows and some yearling steers grazed at the timberline on the far side of the field, with three does and a fawn nearby. On his right, two coyote pups chased each other in circles, romping through the tall grass while their mother watched on, ever alert to any danger to her brood.

Smoky caught up with Brad where he had reined in to survey the pastoral scene ahead. The mother coyote immediately herded her pups out of sight, and Smoky, interpreting this as a challenge, took out after them on a dead run. Brad loosened the reins so Skeeter could graze while he leaned back in the saddle and smiled, awaiting the inevitable outcome of Smoky's "attack." In a split second after Smoky followed the coyotes into the forest, he came running back out with his stubby tail tucked between his legs, yipping loudly. He had almost reached Brad when he looked back over his shoulder at the coyote pups who were again playing just as they had before.

Smoky glanced toward Brad, then apparently decided to give chase once more. This time he was out of sight in the trees for a few moments longer than before and Brad tightened the reins to prepare for a rescue mission just as he spotted Smoky emerging once more with the female coyote close behind. This entire scenario was typical of the manner in which coyotes, and wolves, lure their attackers into chasing them into their own territory where they immediately become the predators. This time Smoky seemed convinced.

"Hey, there, Smoke! What are you, the *chaser* or the *chasee*?"

Without acknowledging his master's voice, Smoky dropped in behind Skeeter and meekly followed Brad when he loped across the meadow to find a different trail back to the lake.

Smoky seemed to forget the shameful episode with the coyotes because he soon resumed his rabbit chasing when they were almost out of the wooded area and were approaching the bait store. Brad tied Skeeter to a makeshift hitching post at the end of the building and entered the front door with the intention of buying a snack of some sort to salve Smoky's recently bruised ego.

Two men were standing by a bin of worms, scooping night crawlers into small cartons. Brad overheard their discussion regarding a red Ford pickup belonging to a plumbing supply place that had been dumped into the lake the night before.

The store owner, Gumpy, was a grey-bearded Willie Nelson look-alike who spoke up while he tallied their purchases on an ancient cash register.

"I figure that's somehow tied in with somebody stealin' my tractor in the middle of the night. They must'a needed a transport out of here." He shook his head, puzzled. "They could'a just asked me. I'd have drove them into town. Could'a just asked…"

Up to that point, Brad was listening, yet not listening, until mention was made of a tractor.

"Wouldn't happen to be a small John Deere with a post-hole digger on the back, would it?" he asked.

All three men directed their attention toward him.

"Sure would," Gumpy said. "You know something about it?"

"On my way into Bear Claw this morning I saw what could have been your missing tractor. It was parked under a tree right at the edge of town."

"Well, I'll be damned!" Gumpy said. "Wasn't wrecked or nothing?"

"Didn't appear to be. Just sitting there like somebody left it while they went on into town."

The fishermen resumed their shopping and left, still muttering about the crazy things people do. Brad selected a small bag of candy for Smoky from of the meager selection, then mentioned to Gumpy that he had to go back to Bear Claw that afternoon.

"I'd be glad to give you a lift if you need to pick up your tractor. Unless you have a flat-bed you can haul it on…"

"Nope, nothing like that," was the reply. "Just have to drive it back home. If that is my rig, and sure sounds like it is, I'd appreciate a lift."

Brad agreed to stop by on his way into town, then he tossed some candy to Smoky and climbed aboard Skeeter before heading back to the cabin.

Doug was awake but still in the hammock.

"Have a good ride, Bud?" he yawned, then raised himself onto one elbow while struggling to keep from tipping over. "You should have seen what pulled in to the cabin just east of us a few minutes ago. A god-damned limousine! Imagine somebody coming out here in a *limo* to go fishing? Maybe the butler baits their hooks for them!" He nearly rolled out of the hammock with laughter before settling back to close his eyes and cover his face with his hat.

"Takes all kinds, Doug. Takes all kinds…"

* * *

Homer suggested they return to their motel room and call Papoose but Orville rejected the idea.

"Those goons must have seen where we was staying so I'd rather not go back there right now. Besides, I don't want that desk clerk listening in on me."

"How about the phone at the service station, Orvie?"

"That sounds like our best bet. Hope he's got his cell phone with him, though. We don't have time to leave messages and wait for a call-back. Besides, Maria's house might even be bugged…"

Orville was relieved when Papoose answered on the first ring.

"Yeah. Papoose here."

"This is Orville. We gotta talk…"

There was such a long pause, Orville thought they had been disconnected. Finally Papoose asked, skeptically, "What now, Dude? You never call unless it's trouble."

"*Major* trouble. The big boys from L.A. are here and they want the bonds. Now!"

"Tough shit, Dude! You already claimed the cowboys stole 'em, right? Why not blame it on the Hastings?" He paused. "They *are* dead, ain't they…?

"Yeah. Sure. But that ain't our problem…"

Orville went on to explain how the man he and Homer murdered was actually someone sent to spy on them by the big boss in California. If those thugs ever somehow found out who really killed their man, that would be the end of the Stokes brothers. They'd be better off if it really had been a feebie, he concluded.

"Only way I see," Orville continued, "is for us to turn over the bonds to these guys and get them the hell out of here before they find out the truth."

"But won't the mob men think you been keeping the loot for yourselves all this time?" Papoose asked. "How will you explain that?"

"Already did. I told them you, not by name of course, heard we'd been set up by the men who sold us the bonds in the first place, and that for twenty percent you could get them back."

"Twenty percent?"

"That's right. Just like we agreed in the first place. Anyway, if we can turn over eighty percent of the bonds to them by tonight, I think they'll leave and just maybe Homer and me can get away. We been broke before, but never *dead*!"

Another long pause.

"I got to think this one over. How about I call you back?"

"There's no time, Papoose! We gotta get out of here *now!* If you pick us up as soon as possible, we can still get the loot back to these thugs in time..."

"Pick you up? I'm afraid to ask, but what's wrong with your car?"

"Long story. No bus out of here 'til after four o'clock. How about it?"

Another pause.

"Will you stay away from me if I do this one last thing? You got to swear to it!"

"I swear. This is it..."

The Stokes sneaked back to the motel and approached their room from the back of the building. After convincing themselves they were not being watched, they entered and locked the door. At checkout time,

Orville slipped quietly around to the office and signed the credit card voucher, then he and Homer circled through the alley to wait for Papoose at the service station as had been agreed upon. In lieu of their present situation, there was no further mention of shopping for clothes so their "luggage" consisted solely of Homer's tool kit and the California license plate.

Their trip to Denver was fairly uneventful, and definitely silent. The only exchange of words was a statement from Papoose that he would keep his twenty percent and turn over the rest of it to the Stokes so they could save their asses with the L.A. group.

"But what about *us?*" Homer whined.

Orville reached over from the back seat and pounded the top of his head with his fist. "Let's figure a way to get out of here alive, you moron! Then we can talk *money…*"

Papoose explained that Maria was in Boulder at a realtor's seminar of some kind so it would be safe for them to hook up with Pinto at her house and "divvie up the booty," as he put it. On the way, Homer spotted a blue 1987 Plymouth two-door parked on a side street on the outskirts of Denver and asked to be dropped off at the next corner.

"Got everything you need?" Orville asked when they pulled over.

With a smile, Homer held up the small tool kit and his license plate as they drove away.

CHAPTER 25

When Brad arrived back at the cabin, he noticed Doug was no longer in the hammock. He was not at all concerned because the pickup-camper was still in the garage, so he went straight back to the shed where he proceeded to install the part to the generator and get it started. Smoky was waiting on the porch when he circled past the garage and opened the front door.

"What's the matter, Smoky? Old man won't let you in?"

Due to the structure of the cabin, there were no actual areas where a person might be concealed so Brad made one short tour, including a view of the loft, and called out Doug's name several times. As he passed through the living room, he tossed the empty box from Smitty's Hardware onto the coffee table before returning to the porch and scanning the area around the pier. Actually, this was more of an automatic gesture than any actual belief that Doug had walked away, especially with transportation available. There was a standing joke in the Hastings family that Doug never went anyplace on foot unless he absolutely had to. He even hated to walk from the house to their horse barn when he was at home, but Brad always jokingly refused to "play valet" and bring his mount around to the front door, so that was one hike Doug could not avoid.

Back in his pickup, with Smoky on the front seat, Brad approached a few people who were walking toward the lake or away from it. While trying to sound casual, his concern became more evident when each of them insisted they had not seen his father all afternoon. The next stop was at the bait shop. Again, this was a long shot because of the distance from their cabin, but he concluded that someone might have come by and taken him along to pick up a six-pack. Still, Doug should have left a note, or locked the place, or something. Even if he decided to ride into town with one of the other cabin inhabitants, it was definitely not like him to leave without a message for his son.

From the bait shop, where no-one had seen Doug that afternoon, Brad decided to call Tooley to check whether he had heard anything.

When Mrs. Olsen called Tooley to the phone, his voice immediately expressed concern.

"Yeah? That you Angie?"

"Nope. It's me, Brad."

"What's up? Didn't figure to hear from you 'less you had a problem…"

"Well, in a way, I do. Doug call you today?"

"No. Ain't talked to him since the two of you left for Estes Park. He disappear? Maybe you been too rough on him and he needed to get away for a spell."

"That I could understand, but you know what? He's been coasting along pretty damned well on just a few brews a day, and maybe a glass of wine sometimes, so even if he wanted to go on a toot, he'd sure as hell go in his own truck. That's what worries me, Tooley. His rig is still at the cabin, the door wasn't locked, and he never left a note."

"So where was you when he left?"

"In town. Had to pick up a part for the generator at Gorman's cabin. When I got back he was gone."

"You check in town to see if he coulda rode in with somebody else? I'll just bet you'll find him bellied up to the local bar with a drink in each hand! You gotta remember, it's hard to trick an old dog, 'specially a thirsty one, so just ease him back to dry ground as fast as you can! Main thing is to keep him out of jail. Call me when you find him. Any way to reach you if he calls?"

"Not really. You've been up here fishing, so you know where Gumpy's Bait Shop is. I'm using my cell phone now but it keeps cutting out on me. There's a booth out front and it's the only one there is here at the lake, so if for some reason you can't reach me, just leave a message with Gumpy and I'll call you."

Smoky seemed to sense something was wrong because he lay quietly on their way into Bear Claw and his only response to being rubbed behind his ears was a brief wag of his stubby tail.

"Sure hope the old man's just sopping up a few brews like Tooley said. Except for his talent for getting himself arrested, he's been doing okay most of the time. Guess he can still do it. Right?"

Smoky gave another short wag.

* * *

This time, after leaving Golden, the Stokes stayed on I-70 until they reached CO-119 just a few miles south of Central City. No time to take the slow road through the canyon. They had gassed up the Plymouth and picked up some burgers at a Wendy's drive-in, so they had no reason to stop until they reached Little Bear Lake. Orville drove this time while Homer hugged THE BOX MINUS TWENTY, as they now called it.

"Think they'll give us any trouble, Orvie? Suppose they'll just take the bonds and go away?"

"All we can do is hope. If they don't decide we maybe kept the extra twenty percent for ourselves, we ought be okay."

Both brothers were hesitant to get out of the car when they reached the cabin. With all of the drapes and venetian blinds closed, the house looked deserted, but the Stokes knew they would never be that lucky, and this was confirmed when they spotted the rear bumper of the limo at the far corner of the building.

Orville reached for THE BOX MINUS TWENTY but Homer continued to hold it close to his chest as they approached the front door.

The Third Man, with a ham sandwich in his left hand, let them in and pointed toward the kitchen with the .38 revolver in his right hand.

At first glance it appeared that only the four men from L.A. were in the room but when they stepped aside for Homer to place the bonds on the table, it was obvious there was a fifth person present. A man, with his back to them, was blindfolded and tied to one of the kitchen chairs. The veins in his neck protruded and his face was distorted as he thrashed around in an effort to remove the duct tape covering his mouth, so his identity was not immediately apparent to the Stokes.

"What the hell's this?" Orville finally asked. "Somebody try to break in?"

At that exact moment, the brothers both recognized the prisoner. It was Doug Hastings! Homer grabbed the edge of the sink and looked as though he might collapse. Orville stepped over to support him and to frantically search for something to say. For one thing, in flash backs to their few encounters, he could not recall if either of the Hastings had ever actually heard their voices at any time in the past ten days.

Scar-face straddled a wooden chair and leaned his chin on his crossed arms. He nodded in Doug Hastings direction.

"Just a little *protection* in case that Denver friend yez mentioned didn't come through, if there was such a person. We caught this cowpoke asleep at that cabin next door, where yez said. We was gonna search the place, but the limo's too easy to spot so we come back here to wait for the two of yez and thought we'd go back later if need-be." He pointed toward the table where Morty was already cutting the tape off of the Acme Boot Box. "Guess we could'a waited, but no harm done…"

With the bonds stacked in piles of ten thousand dollars each, it was immediately apparent that twenty thousand was missing.

Before anyone could mention the discrepancy, Orville blurted, "Remember, we already told you it cost us twenty percent to get it back? We're damned lucky he didn't keep the haul for hisself…"

Morty smiled, wryly, "Guess they knew what'd happen if they tried to pull something like that, huh?"

Orville was still keeping Homer from collapsing, and at the same time trying to figure a way to get Doug released without any interference from his son. They sure as hell couldn't take a chance on these goons getting together with Brad Hastings, and maybe finding out about what happened to their three-fingered friend.

"Guess you can drop this guy off at his cabin on your way out of here, right?" he asked, hopefully. "You got the bonds now, and we ain't even askin' for a cut for all the grief we went through."

Scar-face rose to his feet. "If we let yez *live*, that's your *cut*! Yez shouldn't have lost 'em in the first place…"

Morty gathered the bonds and stuffed them into an alligator briefcase. He looked from one to the other of his cohorts, then pointed at Doug. "What about that ransom note? Might be cops all over the place by now! We'd better haul ass…"

This was too much for Homer. His knees buckled and if Orville had not slid a chair under him, he would have sprawled on the floor next to the sink.

"Ransom note? Cops?" Homer said weakly. "Orvie?"

At a signal from Scar-face, his three companions joined him in the living room. Orville and Homer strained to hear their conversation, but all they caught was the last part of Morty's suggestion, "We can just dump 'em and take off…"

"Orvie! Was that a *him* or a *them* they're gonna dump? You think they mean dump, like in kill?" Homer gasped, grabbing Orville by both arms.

"Either way, we got to stop it somehow. We can't take a chance on tangling with Brad again, and we sure as hell don't want to be on the dumping end of their plan, whatever it is."

Scar-face came back to the kitchen alone and looked first at the Stokes, then at Doug. The others could be heard leaving through the front door.

"We'll let yez have the cowpoke. You two fucked up all the way, so now we figger it's up to yez to get out of it any way yez can…"

Orville helped Homer to his feet and the two followed Scar-face out onto the porch. Orville hoped if they looked pathetic enough maybe the man would take pity on them and handle the situation some way so Doug could not identify the Stokes as part of this ordeal. It was just approaching dusk and Orville could see several cars parked near the lake with their lights on. Men were milling around and blinking lights identified two of the cars as law enforcement vehicles. His first thought was that this was somehow tied into Doug's kidnapping, then he saw what looked like two men dragging something up onto the small pier at the foot of the hill. He nudged Homer and nodded in that direction.

"Orvie…"

"Yeah. I know." He quickly stepped forward and shook hands with Scar-face. The others were already in the limo. "Don't worry about a thing. We'll clean up this mess. Just tell your boss we're sorry about everything. Maybe next time…"

He struggled to keep from blurting, "So just get the hell out of here!"

When the limo came around the corner of the cabin and headed down the trail toward Little Bear Drive, Orville gripped Homer's upper arms so tightly his brother yelped in pain.

"Sorry, Homer. I'm just praying they get out of here before they see what's being pulled out of the lake."

"You thinkin' what I'm thinkin', Orvie?"

"Gotta be. But how come nobody's looking for Doug?"

CHAPTER 26

When Brad reached town, he decided the most likely place to find his father was at the Bar&Q. He parked in front of the place and stared through the front window at the smattering of customers, some playing pool and two or three standing at the bar. With the rodeo over, the place was practically deserted, and it was immediately evident that none of these men was Doug Hastings.

Something poked Brad between his shoulders.

"Hands over your head, Pilgrim. Y'all under arrest!"

Brad recognized the voice. Laredo.

"Your John Wayne imitation is still pitiful! And *no*, I will *not* put my hands over my head. In case you haven't heard, my doctor won't allow it!"

Brad turned around to face the man he considered one of his very best friends. They first met when Brad was a deputy sheriff in Alamogordo, New Mexico, and the FBI had assigned Laredo to settle some disputes, including a couple of murders, on the Mescalero Indian Reservation. Their last encounter had been just three or four weeks ago when Laredo was instrumental in providing a protective custody arrangement for Tooley's daughter Angie and her husband. Brad knew any conversation regarding their whereabouts was taboo, so he simply shook hands with his friend and punched him in the arm. Smoky laid back his ears, unsure of the reason for Brad's action.

"Gary said you were coming up here for a couple of days. Doug and I already caught all the fish in the lake so you're just wasting your time!"

Laredo's Wrangler jacket and pants, scuffed roper-style boots and three day growth of beard, as always, belied his part-time role of federal agent. He grinned wryly and grabbed his arm as though Brad had punched him too hard.

"Watch it, there, youngster! At my age, I bruise easy. And speaking of age, where's that old man of yours? Y'all keep talking about him, but he's never around. Is he hid out somewhere?"

"Funny you should ask," Brad said, trying to mask his concern. "I came into town thinking he might be here. This afternoon while I was running errands, he disappeared. Our friend Tooley convinced me he must have ridden into town with somebody from the lake, but right now I'm getting more than just a little bit worried."

"Any reason for him to take off without saying something?"

"Not really." Brad paused. "But he's still on probation after his stretch in Arizona, and like I told you before, he does have kind of a drinking problem. It hasn't been too serious lately, and he sure as hell wouldn't have to sneak off without telling me if his sobriety got too hard to handle. Besides, his pickup was still at the cabin and none of the fishermen saw him leave…"

"Tell me what he looks like, Brad," Laredo said solemnly, "and I'll comb one side of the street and y'all take the other. Between us we can cover this burg in ten or fifteen minutes. If we don't find him, let's head for that lake of yours and I'll just bet he's sitting on your porch right now wondering why y'all ain't come back yet!"

"Sounds like a winner…"

It was actually less than fifteen minutes before the two men met again at the Bar&Q. Their expressions, including shoulder shrugs from both men, indicated that neither of them had located Doug. Their sole conversation consisted of Laredo's agreeing to follow Brad back to the lake.

Early evening was settling over the area when Brad pulled onto Little Bear Drive with Laredo's rented Dodge SUV right behind him. As they approached the turnoff to Gorman's cabin, Brad pulled over to make room for a black limo to go past him on the narrow Little Bear Drive and to check out a cluster of cars parked next to the pier. Because of the flashing lights on the local sheriff's car, he and Laredo both stepped out of their cars just as two men on the pier were pulling a body out of the water.

"Oh, Jesus!" Brad said under his breath. "It can't be…"

Laredo grabbed his arms from behind and pulled him back.

"Let me take a look first. Could be anybody."

Brad wanted to follow him but his knees felt like they would buckle if he took a single step, so he leaned against the door of his pickup and waited. And waited. Smoky looked up at him, then lay at his feet.

Laredo waved to him from the pier and shook his head "No" before carrying on a brief conversation with the local law enforcement people. Brad climbed into his truck and leaned his head against the steering wheel.

"Thank God…"

Laredo approached just then and patted Brad on the shoulder.

"Some guy who's been in there a week or so. Just floated to the surface this afternoon. Ain't nobody y'all know, but I think I have a hunch."

"You know him?" Brad asked when he got his voice back. "How come?"

"I didn't get a good look at the body and don't want to get into anything with the local law, but I have my suspicions…"

Brad closed his door and leaned out of the window.

"Just follow me. We'll check out the cabin and like as not you're right. Doug'll be having a fit 'cause I didn't get back when I was supposed to."

Because he had no key to the cabin, Brad had left the door unlocked. The two men entered and while Brad called out his father's name and scoured the place for signs of why he had disappeared, Laredo snooped through the kitchen and living room.

"Think y'all better have a look at this, Brad. Piece of paper I found on the floor by the coffee table."

"What is it?" Reading Laredo's expression Brad reluctantly reached for the paper. He assumed it was the instruction sheet from the generator part until he saw it was hand-printed in big block letters.

It read: WE GOT THE OLD MAN. YOU GOT OUR PROPERTY. IF YOU WANT TO SEE HIM ALIVE AGAIN, PUT THE BOX IN THE HAMMOCK AND DRIVE AWAY. WE'LL LET HIM GO WHEN WE GET BACK WHAT BELONGS TO US. WE MEAN BIZNESS.

Brad was stunned. He looked at Laredo then back at the note.

"What box they talkin' about?" Laredo asked. "Y'all got something' you ain't supposed to have?"

"I haven't the faintest idea what they mean. That's the God's honest truth. Doug mentioned the other day something about a 'boot box' that he thought was mine, but with my mind so fouled up after the accident, I didn't pay much attention."

"Anybody who might know?"

"Only friend we've got around here is Tooley, Angie's dad. He used to be a rodeo clown and now he's got a sheepdog act. I doubt if he knows any more than I do about this 'box' thing but I could ask him. You got a cell phone? Mine's been acting up lately."

"Yeah, in the Dodge. I'll get it…"

The call to Golden proved fruitless. Tooley had borrowed a car from the Olsens and left for Little Bear Lake immediately after he talked to Brad.

"No way to tell if he heard anything," Brad said, dejectedly. He plopped down on the porch steps with Smoky on one side and Laredo on the other. "He'll be here before long if he left right after I called. Let's hope he knows something about this damned box, 'cause I sure as hell don't…"

"You think they left that note since y'all was here earlier?"

"I doubt it. It probably just fell to the floor when I tossed that empty carton on the table."

"Can y'all remember what it was your dad said about a boot box? Maybe we can look for it..."

Brad tried to recall. "Seems like he said it was in the horse trailer, or something. Sounded kind of crazy to me at the time, but like I said, my mind was playing all kinds of tricks on me so I didn't think any more about it."

Laredo got to his feet. "Let's check it out. Could still be around some-place, but damned if I can figure why it'd be important enough to kidnap somebody to get it back. Why'nt they just ask y'all for it?"

The two men thoroughly searched the horse trailer, Doug's camper and the cabin with no success. Skeeter was hobbled at the rear of the cabin and by the time Brad led him to the lake for a drink of water, he noticed all of the cars except for a single vehicle from the sheriff's department had already departed. He was just returning toward the cabin when Tooley pulled up beside him in a white Nova.

"Hey there, Bud! I see somebody on your porch up ahead. You find Doug okay?"

"Nope. Not yet, Tooley. I take it you didn't hear anything, either. That's my friend Laredo, the one that helped Angie and Chip. Come on up there and we'll try to figure this thing out..."

* * *

The Stokes watched as their precious BOX was being hauled away from them forever. Fear soon replaced their depression when the limo driver slowed down near the cluster of cars as though the occupants were checking out the center of activity. Homer and Orville clutched each others' arms and Homer started moaning, then they both sighed with relief when the limo swung past two approaching vehicles and continued along Little Bear Drive to disappear out of sight.

"Should have knowed they'd steer clear of the law but they sure as hell gave me a scare. How about you, Homer?" Orville entered the cabin with Homer following. "With them dark windows they probably never saw nothing, anyhow."

They stood facing each other in the living room. "We still gotta figure what to do, Orvie. Right?"

A crashing sound sent them charging through the archway into the kitchen to find Doug on the floor, still tied to a chair and struggling to rub the duct tape from his mouth. Together they managed to set him upright but he still fought against the ropes.

"Wish we could talk to Papoose," Homer whined. "It ain't our fault everything we try turns sour! If we could have got out of here just one day sooner with them bonds, before we had to hide the box and dump the body, we'd never have had to go through all that shit at the rodeo. You realize I coulda got myself killed that day trying to get rid of our witness? A yokel who don't remember nothing nohow…"

Orville grabbed him by the arm and pulled him out onto the porch. "The man's *mouth* is taped up…not his *ears*! 'Til we decide what to do with him, just keep your own trap shut!"

"Can't we just leave him here, Orvie? You promised we'd go to Mexico. Why not just take off right now?"

"When I made that promise, I figured we have some kind of a bankroll. Right now we got nothing…"

They returned to the kitchen where Homer fumbled around trying to make sandwiches with odds and ends he found in the refrigerator.

"Think we ought to feed him something, Orvie? Now that it looks like we're about as screwed up as we can get, there's no use making it any tougher on him than need be. Right?"

"I suppose so, but let's think on this a bit more. If you take off the tape to feed him, he's gonna yell his head off…"

Doug nodded his agreement and appeared about to tip his chair over again.

"You might be right, Homer. About leaving him here, I mean." Orville straddled a kitchen chair and leaned on the imitation cane back while he nibbled nervously on a slice of cheese. It had no more taste than a hunk of wax. "Soon as it looks like all our neighbors are settled for the night, I think we'd best get the hell out of here. We can be long gone before anybody knows we've been here. Sure as hell they'll start searching these cabins by tomorrow when he don't show up…"

In protest, Doug started rocking back and forth in his chair, shaking his head "no."

"Least we could do is take him outside to pee before we leave him tied up for the night, ain't that right, Orvie?"

"You'll have to let his hands loose. I sure as hell ain't helping him pee, but I guess between us we can keep him under control with both his legs tied. After all the times we tried to ice him and his kid, we owe him that much. They didn't really do nothing *wrong*…"

Homer grinned. "Except survive!"

CHAPTER 27

In Gorman's cabin, Laredo stood with his hands clasped behind his back and stared through the front window toward the lake. Tooley leaned back with his hips on the windowsill. Brad paced.

After several minutes, Laredo turned to face Brad.

"Anything different happen in the last week or so to indicate your old man might be in some kind of trouble?"

Brad shook his head. "Nothing special. There were a few strange incidents but no reason to think they were tied into something like this…"

Tooley walked out onto the front porch where he stood for a while and appeared to be checking out their section of lakeside properties. He disappeared for ten or fifteen minutes, then returned to stick his head in the doorway.

"Who owns that place next door, Son? The one with a blue Plymouth parked out front…"

"Damned if I know, Tooley. I never paid any attention. Doug mentioned something about a black limo over there, but I don't know about any Plymouth. Why?"

"Just curious. A half-block away from the Olsen's where I been staying in Golden, a blue Plymouth like that one was parked in their driveway just this afternoon. Smoky was with me when I walked past their cabin just now, and he kept kind of whining when we turned around and started back.

There could be a million blue Plymouths, Tooley," Laredo suggested. "No reason to think it's the same one."

"Suppose not. Sure weird, though, the same jerks that drove away in it have been hanging around for a week and every time I see them, they've got a different car!"

"Anybody you know, Tooley?" Brad asked.

"Not sure, Son. Only person who looked familiar was the joker with the brace on his neck. Sure resembled that gunsel who caused your accident…"

Brad laughed. "No chance of him tangling with Doug. Ever since that day, Doug's been threatening to annihilate him on sight!"

Laredo stared intently at Tooley. "Anything suspicious about the man, except for all the different cars?"

"Just weird goings-on with some Injun who's shacking up with the woman that owns the house." Tooley looked sheepish. "The Olsens know all the neighborhood gossip. I used to sit out on their porch and read the newspaper and when I asked about them people down the block, that's what they told me."

"Anything else?" Laredo probed. "What about all those cars?"

"First it was an old grey Chevy, like the one sittin' next to Doug's horse trailer one evenin' during the rodeo. Then I noticed it circling past us when Brad and me was loading Skeeter the night him and Doug pulled out of there for Estes Park, but I never thought nothing' about it at the time."

Brad pulled Tooley over to sit beside him on the sofa.

"Grey Chevy? That's what the gunsel and his brother were driving when they left the hospital that first day." He looked from Laredo to Tooley. By way of explanation, he added, "I have no problem remembering things *after* the accident."

Laredo dragged a chair over next to the sofa and sat facing the other two men.

"Any reason for them to be parked by your dad's horse trailer, Brad? Or watching y'all load up to leave? Seems they were damned interested in that trailer, if y'all know what I mean…"

Brad, thinking of their earlier search, nodded. "No reason that I know of, except somebody looking for a box, maybe. But what about all the other cars, Tooley? Even if that isn't strange enough, can you think of anything else suspicious?"

Tooley looked thoughtful for a minute or two, then added, "Not really. It was just that there was a white Isuzu for a day or two, then a red pickup truck…"

"Ford?"

"Yeah, Son. Some kind of printing on the side."

Brad sat back and frowned. "Well, I'll be damned!"

"What?" Laredo asked. "Y'all onto something?"

"Something. But damned if I know what!" He stared across the room for several minutes before continuing. "When Doug and I were in Estes Park we heard about a white Isuzu that blew up in Boulder that same morning *and the driver had a brace on his neck*! So what do you make of that, Mr. FBI man?"

"Hmmm. I guess I'll be damned, too!"

"Wait. There's more," Brad said, suddenly excited. "Sometime after our camp was raided down by the pier the other night, a red Ford pickup got dumped into the lake and a tractor was stolen by somebody needing a ride back into town! That's got to be just too much of a coincidence. Right?"

"Know any reason these people been tailing y'all?" Laredo asked.

"None that I know of, except after getting that ransom note, I figure it has something to do with whatever's in that damned box. Any ideas, Tooley?"

"Not a clue, Son. Not a clue."

The three men remained silent. Tooley paced the floor. Laredo stared out the window again with Brad looking over his shoulder, watching the cabin lights around the lake disappear one by one, until only the reflection of moonlight on the lake was visible in the darkness. He went into the kitchen to brew a pot of coffee and by the time it was ready, each man had resumed his place in the living room and they faced each other glumly.

"So what now, Laredo? You're the expert at this kind of thing. It never occurred to me that Doug might be held right here at the lake. Maybe even in that cabin Tooley mentioned. How would you proceed with something like this?"

"By rights, we're supposed to notify the local law and tell them what's happened, get a search warrant, *then* start looking."

"That's not what I asked. I said how would *you* proceed? I know you've been in hot water more than once for taking things into your own hands and to hell with FBI policy! Since this hasn't actually been reported to anyone, what can the three of us do to try and find Doug before these bastards kill him like the note says?"

Tooley jumped to his feet. "You didn't say nothing' about threats to kill him! That what the ransom note said?"

Brad grabbed his arm and pulled him back onto the sofa.

"We're just hoping to find him, or the goddamned box, before they do something stupid. Don't worry, Tooley, you know my old man. He's too tough to let a few weirdos get the best of him…"

Tooley collapsed back onto the sofa and hung his head. "You're right. If I know that old scoundrel, he'll come out of this smelling like Pete Rose…"

"First thing we need to do," Laredo began, getting to his feet, "is sneak over to that cabin and take a look. Another thing, y'all mentioned a limo. Remember when we first got here, Brad? Just about the time we slowed down next to that bunch of cars, a limo went past us on its way out of here. Just in case they're tied into this thing, it's best we don't wait on any damned procedure or it might be too late to follow up on the couple of leads we do have."

"So…?" Brad asked.

"So, let's haul ass and see just who's at that cabin next door. Okay?"

While they made preparations, Smoky ran in circles around Brad, wagging his tail excitedly.

"That's the *waggiest* damned dog I ever seen!" Laredo said, grinning, on the way out to his car.

Armed with two small flashlights and a .38 Special Laredo retrieved from the glove box of the Dodge, the three men and Smoky lit out through the dense timber behind Gorman's cabin and followed along the edge of the trees until they were directly behind the object of their inspection tour.

"The place is dark so that'll make it tough to see what's going on inside, but let's give it a try," Laredo whispered hoarsely. "Just shut off the flashlights for now…"

Laredo led the way with Brad helping support Tooley as he stumbled along in the dark. When they reached a point about twenty yards from the cabin, Smoky began whining softly and suddenly darted on ahead of them toward the back door of the building.

"Call him back," Laredo hissed. "He'll give us away…"

Brad called Smoky's name softly, but the dog refused to leave the railroad ties that served as a porch at the rear of the building. When the men approached he lay there, still whining softly, with his nose against the door.

"Doug's either here now, or has been in the last few hours," Brad whispered to Laredo. "Let's bust the door down and find out what the hell's going on…"

Laredo held up his hand and motioned for them to stay back. He had one of the flashlights and Brad watched him approach each window in turn, briefly aiming the light into one room after another. At the third one he paused, turned off the flashlight and returned to where Brad and Tooley waited at the rear entrance.

"Looks like somebody's on the sofa in the livin' room. Can't tell if it's your old man, Brad, but whoever it is, he's trussed up like a Thanksgiving turkey, so chances are it's him.

Brad charged toward the door as though to break in by sheer force but Laredo stopped him before he could slam his shoulder against it.

"Cool it, Brad," Laredo warned quietly. "Whoever's in that front room looks to be okay for now, at least. If y'all go bustin' in there like a Brahma on the rampage, he might just get killed during the fracas. Let's think on this for a second…"

Laredo led them to the living room window where Brad peeked through and confirmed that the man on the sofa was, indeed, his father, but it was impossible to determine his condition. Further inspection proved that the blue Plymouth was no longer parked in front of the cabin so at that point Laredo motioned for Brad and Tooley to wait by the rear entrance while he broke down the front door.

Brad kept expecting a crashing sound and was barely able to remain inactive as the silence continued for what seemed much too long. Just as he was about to slam his way into the cabin from the rear, the door opened and Laredo stood there, flashlight in hand, with a big grin on his face.

"Enter my humble abode, gents! My friend in the front room is too tied up to greet anyone at the moment, but y'all are more than welcome to come meet him." He stepped aside and made a sweeping gesture with the flashlight. "Oh, by the way, he appears to be in pretty good shape but from the noises he's making, I'd step back out of the way when y'all turn him loose. That's one *eye-rate* human being!"

Smoky had already raced past Laredo before Brad and Tooley could get through the doorway. Tooley grabbed Brad's arm and pulled him around so they were facing each other.

With both hands raised above his head, palms facing Brad, Tooley chuckled, "Give me a high ten, Son. Looks like we done it!"

Doug's hands were tied behind his back and attached to the rope around his feet in such a way that any attempt to hop around would have tripped him and resulted in a fall on his face. Tooley held the flashlight while Brad rushed to untie Doug who kept shaking his head violently and rubbing his mouth against his shoulder in an effort to dislodge the duct tape. Brad removed that obstruction first and it was like releasing a volcano.

"Where'd them sonsabitches go? I'll kill the whole damned outfit!" Doug exploded. "They ain't only a bunch of thieves, the bastards been trying to kill Brad and me 'cause they think we know something about a *murder…*"

As soon as the ropes were removed, Doug jerked the blindfold from his face and stared around the room, as though expecting to see his captors still there. He tried to stand but he had been immobile for too many hours and his legs collapsed, which frustrated him even more so he kept ranting and raving about the men who grabbed him at Gorman's cabin.

"I was still asleep in the hammock when they stuck me with a needle and flung a bag of some kind over my head. Last I remember was them haulin' me off in a car that smelt like new leather and bad bourbon." He looked from one to the other. "So where in hell *are* we, anyway, Bud?"

Brad sat beside his father and explained that they were in a cabin only a few hundred yards from Gorman's. They had not turned on the cabin lights for fear of detection, so with the beam of Tooley's flashlight, Brad introduced Laredo to Doug and explained why Tooley had joined them. Doug listened intently to the part about the ransom note and how they had finally guessed at the identity of the abductors, until Brad came to the part where the man with the neck brace was tied into the overall picture. At that point, Doug jumped to his feet yelling every obscenity known to man, and managed to charge around the room without falling with his fists waving in the air. The three men stood back and allowed the tirade to subside before Brad grabbed his father by the arm and pulled him back onto the sofa.

"Whew!" Laredo smiled. "For a while there I thought we'd have to hogtie this man again so's he wouldn't self-destruct!"

Smoky had run to Doug's side immediately when they first entered the room, but during the rampage he ducked behind Brad and remained there until things quieted down.

"What say we get out of here before them kidnappers come back?" Tooley suggested.

"Let 'em come!" Doug shouted. "I'd love to get my hands on that slimy little bastard. He won't need no neck brace 'cause I'll tear his fuckin' head plumb off his shoulders!"

Brad gathered up the ropes and tape before all of them slipped out through the back door. "Let them try and figure how he got away…"

Laredo suggested they not waste time going back into the woods so they cut straight across through the wet tall grass and sagebrush. Once inside Gorman's cabin, they turned on the lights and settled back in the living room where they looked at each other with a touch of pride and more than a little concern.

"So what now?" Brad asked of no-one in particular.

Each one, in turn, shrugged and silently shook his head.

Doug was the first to speak. He was more calm now but the muscles in his square jaws still bulged each time he paused between sentences and gritted his teeth in anger. Brad rubbed his cheek. Tooley paced. Laredo stared through the window.

"When I came to, them bastards had already tied me up and blind-folded me. They acted like I wasn't even there. They talked about some stolen bonds that the Stokes were supposed to have bought with money belonging to these guys, and then lost 'em before they could be delivered to L.A. From the way they talked, it sounded like they thought Brad and me was somehow responsible for all of this!"

"Stolen bonds?" Laredo asked. He looked thoughtful, then just nod-ded his head.

"Anything else, Doug?" Brad asked. "You said something about a murder? I thought this was all about that box. Now I really *am* confused."

"Near as I can tell, they think we already knew about some yahoo they killed, then they blamed us for stealing their bonds. Go figure."

"You ever find out who the Stokes were?" Brad continued.

"Knew the name right off, from the hospital, and figgered one of them was that bastard from the rodeo. I'm thinking now that it weren't no accident you almost got killed that day, only the gunsel didn't figure to get hisself hurt at the same time." Doug clenched his fists and pounded them against his thighs. "Sure like to get my hands on him jus' one time! It'd be worth spending some more time in the pen just to kill that mother-fucker…"

"You hear any talk about all the different cars they had?" Tooley inquired. He still seemed intrigued by the strange collection of vehicles.

"Nope. Not at first, but after a while two other men showed up and my guess is it must've been them Stokes. Sounded like they brought the bonds with 'em, but they said some con in Denver kept part of the loot for his part in gettin' it back. When the first bunch went into another room, I heard these two whispering about a man named Papoose who's been helping them find some damned box, then try to get rid of Brad and me cause we knew about a murder they committed. They did say they'd had a little bad luck with their cars, whatever that means."

"You say they mentioned somebody named Papoose?" Tooley interrupted. He looked at Laredo, then Brad. "That must be the Injun I was tellin' you about!"

Doug and Brad exchanged glances. "Indian!" They said at the same time.

Taking turns, they explained about the night they were stopped on the highway by an Indian they thought was having car trouble. Brad also recalled seeing that same person at the rodeo grounds near the pizza concession and later at the café when he was making a call to Gary in Phoenix.

"I'll just bet that beer he gave me was supposed to knock me out so I'd wreck our rig, huh, Bud? I told you I didn't drink nothing else that night!" For the first time Doug sounded a bit more cheerful. "Good thing Smoky spilt the rest of it..."

"Y'all hear any names, Doug?" Laredo asked.

"Out of the ones who grabbed me, I only remember the name 'Morty' but they said something about a missing man named 'Three-fingers'. That mean anything?"

Laredo again only nodded.

"These Stokes, if that's who they were, did they call each other by name?" It was Brad who spoke this time.

"One of them, the whiner, called the other one 'Orvie'. That's all I remember..."

"That's them, all right," Tooley interrupted. "When the accident happened, I 'member the announcer called for somebody named Orville to come to the chutes 'cause his brother was hurt!" Each of the men remained silent, apparently mulling over the information that had just been exchanged, while Brad went into the kitchen and brought back a platter of snacks and some cold beer.

"What now, Laredo?" he asked when he placed the food on the table. "Who do we go after first, the Stokes or the goons in the limo?"

"Before we do anything, I'd like to hear a bit more about the bonds. Anything else that might help, Doug?"

"Just that the Stokes were told about the deal by two men they met in jail in L.A."

"That enough to go on?" Brad asked. "Can you arrest them for handling stolen property, too, besides the kidnapping?"

Laredo took a sip of beer and leaned back in his chair, smiling. "I don't think that'll be necessary..."

"Why not?" the other three men asked in unison.

"First of all, the bureau'd already been tipped off about a batch of counterfeit bonds..."

"All this shit over a bunch of phony paper?" Doug blurted. "How come the mob guys didn't know that already?"

"The two men in the L.A. county jail were the actual counterfeiters and they needed a couple of patsies to take the phony bonds off their hands since they were headed for prison, anyway. Seems to me like your Stokes brothers just about fit the bill. From what we know now, they're about stupid enough to fall for this scam."

Laredo nibbled on a slice of kielbasa before continuing. "The bunch that Morty and Three-fingers are tied in with aren't too swift, either. They work for a man named Salvatore who's been known to eliminate anybody dumb enough to call him *Sally* to his face. And by the way, the body they drug out of the lake was Three-fingers himself, and the way I figure it, he came to check on the Stokes' progress and got killed for his efforts. What I don't understand is why they thought Brad or Doug knew anything about the murder."

"You know what?" Brad said. "A strange thing happened the other day when I was jogging around the lake. There was a boat anchored out a ways and it flashed through my mind that it looked familiar. I soon forgot about it, but I'm wondering now if maybe I actually saw them dump the body and because of my amnesia I never remembered it! Suppose that's possible, Laredo?"

"Sure possible. But since y'all can't testify on what you *might* have seen, even murder'd be hard to prove."

"You tellin' us these gunsels are getting' off scott free?" Doug jumped to his feet and glared down at Laredo. "They tried to kill me and Brad. They kidnapped me. They murdered a man, even if he was one of the bad guys. And now you ain't gonna do nothing?"

Laredo rose. He walked over to the window and stared out for a few minutes before turning to the three men who were waiting for his answer.

"Think about it. What happens to the men who kidnapped Doug when they return to L.A. with a bunch of counterfeit bonds that their bosses put up good money to buy? And what happens to the Stokes when those same men realize all they've been put through because a couple of wannabe gangsters hustled them into buying these same bonds? Maybe they'll even figure out what really happened to their man Three-fingers. See what I mean? The way I look at it, every one of them will get what's coming to 'em and the government won't need to spend a dime tracking 'em down to convict legally!"

CHAPTER 28

After a day and a half of fishing, Laredo said his goodbyes and left for the FBI meeting in Denver. Tooley returned to Golden to pack up and leave for the rodeo in Elsie, Nebraska. Doug and Brad said their goodbyes on the front porch of Gorman's cabin.

"You sure you won't come on up to Billings with me, Bud? Promise I won't let no more gunsels try to kill you! We can do a little team roping…"

"Not this time, Doug. I'm going to stop over in Reno and spend a couple of days with Valerie Hummel. Remember, I told you about meeting her when I ordered my new boots at their leather shop?" He paused, choosing his words carefully. "I was kind of hoping you'd come home with me. I'd still like you to run my spread for me…"

Doug stared out across the lake. "I told you once if you had something like this in your part of New Mexico, I might consider it." He hesitated, and his voice was slightly hoarse as he added, "Maybe at the end of this season, I might just do it anyhow."

* * *

Before they had left the cabin, the Stokes tried to make Doug as comfortable as possible on the sofa in the living room. Orville even went around trying to wipe away any fingerprints they might have left, and then gave up the project as hopeless.

"Let's just get the hell out of here. Somebody'll come searching when this cowpoke don't show up today."

"You sure, Orvie? We could give them a phone call from somewhere down the road…"

"We'll see, Homer. First off, we need a bankroll of some kind, then we'll head south."

"What you got in mind, Orvie?"

"You drive. I'll give directions."

Two hours later they pulled into Maria's driveway and stepped out of the Plymouth. Before either of them could go any further, Papoose and Pinto came out onto the porch, hands on their hips, looking menacingly at the brothers.

"Yes?" Papoose snapped. "What now?"

Orville cleared his throat, tried to speak, then cleared his throat again. "We're finally square with the L.A. people and all we need now is some *getting' away* money. Since you got your share of the bonds we agreed on, and we got *nothing*, we kind of thought maybe you'd be willing to help us out one last time…"

"Why should I?"

"'Cause if you do, we'll leave the country. Go to Mexico. Promise to never ever come back to Colorado…"

Papoose did not move but he appeared to be considering the offer.

"You gotta understand I won't get nothing, myself, 'til the fence is convinced the bonds are authentic, but it's worth a few bucks to me to never have to deal with you again! How much you have in mind?"

"Two, three hundred maybe?"

"And you'll *never* come back? I'll never hear from you again? *Ever*?"

"Promise!"

Papoose stepped off the porch and walked toward Orville. He took a roll of hundreds out of his vest pocket, pealed off four of them and put the money in Orville's hand, then added one more.

"*Promise*?" Papoose asked.

"Promise," the brothers replied and scrambled to get back into their car.

Just before they drove away they heard Pinto exclaim, loud and clear, "Thank God!"

THE END

About the Author

Jane Burnett Smith was raised on a cattle ranch in Montana, was a professional bronc rider for 15 years, performed in western movies as an extra and stunt double; served as a staff sergeant in the Womens' Army Corps, dealt blackjack in Reno, Nevada, taught creative writing at two junior colleges in Phoenix; Arizona, published several textbooks in Spanish and is a member of the mystery writers' organization *Sisters in Crime*. Before retiring in Tempe, Arizona, she worked 10 years as a medical transcriber. Smith now lives near her daughter and family, and spends time each year with her son Loren and his family in California.